T0414288

Path of Totality

P. Clauss

WESTBOW
PRESS®

A DIVISION OF THOMAS NELSON
& ZONDERVAN

WestBow Press books may be ordered through booksellers or by contacting:

WestBow Press
A Division of Thomas Nelson & Zondervan
1663 Liberty Drive
Bloomington, IN 47403
www.westbowpress.com
1 (866) 928-1240

ISBN: 978-1-9736-7886-1 (sc)
ISBN: 978-1-9736-7885-4 (hc)
ISBN: 978-1-9736-7887-8 (e)

Library of Congress Control Number: 2019917586

Print information available on the last page.

WestBow Press rev. date: 11/13/2019

Dedication

To my loving husband, David,
Thank you for your encouragement and providing inspiration.

Contents

Acknowledgements

Many thanks to my patient and encouraging editor, Kathy Locatelli.

And deepest gratitude to my talented and creative daughter, Stephanie Thomas, who incorporated my ideas into the cover design.

Prologue

Near Future

He watched the news channel in horror. More people – no – specifically, children from birth to prepubescent ages were dying worldwide. He hovered over his computer as he intently keyed in different search parameters. He sought data on the distribution pattern of this strange new illness that suddenly appeared only months ago. He finally found an animated representation of the data from all the nations' health organizations as well as WHO, World Health Organization, on what was being called a plague. He watched as the image of the flattened world at first had pinpoint spots of red at each of the major cities then blossomed outward to eventually meet the others in the same land mass. The final result, excluding Antarctica, was a totally red world. Blood red.

He knew this was not the distribution of a naturally occurring pandemic. The pattern was frighteningly familiar, as he had worked out the exact data on a theoretical distribution system for a beneficial biologic less than a year before.

He dropped his face into his hands and groaned a guttural cry from his heart and spirit. He suddenly suspected where this virus had come from.

As he forced himself to take deep, cleansing breaths to re-center his mind and thoughts, he felt his frantic heartbeat slow down to a more normal rhythm. Absent-mindedly, he rubbed his grey- and black-whiskered cheeks and chin. Even though he was usually a stickler for a clean-cut, professional appearance, he hadn't even noticed his disheveled state as of late. This crisis had taken his life and everyone else's and thrown them into a cruel blender of circumstance.

He suddenly sat back in his chair. "It can't be. It would be affecting the wrong age," he declared, feeling he jumped the gun on thinking he knew what was going on. "Anyway, he promised he was done with it. That it wouldn't happen. I told him that what he was seeking was playing God, that it was unnatural."

He had a sudden thought. He, the King of Tech, could find and do anything if it had to do with technology. He was a multi-billionaire because of it and had been living a wonderful life with his family. His beautiful children, all whom had grown into adults he was proud of, had gifted him with grandchildren who were his joy. Grandchildren, all who greeted him with open arms and bright smiles.

"Used to," he groaned again as tears filled his eyes. "Nothing saved them. None of my fortune could save them." The memories of each one of them dying were indelible in his mind. How he had to comfort their grieving parents as his heart broke over and over again.

He dashed tears from his eyes as he pulled his thoughts from his grandchildren. He had to know what happened. He had to know what killed them and the rest of the children. He keyed in a new search and used whatever he could to hack into any data source to find it.

Soon, he had his answer. He stared at the screen as he clenched and unclenched his fists on top of his desk. The faces of his grandchildren flashed before his eyes. Smiling, innocent, their amazing simplistic view of the world…He slammed his fists on the desk, nearly annihilating his keyboard. *They are gone, gone,* he cried in his heart and mind. *They are lost forever! And he killed them!*

His grief quickly morphed to anger. Fierce anger. He grabbed his smartphone. So intense were his emotions, he couldn't even talk to have the AI call the number for him. He hit the speed dial link to the person who he knew was the cause. As he waited for someone to answer, he swiveled his chair around and leapt out of it to furiously pace around his large home office space. Suddenly, he stopped in the middle of the room in shock, as he thought, *He actually answered!*

"You lied to me!" were the first heated words out of his mouth when he heard a voice. "What have you done?!"

"Oh, dear brother," the silky smooth voice replied back. "My bosom companion. In what way have I lied to you? What on earth do you think I've done?"

"You released AE253, didn't you?!" A pause stretched out several seconds. That was all he needed to know that he was right.

"Now, why would you think that, dear brother?" the voice finally spoke with caution – a sharpness under the silk.

"The distribution pattern is one we mapped out when you told me it was for a beneficial biologic. That was before I found out that it was for an Age Enhancement virus. I told you it was defying nature and dangerous," he answered with clipped, fierce tones.

"Ah, but, dear brother," the voice had strength again. "We know from epidemiological studies that that distribution pattern from large population centers is typical for a pandemic scenario with any virus or disease."

"Not starting at all population centers at the same time!" he growled into his phone in reply. "And why is it so selective to kill children up to puberty?"

"That age is weak and susceptible," the voice was smooth and dismissive. "How can you blame AE253? It's a vaccine and those ages were not the targets at all. It would not have affected them."

"It's a live vaccine that was made from a genetically altered virus! If you had gone through the safety studies, you may have found that as a possible problem. But you didn't want to spend that kind of money. You promised me you discontinued the research and destroyed it!"

"Really," the voice was exasperated now. "Why are you so insistent that it is a result of the virus in the vaccine?

"Not only are children more susceptible, but so are the elderly when there is a disease outbreak." He gripped the phone tighter. "So how do you explain the data which show that in the same time period as the emergence of this plague, there has been an unprecedented lack of elderly deaths?" He barely registered the popping sounds of his screen protector when it shattered as his grip tightened even further on his phone.

"Ah, I see," the voice sounded pleased. "So it does work." It was a whisper, but the phone picked it up clearly.

"You did release it! You monster!" he shouted into the phone.

"Ah, now, come on. What an accusation," the smarmy voice continued. "I told you I quit pursuing it. There has been no more testing. No more pursuits for approvals. How could I have purposely released it? I know better than that."

"You bet you should know better than that! You are a high-ranking research doctor. You are the head of multiple projects. You are well regarded and well known for your expertise."

"So, it must have been an accident," the voice reassured.

"Oh, come on, an accidental exposure would have a different distribution pattern! And you know that!"

A heavy sigh came over the line. "No matter now, it's out. Humanity will now change due to longer life expectancy." He sounded like he was patting himself on his back.

"You fool!" he shouted at him. "You have killed humanity!"

"Ah, dear brother, those that are alive will exist forever now."

Before he could voice a rebuttal, his eye caught the action on the screen. It had changed suddenly from newsfeed about the plague to videos of warfare! He read the banner at the bottom of the silent screen. After he closed his eyes and took a deep breath, he spoke again, surprised that his voice was so steady.

"Brother, mine," he said sarcastically. "You need to check the newsfeed. Humanity will unlikely survive to live long enough to reap the benefits of AE253."

A silent pause was all he heard for a while. Then he heard voices in the background. He knew his brother had activated his newsfeed. "Oh, my…" his brother's voice trailed off. As he listened to see if his brother would have any further reactions, he also turned to watch on his end as the news agencies were frantically trying to cover the many battles that erupted while nation started fighting nation.

The governments of the world had reacted to the shock of so many young lives lost and had quickly escalated from finger-pointing to war. He fell back into his chair and slumped over. He was utterly spent. He was in such an emotional and mental turmoil, he didn't know what to think or say.

He heard a voice calling his name coming from his phone he had thrown onto his desk. He reached over to activate the speaker. He didn't have the strength to pick it up again. "What do you want," he stated listlessly rather than questioned.

"Look," the voice was pleading. "This was not expected. Actually none of this was expected. I was ordered to release it. No one had any idea it would affect the young or that nations would go to war!" The now panicked voice stopped for a very lengthy pause. He knew his brother was waiting for him to say something.

"Who wanted it to be released?" was the only thing he could muster enough energy to ask.

"The powers that be, brother, the powers that be," the voice pleaded for understanding, to be absolved, forgiven for any wrong.

"Shut up!" he shouted as he reacted to an obvious lie. Rage filled his senses and jump-started his energy. "You are the powers that be with anything biologic!"

"Believe me, there are more powerful people than me," was the whimpering reply. "Come on, between the two of us, not only brothers but twins, and with our areas of expertise, we can formulate some sort of plan…"

His thoughts were still whirling. His last flare of fury didn't have enough fuel to maintain. He threw his head back on the headrest and pointed his chin at the ceiling. He drew in deep breaths as he tried to order the maelstrom in his mind. He heard his brother pleading for some sort of response. "I'm thinking," he said abruptly. "Just. Let . Me. Think."

Suddenly, out of the mists of chaos, a germ of an idea started to emerge as he considered what they were up against and what they needed to do to start the process of trying to save humanity.

"Okay," he started. He heard his brother respond right away. He ignored the insincere simpering of thankfulness that poured from his phone's speaker. "This is for humanity. Not some award or some place in history that you seem to be driven to achieve. Simply, humanity."

"Yes, humanity," the voice over the speaker echoed him. He lifted his head to look at his phone. Somehow, when his brother said it, it seemed to have a dark quality to it.

Chapter 1

Far Future

Sally figured she had had a normal childhood in the era they called the "Great Golden Age." At least normal in the sense that she was one of the many children whose parents had died off-world and was raised by the Society.

The Society. The fabric of their lives. The reason for their existence was considered perfect as governed by technology. No poverty. No hunger. No want. Through this technology, their lives were carefully watched and managed. Their living spaces and work areas were completely safe. Food and items were delivered directly to their door. The artificial atmospheres in the Complex so homogenous it was hard to tell which country zone you were in, much less which planet you were on.

She still remembered that when she was in her teens, she would strain to look out of the shuttle's windows to get the briefest glimpses of the sky, mere slices between the tangle of enclosed bridges that connected the massive buildings that made up the Complex. Her mind suddenly skipped away from any thoughts of the outdoors as if the very thought was toxic. Subconsciously, she knew that going outside was strictly prohibited because of the dangers of being exposed to the TEENA virus that had appeared centuries ago and had triggered the World Viral War.

Other memories came to mind, replacing the ones of her younger days when she was curious about the outside and dreamed of leaving the Complex. She thought of how as an adolescent she had been tested like everyone else in her education level. The educators and administrators had interviewed them extensively and, with their test scores, placed them in specific advanced educational programs to fit their talents. They had been prepared throughout childhood for this testing and placement. It had been emphasized that this was done so that they could be placed in the work force with a position that best suited them. The ultimate goal was to be a useful part of the Society.

She sighed deeply as she thought, *We have shelter, we have food, we can have anything we want, and we have purpose. We have everything. But why does it seem empty?*

As she sat in the transport while it sped through the maze of tunnels through the Complex, she didn't understand why her mind was wandering. Why she was suddenly thinking that her life up to this point was rubber-stamped like so many of the young adults her age. It all seemed to be monochrome in activity and construct.

Sighing again, she looked around at the variety of people with her in the shuttle. They had various shades of skin tone, eye color, and hair color. They wore bright outfits of oranges, yellows, reds, and blue-greens. She herself wore a flowing robe of bright yellow with bright green and blue swirls. The interior of the shuttle was absolutely clean. No dust, no litter. The shuttle was made up of a white plastic material, but the seat cushions were patterned in geometric shapes of subdued tones of dark reds, blues, and greens. The color of her world wasn't monochrome.

No, our world is not monochrome. Just our lives, she thought morosely as she sighed again then changed her expression suddenly to smile into the camera pointing at her.

"Are you feeling okay?" the synthesized female voice came through her comm, an embedded device below her right ear. In the Society, it was the means for personal communication with the Society and with the other inhabitants in the Complex. "You seem melancholy today."

Before the computer could book an appointment with a doctor, Sally answered cheerfully, "I am fine." She brushed her short, gold blonde hair back away from her oval face with both hands. As she smiled brilliantly, she sat up with her sea-green eyes wide and bright. She knew how to fool the technology. "I am very well. I was sighing reflectively over my wonderful childhood."

"Oh, that is good." The voice sounded appeased. "I am glad you have good memories! Have a nice day."

"I will," she assured the computer. *I'm glad you don't read thoughts like so many think you can,* she thought to herself. She learned early in her life that the supposed thought reading by the Society was a computer watching body language and, with complex algorithms, surmising the thoughts of the person.

At that moment, she was glad the Sentries didn't immediately take action from those calculations. She was also relieved she was able to think up a quick, essentially truthful excuse for what the computer had picked up. As she continued to maintain the expression of being happy, she mentally kicked herself for allowing her guard to slip.

When the shuttle arrived at her destination, she was relieved to be able to get out and slip into a crowd of people. She didn't want to trigger the Society's interest again as she started to concentrate on what was ahead and try to leave the disconcerting thoughts behind. *After today, maybe things will be better. Maybe things will be different,* she told herself, and she hoped it would be true as she slipped into the surge of her fellow advanced general study students who entered into a large classroom with stadium seating.

Silently, she obediently sat in her assigned seat along with everyone else. There was no chatter. There was no clutter in backpacks or on desks. Discipline was the rule, and everyone had to obey.

Their instructor, always clean-shaven with close-cropped brown hair, stepped into the classroom. He wore a crisp, clean shirt and pants, both in his usual color scheme of subdued earth tones. Sally thought of how he never showed any concern that those colors were considered outdated and drab in the Society.

Personally, Sally didn't care. He was an excellent instructor. His teaching was good, clear, and thoughtful. A thought hit, causing her to sit up even straighter. *He is not monochrome.*

He seemed to look at her as she had the thought. He smiled, then scanned the rest of the classroom. "Welcome, Class, to your last day of formal studies," he started, his deep, rich voice easily filling the room without the aid of sound enhancement devices. "Although all of you have already started working in your appointed fields as interns, this was the final required class of general studies to complete your formal education."

"From here, you will finish your hands-on studies within your internships. Once those are completed, you will be assigned to your lifetime positions for which you have been chosen as full members of the Society workforce."

He smiled at the class again. With his arms spread wide as if he wanted to embrace everyone in the classroom, he announced, "Let us begin our end to this part of the journey!" Dropping his arms to his sides, he slowly walked back and forth in front of the class while he taught the last lesson.

At the conclusion of the lesson, the exit exam was taken on the computer interface at each of their seats. No one moved until all the tests were logged in. Once they received the signal from the computer, they all stood up and started to file out of the classroom for the last time. Their formal classroom education was completed. As the students started to leave, the instructor was at the door greeting each person as they left.

Bruce Marshall was the only teacher she knew of, or ever heard of, who spoke to each student their final day. Individual attention was frowned upon by the Society. How he got away with this ritual no one knew. But it was known by all the students that he did, and because of that and his teaching style, he was the most sought after instructor in the advanced general studies.

Sally thought about everything he had taught throughout the now finished segment of studies. Somehow, it seemed that he had said things in a way that hinted at something more. It could've been her imagination, but she was curious. She had a strange compulsion to stand at the end of the line. She wanted to ask him a question without anyone to overhear and report her to the authorities.

All the other students had filed out, feeling important and ready for their life's work after their encounter with Instructor Marshall. Sally now stood in front of her final instructor and for the first time realized how tall he was and how blue his eyes were.

"Ah, Sally Delaine," he started the conversation. He glanced around. "The best student I ever had. You will do well."

She blushed at the compliment that rang with truth. No one had ever said anything so important to her before. The Society didn't congratulate anyone over the others; it was not done.

He smiled at her sudden look of consternation. "Don't worry," he whispered, "No one else was put down by that revelation. We are fine."

"Oh," she smiled as her thoughts were in turmoil. "I, I had a question." It was her turn to make sure the room was still unoccupied; she checked that the cameras were off. The computer hadn't expected anything different today and was spending its energies elsewhere.

"It is a good time for a question that needs secrecy," Instructor Marshall said with a smile that definitely reached his eyes.

"Was I that obvious?" she asked with her own genuine smile. She felt somehow close to him. Some kinship she didn't understand. "I was wondering why you weren't so monochrome," she blurted out before she lost her nerve. She was going to specify what she meant when he held up a hand, signaling for her to listen.

"I know what you mean," he said, his voice low as he leaned toward her intently; his eyes were locked with hers. "You see, but you do not understand." He shook his head slightly as her mouth opened to try to speak again. "You can answer it. You need to find the Path of Totality." Continuing to hold up his hand, he turned to exit the room. Looking over his shoulder, his eyes met hers once more. One nod to her, then he was gone.

It took her a moment to react. By the time she left the room, he was nowhere in sight. She slowly walked down the hall to enter another shuttle to go to her place of internship. She felt slightly dazed. The phrase 'Path of Totality' echoed in her mind. Something about it tugged at her, but it somehow demanded secrecy. She made sure to mask her thoughts by fixing her expression in a placid grin. She did not need to trigger the computer again as she pondered this phrase.

By the time she arrived at her destination, she knew she had to find out what it meant. As she exited the shuttle, she wondered who she could ask. *How can I find the path of totality,* she wondered, *if I have no idea where to start?* Suddenly a comment her instructor had said during a lesson came to mind. *'The start of any journey is knowing there is something to journey for.'*

She almost let the reaction to that memory slip through her facade in front of a camera. Instead, she smiled at the staring lens and walked cheerily into the place of her internship.

Chapter 2

He had finished instructions months ago and was fully versed in the rules and expectations of Society. He was fully engaged. He had no thoughts or questions about the Great Society or of the Great Golden Age. He cherished the safety and security of the system and willingly performed in its continuation.

He sat at one of the banks of screens that showed video feeds from monitoring devices that were riddled throughout the buildings of the Complex. He was one of the Sentries that watched the inhabitants. He knew that his section in the massive control room only covered one of the many sectors, a cog in the mighty machinery of the Society. He had aspirations and expectations of moving up in ranks until he was in charge of the entire planet.

He had been on duty and had caught the video feed when the computer flagged the pensive expression of a young woman roughly his age. He was captivated by her short, golden blonde hair that framed an oval face. Her sea-green eyes had looked so far away and distant. He wondered about her and her function in the Society.

He knew the rules keeping him from following her with the devices that were meant to only serve the Society. But, he reasoned, that would not keep him from seeing if he could meet her by chance. As he focused on his reflection on one of the screens, he wondered if he would catch her eye. His broad face, dark eyes, and dark blonde hair may interest her, he thought.

The computer interrupted his daydreaming. It indicated one of the monitors that showed a video feed viewing a scene of a man and woman speaking in one of the squares and surrounded by several people. "Disturbance in city square number 20," the female voice of the Society alerted him.

He could only see them talking in a crowd. It all looked peaceful. "There is right to free speech," he told the computer.

The computer answered, "There are inflammatory words being spoken. These are known to incite riot and disturbances."

He toggled the speaker to listen in on the audio. All he could hear was that the couple was talking about something called the path of totality. He wondered about the words: they seemed somehow familiar but vague, like a distant memory. He was about to cancel the alert when a hand stayed him. He looked up from his seat to see his mentor standing over him.

The older man with graying sideburns, brown hair, and a face that didn't look as if he smiled much gave him a severe look, then toggled his comm. "Square, city square number 20. Take into custody male and female distracters. Disperse mob." He nodded when he got verification of his orders and toggled off his comm.

"Blake," he said sternly. "I know you are new. Learn now: if you ever hear of the Path of Totality, you are to disregard their words and call the security squads." He patted the console. "The computer knows what it is doing to keep the Society safe."

Blake nodded his understanding, then asked, "What is the Path of Totality? It seems familiar to me. Do you know?"

Suddenly, his mentor looked worried but then quickly changed his expression to anger. Before he started to say anything, his expression relaxed and eased into a fatherly smile. "I know enough to know that those who speak of it are pretenders and liars. They seek attention and to cause unrest in the Society." He clapped the younger man on the shoulder in a friendly gesture. "You have promise in this position to serve the Society. Don't risk it," he gently warned as he moved away to watch others in the vast room.

Blake nodded to himself and made a mental note to disregard anything about the Path of Totality. Remembering the young woman, he started to wonder about her and when he would see her again.

Chapter 3

Devon, Bruce Marshall's son, stood well hidden in the shadows of the classroom and had seen his father talking with Sally. He knew his father was only interested in her as a good student and someone he felt was ready to consider the Path.

He had been raised by his parents in the knowledge of the Path of Totality, even under the watchful eye of the Society. His parents were among the few who raised their children without using the Society's resources for child-rearing. Devon knew this gave him a clearer view of the Society by not being programmed by it.

He knew that soon, he would have to make a choice, either to seek the Path or to ignore it and steep himself deeper into the Society. Either way, he knew that he would never consider betraying those he knew to be members of the Path, also called Travelers.

Once Sally had left, he had also left the classroom to find and follow his father. As he moved down the hallways, he didn't consciously realize that he stayed in the shadows and avoided the view of the cameras. Moving around the Complex in this fashion had become second nature.

As soon as he had caught up with him down the hall, his father spoke without turning around. "What do you think?"

This did not surprise Devon. His father had a sense of who, or what, was around him at all times. "She's confused but curious," he answered in a low tone, one that was difficult for the audio, the ears of the Society, to pick up.

"Yes." His father nodded as he slowed the pace to put his arm around his son's shoulders. "An accurate assessment."

They walked quietly until they arrived at one of the many cafés found throughout the Complex in the larger park-like areas. Finding one of the small, round, plastic and metal tables empty, they sat on the small, high-backed plastic chairs and ordered their food and drink with their internal comms.

"How is your internship?" Bruce Marshall asked his son as they waited.

"It is comfortable," the younger man stated obliquely.

His father nodded as their food and drink appeared in front of them. He picked up a cup of steaming coffee and took a sip. "Comfortable is an interesting word," he started, his eyebrows raised with the hidden question.

"The Society chose well for me," Devon intoned. He leaned forward to pick up a sandwich and take a bite out of it. He chewed slowly as if he was thinking about something.

His father nodded and smiled. Devon knew his father had caught the implication of his careful words. He had told him that he was bored. Unfulfilled. "When do you go to your permanent position?" the older man asked as he picked up his fork to stab at his salad and took a bite.

"In a few weeks," Devon said quietly after he swallowed. He took a sip of his cold beverage. "They want me to go to an off-world colony," he announced quietly as he met his eyes.

His father's face fell for a moment. He quickly rearranged his expression. "They must need those of your position out there."

Devon nodded and continued to watch his father as he took another bite of his sandwich. He knew what his father would say next, and he was not disappointed.

"What of your decision about the Path?" The older man dropped his voice lower and held his cup in front of his lips to hide them from view, tactics followed by Travelers to not trigger the Society's interest.

He swallowed his mouthful. "I am considering," he said and stopped. "I'm not sure what to do." He met his father's gaze. "It is so mysterious. I truly don't know what it is or what it means." He also spoke in lower tones as he rested his chin in his hand, his fingers hiding much of his mouth, tricks he knew that would mask enough of his lip movement but look natural. His eyes traveled around, taking note of who was around them. Long ago, he had quit noticing the large rooms made out to be parks with their areas of artificial grass, bordered by fake trees and bushes. By habit, he blocked out the recorded bird song: it had always sounded tinny to him. When his gaze rested back on his father, he asked, "What is the good? Why follow or seek the Path?"

Bruce put his cup down and looked around as his son did, as if he were contemplating a point in a conversation. He picked up the cup again and took a sip. "The end is totality. The path is the process of getting there." He spoke to his son as he continued to carefully modulate his voice.

"What is totality?" Devon asked. Although his expression was calm, inwardly he was anxious for the answer.

After putting his cup on the table, his father gestured by using his hands in a motion to look as if they gathered up something then balled it together. "Totality."

Devon rolled his eyes and huffed. It was the same answer as when he was younger and was trying to seek absolute answers.

"Son," his father stated with patience. He had his elbows on the table with his hands folded in front his lips as he tapped his chin with them. "The Path of Totality is a process. That's why it is a path." He briefly patted his son's hand that was on the table. When he resumed talking, he had repositioned his folded hands in front of his mouth to hide his lip movement. "You must seek it to find your path. And to find totality you must walk the Path."

"How?" Devon was getting frustrated. He straightened up in his seat and leaned back into the sturdy plastic chair.

"There are many who can guide a seeker along the way," Bruce said quietly. "But everyone has his or her own experience of finding the way to the Path."

Devon was getting more frustrated. He was anxious for information to make his decision before he was shipped off-world. He knew he had to calm down or leave before he was noted by the Society. His father motioned to the table. "Eat. Drink. Let us talk further."

Devon nodded as he sipped his drink and ate several more bites from the sandwich on the plate in front of him. As he calmed down, he suddenly realized something. He looked up at his father. He held the drink to mask part of his mouth. "The first choice is to choose the easy path, Society's way, or to seek the difficult path, the one of totality," he spoke in low tones. He was rewarded by a big smile on his father's face as his eyes sparkled.

"Yes, my son, that is the first choice." The brightness was soon dimmed by a shadow of a concern. "But it is your choice. No one can choose this for you."

"The Society tries to..." Devon pointed out.

Bruce lifted a finger "Tries to..." He emphasized. "If you are not aware there is a choice, how can you choose?" he stated logically.

"Then those who haven't heard of it cannot make a choice," Devon said thoughtfully. It was so logical that it was obvious, but he had never thought of it from this perspective.

"Correct." His father nodded.

"I have an advantage," Devon said slowly, thoughtfully. His father nodded. "I was raised in the knowledge of it."

"But that is a danger unto itself," his father pointed out. "It is a familiar, well-worn concept. One that young people disregard in the face of what they know the Society offers."

Devon nodded. He understood the warning his father was giving him. "I must go," he said as he stood. His father stood as well. "I will contact you and mom before I leave." They shook hands. "But even before then, I will visit often."

"I will be looking forward to that." Bruce smiled. It looked as if he was going to say more but decided to settle into a smile again. "Then we will see you soon," he said in farewell.

Devon nodded and smiled before he turned to walk to a transport that would take him to the part of the Complex where his internship was being done. As he arrived at the landing platform, he wondered what his father was going to say before he had said goodbye. The thought left him with an unsatisfied curiosity. As he let his thoughts drift, he soon found himself wondering what Sally was going to do.

He felt as if he knew her from his father's descriptions and telling him about her over the past several months. As he waited for a transport, he wondered what she would be like in person. When the doors opened to allow boarding onto a shuttle, he shook off the thoughts. As he got on board and sat down on one of the seats, he set his mind on his "comfortable" duties.

Chapter 4

As soon as she walked through the automatic doors to report for her internship duties, Sally approached her mentor.

"Ah, Sally," the older woman greeted her. She held a tablet and was scanning through a report displayed on the screen. "You have finished your lessons today. As you complete your internship over these next several months, we will refine your workplace duties in the Society. As you know, you have been approved to work with the ones who cannot control their emotions."

They walked down a long hallway with glass walls on either side. "In the past few weeks, you have been working with the very young." She gestured toward one side of the walkway, indicating a huge room filled with toddlers and preschoolers with their caretakers. "And with the very old." Her other hand gestured to the opposite wall, showing an equally large room where a crowd of senior citizens were under the watchful eyes of several attendants.

"As you know," the older woman continued, "neither can contribute to the Society. Young will grow. The elderly have had their time to contribute and are kept safe until nature has run its course."

Sally nodded that she understood her choices. Even though she had been switching between the two areas, she hadn't settled on which she wanted to devote her life.

The older woman watched her with clear green eyes, waiting for an answer.

"May I have more time to see where I want to complete my internship?" Sally asked quietly. "I see advantages of working with either group. But I cannot choose which one to devote myself to."

The older woman smiled and nodded in understanding. "Yes,

we expected the choice would be a careful one for you." She turned back to the tablet and entered something on the screen. Waiting a moment as she watched the screen, she nodded and smiled as she turned back to Sally. "Yes, as I thought. A few more weeks before you make your final choice have been granted."

"Thank you," Sally replied and bowed. "What should I do today?"

"Let's see…" The mentor tapped her chin with a forefinger as she scanned both rooms. "Let's have you do senior citizens today."

"Thank you, ma'am," Sally said quietly as she walked around the corner to the indicated door.

"Tomorrow plan on the little ones," the mentor called to her before she entered the room.

"Yes, ma'am," she answered back.

When she entered the soundproof room, her ears were assaulted by the high-pitched keening of an old woman lying in a fully reclined, padded chair.

One of the attendants approached her. "Sally, maybe you can help her," she said, her tight smile showed how strained she was. "The medicine we gave hasn't kicked in yet."

Sally nodded and approached the chair while she spoke softly to the woman. The ear-splitting sound continued unchecked. She wanted to put her hands over her ears but instead took a deep breath and sat in a nearby high-backed chair.

Softly, she started singing an ancient lullaby, one that she used for the preschoolers. She continued to sing softly even when the keening didn't stop. After a few minutes, the old woman seemed to hear her as the piercing wail slowly eased into a slow decrescendo into silence. Sally allowed her voice to stay steady and low as the words flowed from her into the quiet air of the room. After several minutes, the woman was asleep.

On the other side of the room, the other elders had gathered around a long table. They had been watching her as she calmed the old woman down. When they saw the ancient one was sleeping peacefully, they started to clap their hands softly. When they saw her look in their direction, they all smiled at her and waved her over to them.

She stood up carefully, not wanting to disturb the sleeping

woman, and slowly walked over to them. She was mystified by their reaction and wondered why they had slapped their hands together in such a fashion.

"You have a beautiful voice," said an older woman.

"Yes," an old man nodded in agreement. "You have a voice like an angel."

Sally furrowed her brow, but the older ones did not see her confusion. *Angel,* she thought, *what is that?*

An attendant waved her over. "Ah, thank you," she whispered, "Must have given the medicine time enough to kick in."

"You're welcome." She smiled at the woman. "Why did they strike their hands together?"

"Oh, they do that." The attendant waved it off. "It's because of their years; think nothing of it."

Sally smiled again. Since her curiosity was already piqued, she had to ask, "What's an angel?"

"Oh," the attendant shrugged, "they speak of odd things like that. I guess old beliefs. You know, before the Great Golden Age."

"Oh, I see," Sally replied. She didn't bother to ask if anyone had ever been curious about what these older people were saying and did some research on it. She knew the answer would've been no. Such matters would be frowned upon by the Society because it wouldn't have added anything to the Society. *Or would it?* she asked herself.

Later in her shift, a male caretaker approached her. "Hello, Sally." He stuck out his hand. She shook it politely. "I am Jessie Daring. I will be mentoring you from now on in the senior citizen ward." She nodded toward him but looked around for Emma Tron, the gray-haired woman she had been working with since she had started there. Jessie caught the gesture and explained, "Ms. Tron is the senior mentor over the entire behavioral ward. You will have another mentor with the very young ones. This has been done so as to give you more detailed information and assistance as you decide which way to go."

He gestured to a table nestled in an alcove at the back of the room. As they were walking toward it, he spoke to the computer, "Standing order: Daring and guest." As the ordered items appeared on the table, he sat down and gestured to the other seat. She sat down obediently. "Enjoy." He gestured to the drink and food. He picked up his cup and took a sip. "How's yours?" he asked as he watched her take an experimental sip.

Her surprised smile answered his question without words. "How did you know that this is my favorite?" she asked him in amazement. She was mystified about how he knew she liked this particular flavor of coffee with her usual add-ins.

"I know people." He smiled as he tapped his temple. Before she could react, he leaned across the table and whispered as if in a conspiracy. "Plus, I have clearance to read all that the computer has on you."

"Clearance?" she asked, her expression reflecting the bewilderment she felt. She wondered what details about her were important enough to be kept on the computer. The concept of being part of the Society's database was foreign to her. She had always thought of the Society's involvement being of the moment to meet the inhabitants' needs and not for accumulating data on people. She slowly put her cup down.

"The Society has many secrets," he said quietly as he leaned back into his chair. He glanced up and nodded. "As you get older, you will understand more."

She watched him, careful of her reactions. She wasn't sure what to think about his comments about the Society. Was it a compliment, which is good and is rewarded, or was it a complaint, which is bad and is punishable?

"You can speak freely," Jessie said as he watched her. "We are now surrounded by a field that distorts words and actions."

Sally immediately panicked. "The distortions will alert the computer." She leaned over the table to whisper nervously.

"Ah," was all he said as he crossed his arms over his chest. "I should have said that it transposes images and words over ours so that they will not trigger the computer's algorithms."

She sat with her mouth agape. She had never heard of any tech that could deceive the computer.

"I see you have relaxed your guard," he chuckled softly. "Otherwise you would not have trusted me enough to show that kind of expression."

She closed her mouth. "Why would you entrust me with the knowledge of such a shield?"

"Because we have been watching you," he said kindly without any particular emphasis.

The evenly spoken words shocked her to the core "But why? Who am I to be noticed?"

He gestured to the table again as he picked up his cup. "This shield can only mask so much. We need to proceed with expected activities."

She picked up her cup and took a bigger sip. The warm, sweet liquid helped to soothe her. "What is this about?" She picked up a piece of toasted and buttered bread, her favorite snack. "It must be more than being my mentor."

Jessie took another sip and set his cup down. "It is a mentorship," he said calmly. "Of a different sort." He looked back into the room full of senior citizens. Some saw him and waved. He waved back and smiled. "I will be helping you with the senior citizens. But along with that I will help you understand much of what they will say." He looked to the ceiling and flicked a hand as if throwing out the thought for her to consider. "An interpreter, so to speak." He looked back at her." Any questions?"

She took another sip, allowing the sweet warmth to relax the tension in her body, even though she knew it would be fleeting. As she held the cup in both hands, she considered his words seriously. She knew she would be stepping into dangerous territory if she spoke her true thoughts. Curious to see if she could find the masking device, she glanced up and stared. In a slight recess on the ceiling, a ring of lights blinked randomly.

She dropped her gaze and met his eyes. He smiled at her and nodded. She decided it was worth the risk and asked the first question that came to her mind. "What are angels?"

"Ah," he smiled, took another sip from his cup, and set it back down. "So that is the question we will start with. Interesting." He sat back and folded his hands to rest them on the smooth top of the plastic white table. "Angels are created, supernatural beings that came before man."

"You say 'created,'" she said quickly. After thinking a bit more, she continued. "You imply man was created."

"Yes," Jessie answered, short and simple. He didn't attempt to explain.

Sally waited long enough to see that there would be no further explanation. She saw he was using a communication technique in which information would be given in concise segments as it was asked for. She took another sip then stated, "That is not what we are taught."

"No."

She could quickly see that asking more questions on this line of thought would have her confront information she wasn't sure she wanted to hear. Information that could directly conflict with the teachings of the Society.

"Angels," she took a deep breath and stated again. "Who are they, I mean, their function?"

"They are messengers of God."

"Who is God?"

"The Creator of all things."

She dropped her hands into her lap as she looked down into her cup. There it was, the words she did not want to confront.

Unbidden, a vague memory stirred of an elementary school teacher or attendant who whispered stories to them of God, who created all things. She had liked the stories and the woman who told them. But she disappeared one day, and another teacher replaced her and told stories of talking animals and mythic heroes.

"Ah," Jesse's voice interrupted her thoughts. "You are needed."

Sally looked over her shoulder to see an attendant standing patiently nearby. She could see the old woman flailing in her chair and starting to become more vocal. She smiled and stood to bow to her mentor. "Thank you for your insight. I will consider it," she said brightly as she masked the inward turmoil the short conversation had caused.

Jesse stood and bowed as she turned away to enter into the main part of the room again.

The attendant whispered to her as they walked to where the old woman was. "I am sorry to interrupt your conversation," she smiled tensely. "Apparently the medicine didn't last as long as it should have. Perhaps you can calm her."

Sally smiled back at her. "I am happy to try to help. Perhaps she will find peace again."

She was prepared to focus her attention on the old woman and sing a lullaby when she sat down in a chair next to her recliner. Before she could start, the woman grabbed her arm and pulled up her frail form to look at her through milky eyes. "Find the Path of Totality," she whispered hoarsely. After Sally fought to control her surprise and nodded, the old woman fell back into her chair, her energy spent.

Sally rubbed her arm where the woman had grasped her with an unexpected strength. Pondering her sudden statement about the Path, she gently picked up the hand that had flopped near her in the chair. Acting like nothing happened, she patted the old woman's hand as she sung the lullaby. The woman squeezed her hand as she turned her head to look at her with tears in her aged eyes. Slowly, she smiled as her eyes closed and she fell into a gentle sleep.

After singing a few more minutes, Sally gently laid the arthritic hand on the woman's lap. She decided to think about the strange happenings of the day later when she was alone. Slowly, she stood up and walked over to a group of senior citizens. She distracted herself by talking with them and caring for their entertainment and social needs, which took up the rest of her shift. She enjoyed hearing their stories and quaint ways of speaking. She pondered their talk of past events and wondered how much was true and how much was fantasy.

After her shift was over, she started to think about what Jesse had told her and the old woman's declaration as she rode in a shuttle to her living space. Her thoughts wandered from them to Instructor Marshall then to focus on what 'the Path of Totality' could mean. She smiled as she realized that her life seemed a bit less monochrome.

Chapter 5

She felt strange not going to the classroom the next morning. All her life, she had been in classrooms. Now, she was past that point in life. She arrived at her place of internship and was met by a young woman, slightly older than she. She was her mentor for the preschool children.

The day proceeded with high-energy charges hollering, screaming, and running around. She patiently taught them the ways of the Society and introduced them to their letters, numbers, shapes, and animals. Nap times gave her and her mentor time to talk. The conversation never strayed from the care of the preschoolers.

She was surprised to realize that, as the day wore down to the close of her shift, she started to detest the rules of the Society. She enjoyed seeing the children express their free spirits unhindered by the strictures soon expected of them by the Society. She wondered why, after the weeks of working with the young, she felt this way now. *Is it because of the permanence about making a decision on my life's purpose?* she wondered. *Or is it because of the odd encounters the day before that enhanced how I feel right now? That somehow my life is missing something? That it seems flat and monochrome?*

As she picked up the floor that was strewn about with thick plastic pictures of flowers and plants along with small plastic models shaped like different animals, she wondered about teaching the children about them. All they ever saw were the artificial plants in the parks and the acceptable pet animals such as dogs, cats, rabbits, and the occasional pocket pet. She wondered if there were still cows, sheep, pigs, and chickens.

She laughed at herself. *Of course, animals are still around,* she thought. *We still have meat to eat that come from them.* Then her thoughts fell dark as she walked to a window that showed the barest strip of sky but not the ground. *Where do they keep them?* she thought as her mind brought back Jesse's words. *"The Society has many secrets."*

She ran her fingers through her hair as she shook it back out of her face. She made sure her face was happy and smiling as she turned back to the children where she knew the cameras would see her expression.

At the end of her shift, she walked down the long hallway between the very young and the very old on her way to her living space as she continued to ponder the situation. She knew the role of the caretakers and teachers of the young was very important in getting them ready for the Society. But, she was having the first questions about the Society. Could she truly be the one to train these free spirits in the confines of this life? She looked across the hall at the senior citizens. They had lived through the Society. Could they teach her how to navigate the waters of the Great Golden Age for the remainder of her life? Or, she thought further, could they teach her more?

On her way home in the shuttle, she decided to still wait the allotted time for her choice, but she was starting to become more sure that she would choose to care for the elderly.

****

He sat in his secret room in the dark. *It is time,* he thought as he triggered his view screen to tap into the Complex's surveillance system. *It has been long enough to see how she is turning out.* He ordered the computer to find the person of interest and found her working with the elderly.

After watching her for several minutes, he commanded the computer again and brought up her records. Reading through the education reports and internship reviews, he caught up with her life. He nodded slightly as he thought, *I knew she would be worth keeping alive. She is fast becoming a useful part of the Society.*

A voice full of dark intent and evil mocked him. "Useful part of the Society," it sneered. "She is dangerous. Once she knows what she can do, she will destroy your perfect Society."

The old man shook his head at these words. "There are no more

Travelers. The last Cleansing took care of them all, either by killing them or reconditioning them. There would be no reason to destroy the Society. It is Utopia!" he reasoned with his dark master.

"You gamble with the success of everything. You risk losing your control of humanity, you risk destroying my rule over mankind...all through keeping her alive!" The voice hissed threateningly.

The white-haired head shook decidedly in denial of the allegations. "Everything is under control. And it will remain under control," he said as he snapped off the monitor. He had seen enough to know things were still on track.

He felt the presence of evil move on as he sighed. He knew he would leave a few of his minions behind to watch and report back to him. Clenching a shaking hand, he took in another deep breath and released it slowly. He scanned his menu of concoctions on the screen on his table and ordered one of them to be delivered to him. When it appeared, he smiled, knowing that it would dull his fear and guilt with a sense of giddy happiness. Popping open the vial, he gulped it down and sent the empty container back for recycling.

Leaning back in his chair, he waited for the effects to kick in as he sat in the dark. *She's definitely good with the elderly,* he thought suddenly. *I wonder if she could take care of me...*

****

After working the allotted weeks to make sure of her life choice decision, the day arrived that she officially committed to working with the elders. That day, Sally decided to walk home instead of taking the transport. She had a lot on her mind as she let her feet carry her through the maze of hallways.

When she snapped out of her wandering thoughts, she looked around and found herself in the brightly decorated Hall of Graffiti. She looked at the bright colors making up swirls, letters, and figures. She usually liked to take her time to find the minute details each artist would leave and look for something new that hadn't been noticed before.

But today, she looked at the whole. She immersed herself in the artists' talents and imaginations as she stood still and looked at the graffiti that covered the walls, floor, and ceiling. After taking it all in, she pondered the word graffiti and wondered about its origin, then her mind considered how each individual of the Society was free to express themselves in all forms: art, literature, and music.

She started walking again, no longer noting the bright colors and artistic talents as her thoughts became sober. She thought of the Society. *Everyone was housed, fed, and had everything attended to. Everyone had a purpose. Life is good but...*she let her thoughts trail off unfinished.

She turned the corner to go down another hall that was full of photographs. This was another place that she liked to take time to visit and study the pictures. But she didn't notice them as her mind was occupied in trying to grasp something that was elusive.

She should be happy, but she wasn't completely happy. She wasn't fulfilled. "Monochrome," she whispered to herself. *I still feel monochrome*, she thought, not wanting the hidden microphones to pick up any further hints on her state of mind.

As she continued to walk from one hallway to another, she idly wondered if what she needed was a mate. *Is that what I need to make my life complete?* she thought to herself. Somehow deep inside, she knew that wasn't the full answer.

****

Blake was in the control room watching her on one of his screens. He had seen the completed purpose of life form for her pop up on the computer and smiled. He saw how she had worked with the elderly, and she was good. They loved her.

He smiled again to himself as she stood in the Hall of Graffiti and looked around. He liked that. He also enjoyed seeing the works in that hall. He pulled his attention from her as he checked his other monitors, making sure he was doing his job while he tracked her walking through the Complex. When he turned back to her, she had turned into the hall of photos. He frowned slightly when he saw how she didn't even look at them. Her expression bothered him. As he debated about instigating the analysis mode of the computer, his stomach dropped as he heard her say a word that he thought sounded like 'monochrome.'

He leaned forward and watched her intently as he wondered

what she could mean by that in their world full of color. He saw her expression clear of any confusion or stress as she continued to walk through the Complex. He rubbed his chin as he still wondered whether to involve the computer or not.

"Mooning over her again?" His supervisor's voice startled him. He swiveled his chair around to find the older man standing with hands on hips staring at him then glancing at each of the monitors in turn.

"Uh, not exactly," he stammered then clicked into reporting mode. "For a moment her expression seemed to be not in accordance with the Society's protocol." He thought about the whispered word and decided not to report that. *What basis could be named to report it?* he thought to himself in justification.

His superior leaned toward the monitor to watch the young woman walk the halls. After a few minutes, he was satisfied. "Not to worry," he proclaimed. "We all have pensive moments. The important thing is that they do not linger. Then the attitude can potentially be harmful to the Society."

"Yes, sir," Blake saluted his superior then swiveled again to face his monitors. He made a point to intensively study each monitor, proving he was doing his job.

Soon he heard soft footsteps as his superior moved away. Inwardly, he sighed. *Monochrome*, he thought. *What could that mean?* His curiosity was piqued, not because he felt it was a danger to the Society, but simply a need to know what she had meant.

Chapter 6

Trevor sat back into his chair with a deep, relieved sigh. He ran his long-fingered, tanned hands through his short-cropped, graying, brown hair. He had been watching the Sentries. Long ago, those of the Path had infiltrated the Society's control room to keep up with what they were doing. He was currently on duty in their own secret control room they called the Watchers' room.

As he picked up his mug of hot, black coffee, he shook his head slightly as he thought of the emerging situation. As he took a couple of sips, he continued to watch the boy watch the girl. Triggering his comm link keyed into the Travelers' frequency, he contacted Bruce Marshall, Sally's previous instructor.

"We need to speed up with the timetable on Sally," he said, keeping his voice soft and low. "There is someone in control who is watching her with too much interest."

"Roger," Bruce's voice answered back.

"And, Bruce," he asked, "how is Devon?"

After a long pause, he answered in an even softer tone than usual. "He is undecided."

Trevor shook his head as he knew the other father's anguish. "Growing up with knowledge of the Path makes it harder," he said as an explanation.

The other voice sighed. "I know. It is harder for them to see the importance. They take it for granted."

"Yes," agreed Trevor, "that is it exactly. But they have to choose for themselves to join and continue on the Path."

"Exactly," Bruce said quietly. "And some don't."

"Too true," Trevor said sadly as he looked at the picture of his family that was propped up on his narrow desk under the bank of monitors. His youngest daughter had left the Path. She had never betrayed them. But he had not heard from her in years. He hoped her life on one of the off-world colonies was successful and happy.

"May Totality be yours, brother," Bruce said.

"And yours," Trevor answered as he turned his attention back to the screens. As he sat back and continued to sip his coffee, he wondered how Bruce was going to approach the girl to see if she would decide to join them.

****

Bruce was wondering the same thing. He was sitting in his recliner in his apartment. His wife wasn't home yet, so the silence of their small, personal habitation helped him think.

The situation with his son already weighed heavily on him. In addition to this, Trevor's asking about Devon brought Bruce's worries to the forefront, threatening to distract him. He did not want the concern about his son to interfere with his choice. With all this on his mind, and knowing the choice of who would approach Sally at this critical time was of the utmost importance, he decided he needed to walk the Path. He knew many times the One on the Path would give them instruction if they would seek him and truly listen.

To anyone watching, he looked as if he were sleeping in his recliner. His chin dropped to his chest, his eyes closed, his arms folded across his lap. His relaxed posture hid a deep, intense connection to the Path and the One who walked it. In this way, he communed, learned, and was filled with insight.

Right before his son came home to visit, he opened his eyes and sat up. His expression exuded a deep inner calm as his eyes shone with new hope and joy. He had been given a plan, one he would have never thought of. He was glad he didn't have to wait long for Devon to come for a visit.

****

The minute Devon stepped into the room, he knew his dad had been communing. He frowned slightly at the expression of peace and joy that radiated from his father's face.

31

He was happy that his dad could so easily enter the Path, but he was jealous that he could not. The others had told him to try; and to keep trying. They had made it sound as if it was so easy to do. He had tried, more than once, but somehow was always barred.

When he brought it up with his mother, she had told him that it was probably because he didn't fully believe. He had reacted to this by asking, "How can I believe what I cannot see?"

Her reaction was a slight shake of her head and to tightly hug him. "You must believe that you will see," she had whispered softly to him.

He was still pondering that concept. He could touch the Society, he could feel the Society, he knew what Society could and could not do. This Path was a mystery. It was unknown. It seemed unpredictable. How could he trust in that, much less believe?

With these thoughts and memories engaging his mind, he was totally derailed when his father hugged him tightly and whispered, "You will help someone find the Path."

After a shocked intake of breath, he pulled away angrily. He almost shouted at his father but stopped in time so as to not alert the computer. "You know I cannot do that." The clipped words came out between clenched teeth.

His father was unfazed and continued to smile. "Yes, that was the expected reaction."

The calm words hit Devon's anger like cold water. As it died down, it was replaced by fear and anxiety. "Who said?" he whispered, fearing the response.

"The One on the Path," his father said gently.

The mix of emotions that suddenly flooded through Devon confused him. His disbelief battled against happiness that he had been noted and a fear of hoping too much.

"You need to teach someone else the Path so that you can understand it better," his father continued to explain.

"Why can't an older one, with more experience, do this?"

"Because you are chosen."

Frustration hit Devon. "Why won't the One talk to me?" he demanded angrily. "I know all the teachings, but I cannot join the Path. I've tried."

"Yes, you know the teachings," his father pointed at Devon's head. "But you need to know the teachings," his hand dropped so it was pointing at his heart. "It must sink into your inner depths, then you will believe and see."

Devon sighed. He had been told this many times before, and it still didn't make sense to him. He felt his father's hand on his shoulder. He looked up into his eyes and saw the joyful light that shone brightly. It tugged at his heart, but he didn't know how to respond.

"You will see." His father patted his shoulder. "Wait here for your mother. I will be back soon," he whispered. He turned and left.

Devon collapsed in the recliner his father had just left and could feel the warmth that had remained. He also felt a peacefulness descend upon him for a few minutes before it dissipated. Devon knew that it had been a mere wisp of what could be experienced by those who traveled on the Path. He tried again to commune but was frustrated when the Path continued to stay closed.

After his attempt, he remained in the recliner. As he thought over the task his father had given him, he pondered how he was supposed to proceed. Then he realized the one thing his father hadn't told him: who was he supposed to be helping find the Path?

He stood up to find his father. He couldn't wait for him to come back for the answer and couldn't ask him over the comm. *Might as well try*, he thought, still feeling he was the wrong choice. *I just don't want to mess up someone else.*

****

In the control room, Blake had missed the interaction of father with son, even though he had their living quarters up on one of his screens. He had been totally enthralled by watching Sally taking inventory of her weekly order. By the time he glanced at that screen, both father and son had left and all it showed was empty rooms until a petite, slender woman with short, curly brown hair entered. She started putting away the weekly supplies in an unhurried, efficient manner. He went back to watching Sally.

****

In the Watchers' room, Trevor hadn't missed the interaction. He had thrown up a concealing field around Bruce and Devon in case the Sentries in Control became interested. The intensity of their expressions and their actions would have alerted the Society, even if their words did not.

He sat back and pondered the strange tack Bruce had taken by involving his undecided son. He gently tugged at his short beard as he contemplated the situation. He could see that at the best possibility, both would join the Path. *But,* he thought as his mind turned dark with worry, *the worst would be the loss of two potential Travelers.* One of whom he knew was very important to them.

He heard the door open behind him. Turning in his chair, he smiled at another older Traveler. Getting up, he bowed slightly. "Greetings, Aaron. Watch the young one," he pointed at the screen, indicating which one to his replacement. "He is showing too much interest in Sally."

The other man returned the bow and nodded that he understood. All the members of the Watchers' team were dedicated to each of the potential Travelers. But Sally was even more special. She had been lost to them when she was small. Now that she had matured to the point she could determine her own way, they wanted to introduce her to the Path and clear away the deception of the Society.

For a few minutes, both men watched a monitor showing a dreamy-eyed young man who watched Sally through one of many screens in the massive control room. Before Trevor left, turning the command over to the other man for the new shift, Aaron nodded to him again as he sat down. "Do we need to order an interference?" he asked matter-of-factly.

Trevor turned toward the monitor one more time to study the Sentry. "Not yet. So far he watches. If he makes a move, we must."

The seated man looked over his shoulder at him. "He will. It will be soon."

Trevor pursed his lips as he thought. He knew this brother Traveler had an extra ability to sense people's next moves. He trusted his evaluation. "Order a team to be ready. When he moves, they can act."

Aaron nodded, his expression still not smiling but less stern and slightly pleased with the decision. "I will order it," he said as he turned back to the monitors.

Trevor quietly left the room to go to his rest. The bright light of the sun met his eyes, which were still adjusted to the dim light of the room of the Watchers. He deeply breathed in the naturally pure air and reveled in the beauty of the forest around him. He always enjoyed hearing the animals rustling through the underbrush and the different birdsong that filtered to his ears through the branches and leaves of the many kinds of trees that provided shelter and shade for the pathway he walked.

Stepping barefoot through the thick grass that carpeted the trail, he entered the small village made up of deceptive looking simple huts. Each one was hidden in the shadow of large trees so that from the sky, the forest looked unclaimed and uninhabited. He entered a hut and found his wife weaving along with several other women. They were chatting happily but stopped when he stepped in.

"May I intrude?" He smiled at the women who were present. They were all around the same age as himself and his wife. He bowed his head to each one in greeting. They silently returned his greeting in like as their hands continued to work skillfully at their looms. They were the best weavers throughout the villages. Their sturdy, homespun, loosely woven cloth was used for all the clothes worn by the Travelers.

His wife continued to weave as she spoke. "Of course, Trevor. What news do you have?"

He sat on a stool provided for him in the room. He made his report on activities of the Society and all that he had seen of their fellow Travelers and those who they hoped would join. "Bruce and Maddie are ready to join us in their next step of the journey."

One of the women sighed happily and pressed both of her hands to her heart. Trevor knew she was a relative of the Marshalls.

When she started to weave again, she asked, "What of Devon?"

Trevor hesitated. He wasn't sure if he should divulge everything he had seen. "He is still undecided," he finally said.

His wife looked at him closely. She knew he was hiding something. "What of Sally? She has been lost to us for too long."

"Measures are being taken to protect her and reveal more of the Path to her." He stood, his report made. He knew the women would pass the news to their huts, husbands, and families. "Seek the One on the Path so we all can be on the course to Totality," he intoned.

All the women stopped weaving and pressed their hands to their hearts as they bowed their heads. Before he left, Trevor joined them and entered the Path to seek the One.

Chapter 7

Months had passed since she had made her final decision about her life's purpose. But Sally felt more and more restless. She thought she was fulfilled in her job of caring for the elderly, but she still felt something was missing.

The short conversations she had had about the Path of Totality, first with Bruce then with Jessie, replayed in her mind. She needed more information but wasn't sure how to get it. She instinctively shied away from asking the computer; she felt somehow that it was taboo and would create problems. She tried to ask some of her elderly charges, but their reactions varied from disgust to great sadness when it was mentioned. She looked for Jessie but could no longer find him since her internship had ended. Without any obvious source of information, she just gave up.

One day, she decided to stop at a sidewalk café. As she ate and drank, she let her mind drift. Looking overhead, she stared at a windowed strip of sky several stories up, a mere glimpse of a bright day. Gradually, she became aware of the presence of a person standing quietly nearby.

She cut her eyes to look without moving her head. She saw a tall, young man around her age with curly, dark hair and slightly brown skin. He was wearing a loose, long-sleeved tunic and loose-fitting trousers. The clothes were shades of browns, blues, and greens, but they highlighted his coloring beautifully.

He was also looking up at the strip of the sky. She dropped her head down to look at him fully. When she did, he sensed the movement and looked at her, meeting her gaze with eyes of bright, deep blue.

A sense of being drawn to him surprised Sally. The sensation made her curious. "It is beautiful," she said conversationally.

"It is," he agreed, his deep voice pleasing to her ears. "But a poor example of what can be seen of the whole sky," he added.

She shyly looked down at her meal and took another bite. She needed a distraction as she tried to figure out why she was confused by her internal reaction. She quickly realized she was uncomfortable and intrigued with the statement and the speaker.

"You know you can go outdoors," he said softly. He had made no moves to get closer to her. He wasn't even looking at her anymore as he had returned to looking up at the slice of blue.

She looked up at him in surprise. "The Society hasn't deemed it safe." She shuddered at the thought of what lurked outside. "She protects us. Not only from a dirty, unorganized world, but from the virus! You do know of the TEENA virus?"

She saw that he watched her as she reacted to the idea of going outside. His expression remained kind and understanding. "But that is what is taught to children before they know how to think for themselves," he added in a soft voice that she could still hear but she knew the computer wouldn't be able to pick up.

As she pondered what he said and how he had said it, her curiosity intensified. When he moved slightly closer to her, she was amazed that she felt no concern at all. She simply wondered why this stranger was taking risks by saying things that could be construed contrary to the ways of the Society.

"That is true," she finally replied just as softly. She had to agree with his last statement since she not only was trained to take care of the young ones, but because she had recently been questioning the dictates of the Society herself. She smiled at him, hoping he could see that he could share more with her without worrying.

He widened his smile and nodded. "But there is another path," the man said quietly as his eyes met hers with an intensity she had never experienced before.

The word 'path,' his intense gaze, and the way it was spoken triggered a shock like a flash of recognition through her. She quickly hid her surprise and rearranged her features so that the many cameras wouldn't target her for interest. She met the gaze of the blue eyes with a smile and gestured to the seat opposite her. "Would you like to be seated and have a meal? I am Sally."

"Hi, Sally. I am Devon." His smile, so genuine and pleased, dazzled her. He moved to sit down when another presence intruded.

"Hi, pretty lady," a male voice drawled as a medium-height, young man with dark brown eyes, dark blonde hair, and fair complexion sauntered over to her. "Is this man bothering you?" His words were hard-edged as he stared aggressively at the other man.

Sally was immediately repulsed by the newcomer. She sensed something wrong, very wrong with him. "No," she said firmly as she stared at him. "I invited him to sit down."

The intruder wouldn't look at her. He stared at the other man as if he were daring him to do something.

"Who are you?" she asked sternly, finally grabbing his attention away from Devon.

He bowed deeply in response to her question. She assumed that he meant it to be grand but to her it appeared to be mocking. "I am Blake." He made it sound like she should have known him and his name.

Sally was confused. *Why is he acting so familiar?* she wondered. She had no idea who he was, and his name was unknown to her.

Devon had remained standing as he watched. "What is your business?" he asked Blake. His words were clear and strong but not challenging.

"I wanted to talk to her," Blake replied belligerently.

"Does she want to talk to you?" he asked pointedly.

"Of course!" Blake exclaimed boastfully.

Devon's blue eyes settled on Sally. "You want to talk to him?"

"No," she answered quietly but firmly. "I am already engaged in a conversation with you."

Devon sat down and looked up at Blake, watching for his reaction.

Blake refused to budge, staring at both of them. He seemed to be in shock by the actions of the other two.

"Please go," Sally said as sternly as the Society would allow.

She could see Blake's broad face darken with anger and indecision. It was obvious that he had to deal with an unexpected result from his plan. When several older men silently gathered around, he looked at each of them and reconsidered the situation.

Sally could see that he grudgingly decided not to press the issue. He bowed roughly. "I will endeavor to visit you again," he said, sounding like a threat to her. As he moved away, the group of men parted to let him through and then quietly dispersed.

****

Devon watched Blake storm away. He knew he was going to be trouble. Looking around the park area, he saw that one of the men who had gathered around to silently discourage Blake from further action had followed the angry man. The others had slipped out of sight, but Devon knew they would be close by to help if needed.

He turned his attention to Sally to see that she was deeply shaken by the encounter. Her face had paled, and she shook slightly as her hands gripped the edge of the small, round table. Her now troubled sea-green eyes met his. "I have no idea who that was," she declared with a shaky voice. He saw that she started to nervously bite her lower lip.

He smiled at her reassuringly. "You don't know me, either," he said lightly as he relaxed back into the chair.

She looked at him seriously as she studied him closely. "I know," she finally said. "But somehow you seem safer than he did." She turned to look around the area as if to assure herself the other man had gone. When she settled back into her chair to face him, she seemed slightly calmer. "I don't know why he acted like I knew him. I have never seen him before in my life."

Devon knew who it was and had been forewarned of his intent on Sally. He considered telling her what he knew then decided against it. He didn't want to be distracted from his mission, and talking about Blake would steer this meeting off course. He smiled warmly at her to try to help put her at ease. "He is gone now." Her responding smile was still tense as she continued to look about them nervously. "What are you eating?" he asked to draw her attention to her food, hoping she would resume her meal.

"It is a chicken and pasta dish," she replied as she seemed to notice her food again.

"Ah, I see," he replied. "I like the beef and potatoes meals." He activated his comm to order that and a drink.

As he waited for his order and studied the young woman with him, he thought of how the Watchers had thought they had more time before Blake made his move. Devon had almost been too late. Over his comm that he had toggled over to the Travelers' frequency, he had a sub-vocalized heated conversation with one of the Watchers. "Why did you let him get to her! I thought you had been watching!"

"We are not sure how he got into the area without our seeing him," came the calm reply from the Watcher on duty. "It is good he saw you with her. Maybe he'll think twice before approaching her again."

As Devon smiled at the most beautiful woman he had ever seen, he transmitted back, "I doubt it." He still could see the intense fire in the other man's eyes as he had turned away to leave. He knew that Blake would not give up easily.

As they ate, he talked with Sally about anything that came to mind. Slowly, she began to relax more and started talking easily with him. He steered the conversation to center around her as he drew her out to talk about herself. He knew the basic details of her life but wanted to know how she thought and felt about everything in general.

As they discussed safe topics that wouldn't trigger interest from the computer, he began to wonder. *How did the computer not catch the intense emotions Blake exhibited?* Everyone in the Complex knew that the Society strictly forbade such intense feelings and actions. *Was that person somehow hiding under the radar or was he protected?* he thought with an icy chill.

"I've talked enough about myself," Sally was saying as she drained her drink and requested another. As she waited for the empty glass to disappear and a full one appear, she met Devon's eyes. With a upward twitch of an eyebrow, she signaled that it was his turn to talk.

"Ah," he said as he fiddled with his fork. "There's nothing special about me." He smiled into her eyes. "I enjoy your voice. It's a perfect speaking voice. I bet you are a good storyteller."

Sally blushed as she ducked her head. "The children and elderly do seem to respond favorably," she said modestly. She pointed to him. "You have a grand voice. What is it that you do?"

He shrugged. "I'm in technology," he said, trying to sound interested and excited. "I help keep our world running."

As soon as he said it, the words seem to impact Sally as she suddenly turned around to look at her surroundings as if seeing it all for the first time. "Yes," she said slowly, "our world is all about technology."

She seemed to mull something over in her mind. He was starting to worry that her expression would trigger the computer when he saw the accepted and expected expression snap in. He relaxed as he saw that she was well trained.

She met his gaze with eyes that were solemn and probing. "You had said that there was a path outside," she said softly, her voice modulated below the sensitivity of the computer. He nodded. "You have been outside?" she asked.

He nodded and smiled to mutely answer her question. He thought of how he had enjoyed the world outside the Complex ever since he was old enough to start to venture out, at least, when they knew it was safe enough for him to leave the safety of the compound. He wasn't sure how much he should tell her at this point.

"Ah, so you have? And you have survived. How interesting." Her smile reached her eyes, causing them to sparkle. Then they became serious again. "Have you journeyed the Path?" she asked with even more intensity in her hushed voice.

He hesitated. He saw the impact of his delay when her eyebrows came together and other minute changes in her expression indicated concern. He would not lie to her. He couldn't. Keeping his voice modulated in the safe zone, he explained, "I know of the Path. I have been taught that it is the truth but it will not open to me. I do not know why I am rejected."

Confusion clouded her face then quickly cleared. He could tell this was information she wasn't sure how to interpret. She surprised him when she leaned toward him to ask, "Is your life monochrome?"

At first, he was confused about what she meant as he looked at the splashes of color and texture around them. He looked back at her and saw her watching him intently. Suddenly he understood; she was asking if he felt an internal state that was devoid of color, devoid of light, empty. His mind raced as he considered everything he had done and known throughout his life. Except for his parents and other Travelers, he could see that he could call his state of being monochrome. He nodded and with absolutely no doubt, he said, "Yes, it is monochrome."

She studied him closely, her eyes serious and probing as he met her gaze unwaveringly; he enjoyed the color of her eyes. Suddenly she smiled, "Somehow, I believe you."

Devon experienced an unexpected surge of warmth at the sight of her smile and her trust. As he returned her smile, he thought of how less monochrome his life felt at that moment.

****

In the control room, Blake clenched his teeth as he looked over the shoulder of the on-duty officer. *I should be there,* he thought angrily. *She should be smiling at me!* He watched the monitors as they both stood up from the café table and walked slowly together, deep in conversation. He wasn't on duty so he couldn't adjust the controls to zoom in to read their lips to see if he needed to trigger the audio. Since he was the only one watching them closely, no one else noticed when they disappeared from every screen.

Double checking every available screen in the control room, he couldn't pick them up. "Hey!" he tapped an officer on the shoulder. "A couple just disappeared."

The man swiveled in his chair and glanced at him in irritation. "There are many couples in the sector. Were they causing problems?"

Blake stood silently as he tried to formulate an accurate response; otherwise the computer would pick up the falsity. "No," he had to finally admit. It was a problem for him but not the Society.

"You weren't following couples to watch their interactions, were you?" the man asked sharply, his eyebrows raised as he stared at Blake.

"No, sir! That is against the rules of the Society!" As he spoke, he snapped to stand at rigid attention.

When the other man saw that the computer flagged him as being truthful, he shrugged and turned back to his screens.

Blake knew he had been abruptly dismissed. After looking around the large control room with its banks of screens and silent monitors, he decided to slip out and try to find the couple on his own.

Chapter 8

"You need to go outside," Devon said to Sally as they rode a transport on one of their outings. His face was turned away from the camera, his voice lowered so as to not be easily picked up by the audio.

"But, we can't!" She shook her head slightly with fear in her eyes. Her face was carefully diverted from the view of the Society as well. "It is deadly out there," she whispered earnestly to him. She tried to keep the intensity of her emotions dampened.

"At our age, we can go outside," he insisted. He could tell by the set of her mouth he was not going to win unless he could find another approach.

After seeing each other for a few months, they found similarities and differences between each other's thoughts, feelings, and lives, so that they seemed to fit together like intermeshed cogs. Devon knew this had started as an assignment but realized that it quickly had grown into much more.

He looked away from her as she watched their surroundings speed by with hints and bits of the outside world peeping through despite the massive maze of interlocked buildings and enclosed bridges and walkways. He sighed deeply as he sought a way to convince her.

The older Travelers wanted her to visit outside the Complex. But not only that, he was anxious to show her the world outside. He had been out there so many times, he thought he had grown used to all the wonders outside in the world. But now that he could show someone else, someone to share the experience with, he was anxious to do it.

Suddenly, a thought hit him. He turned back to her and looked into her eyes. When he knew he had her full attention, he whispered, "It's not monochrome." He saw the reaction in her eyes as her face remained passive.

Before they reached her stop, she whispered back, "I will consider it."

He smiled brightly at her as she disembarked. Leaning back in the seat as the transport resumed its journey, he thought of the ways they could use to escape the Complex.

He was so deep in thought that at the next stop he didn't notice who got on. Soon he sensed a disruptive presence and looked toward the source. Seated by the door was Blake. He was slouched over, glaring at him.

Devon kept his face neutral as he watched the other man. He had seen him at times when he was with Sally, but this was the first time he showed up while he was alone. Alarms went off in his mind as his senses sharpened and his muscles tensed. Blake had stood up and was walking toward him. He was ready to spring into defensive mode when the other man sat down across from him and folded his arms across his chest.

"Where do you two go?" Blake asked bluntly.

Devon furrowed his brow as he asked, "What do you mean?"

"When you're with Sally, where do you go?" The other man asked insistently.

"Different places." Devon kept his voice even, the words measured.

"Why can't I find you?" Blake was getting more agitated.

At first, Devon was shocked by the implications of the level of surveillance that Blake was doing. Then he started to wonder when the computer would step in. This interaction was against the rules of the Society.

A sudden thought chilled him to the core of his being. *Maybe he has disabled the link in the transport with the computer. His status in the control room could warrant that kind of ability,* he thought logically as he tamped down his rising emotions. But, to his relief, he saw the camera swivel and move down to face Blake. It was taking readings.

"Shut up!" Blake growled suddenly.

Devon knew it was not aimed at him. The outburst had been

a reaction to the Society questioning Blake's actions through his internal communications link.

"I'm here on official business," Blake growled.

"State your business and security code." The external speakers in the transport had been activated so Devon could hear what was going on.

Devon watched Blake stop cold, as he obviously struggled to decide what would be sanctioned as being official. He could see that the other man was at a loss for words.

Another voice boomed over the speakers. It was not the computer. "Blake, stand down. Leave the transport and report to Control."

Devon raised his eyebrows at Blake as the other man continued to stare fiercely at him with dark, dilated eyes. It was a silent question as to whether Blake would obey. He had seen the other man's face pale, sweat beading on his forehead when he realized he had passed the limit of tolerance.

Blake hastily rearranged his expression and bowed to Devon. "We will speak of this later." He stood up to move next to the shuttle doors.

Devon smiled and watched as the computer moved to standby as the camera swung back to nestle into the corner as they came to a stop. Blake stepped off the transport. But before the doors closed, he turned to face him. Devon had to suppress a shock of surprise at what he saw. He had never in his life seen such a blatant unveiling of hate as was revealed in the other man's face.

He was relieved when the doors closed and the transport continued its route. Keeping his demeanor calm and automatically keeping his breathing even and his heart beat slowed, he pondered the encounter as he waited for his stop.

****

"That stupid child," the director of the control room exclaimed. He shut his mouth as he realized he had said it out loud. They were in a separate room overlooking the main control room. A room that no one but the elite knew existed.

A dry chuckle came from the figure behind him. "It's okay," the old man said as he smiled, his finely lined face folding wrinkle upon wrinkle. "We are not monitored here. Remember, I made this Complex and created the Society. It obeys me."

The director smiled at him, still unable to believe that this old man was not in his eighties as he seemed to be, but was centuries old. "He is trying to ruin it all!" He pointed out.

"Blake is a young man who thinks he is in love," the old man smiled. "Unfortunately, he chose the wrong person."

"Are you sure she is the one?"

"I am certain," he smiled as he reached for his glass. After taking a sip, he continued. "Fortunately, he is watching her closely and may have uncovered something the computer has missed."

"What's that, sir?"

"The Travelers still exist and are interested in her."

"How do you know that? She hasn't triggered any of the failsafes."

"Apparently, they have gotten wiser and slyer over the years. Somehow they must have trained her," the old man muttered, mainly to himself.

"We thought they were all dead." The director looked into the control room and studied all the monitors. "Nothing serious has been flagged in decades. Well, except for the ramblings of a few people about those strange beliefs of theirs."

"They're out there," the old man whispered as he set his glass down. "Did you not note the young man Blake confronted?"

"What about him?" The director looked at the old man, puzzled. "He didn't trigger any failsafes."

"True." The old man pointed at the screenshot of Devon that he had transferred to the big viewing screen in the secret room. With the video and audio were the sensor readings showing the vital signs of the man during the encounter. "Could you be so calm when confronted by someone so hostile?"

As the director re-watched the scene, he now could see what the old man had noticed. "There should have been at least an unconscious response."

"Correct." The old man leaned forward to make his point. "He is a Traveler. And he is very young."

The director sat back hard into his chair. He felt the world as he knew it crumble. "How many more are there?" he whispered hopelessly.

"We may have to go back to the old days of ferreting out believers of the Path," he said calmly.

"Cleansing?" the director asked in shocked surprise. He was clearly afraid he had heard the other man correctly.

"Yes." He sat back and took another drink. "If they convert the girl, she will have to die."

The director turned to stare at the old man. "Because she would bring down the Society?"

The old man merely nodded. "Years and years of playing chess, and we can all be brought down by a pawn," the old man whispered to himself.

The director heard it and was chilled to the bone. Everything he knew, his position, his prestige: it all was threatened.

****

The Watcher drew back in alarm. He signaled another to take his place as he ran to get Trevor. He found him sitting outside his hut leaning back in his chair drinking some cold, sweet water. "Sir," he said breathlessly as the exertion of his frantic run had caught up with him.

"Sit down. Catch your breath," Trevor said as he waved toward a nearby chair. He poured some more of the drink from a nearby pitcher into another glass and pressed it into the other man's hand. "What has you so upset?"

"They are aware," he said after he quickly gulped down the drink.

Those three words froze the smile on Trevor's lips. "How? No." He shook his head in disbelief as he stood up. "Let me see the replay."

After they both ran to the room, Trevor watched the recorded scene unfold. Afterwards, he tapped his chin as he thought. "How long have we been monitoring this room?" he asked for anybody in the room to answer.

"A few weeks," responded one of the Watchers. "We had not

been aware of this room until then. In fact, no one had been in it at all until recently."

"I see," Trevor whispered as he turned away from the screen that showed the frozen image of Devon even though his thoughts had locked onto another person he had seen.

"What do you command?" The other Watchers on duty had turned away from their screens and swiveled their chairs to face him to listen. They all waited for him to speak.

So, he is still alive, he thought in shock. He had to force himself to move past the impact of the face he recognized to make decisions that needed to be made. "Warn the other Travelers in the Complex."

"All of them?"

"All of them," he confirmed grimly as the communication commander went back to his post to send out the warning.

"Contact Devon's parents," Trevor stated as he turned to the on-deck commander of the Watchers. "They need to get their son out along with Sally."

"Should all the Travelers exit the Complex?" the commander asked.

Trevor shook his head slowly. "No, we need to take this cautiously. Right now, the interest is on two people." He saw the commander about to ask him something. "Yes, warn them. The Society is aware of Sally for whatever reason. And Devon is also being watched now." He turned to face another communications officer. "Contact all the villagers."

"What do we tell them?"

Trevor thought for a while, then smiled grimly. "It is almost time."

"Almost time for what?" one of the younger Watchers asked. The others had stopped their work again and stared at him. He could tell they were all waiting for his answer.

"Final Resolution," he whispered.

The words were softly spoken but easily heard in the silence of the room. Absolute stillness met his ears as he turned toward the door to leave. As he stepped out of the room, he heard them snap out of their shock and resume their duties as they obeyed his orders.

As he trudged back to the village, he allowed himself to think about the old man he had seen. He knew where his next stop must be. He made his way to a particular hut at the edge of the village. After tapping at the doorframe, he heard a voice inviting him in.

"Hello, Trevor," an aged but strong voice greeted him. "How may I help you?"

"I have news," he said as he entered the hut and bowed to the speaker who was seated in a wooden chair behind a rough-hewn, wooden table.

A deep-throated chuckle greeted him as he settled into one of the many straight-backed wooden chairs in the room. "What kind of news?"

"I have seen your brother," Trevor said, deciding to get straight to the point.

"Oh, my," the old man sighed as he sat back. "I had wondered if he was still alive."

"He is," Trevor confirmed. He leaned back in the chair.

"If he is anything like when we were younger," the old man frowned at the memory, "he will be a problem."

"There is every indication that he will be," Trevor said quietly as he stood. He had decided that he needed to check on the progress of his team. He didn't want to bother the Wise Man with the other news at that moment. He had given him enough to think about.

"Thank you for the news." The old man nodded at Trevor, then turned toward the fire that burned in the small clay chimney embedded in a section of wall near him.

Trevor stepped out of the hut, leaving the old man to his memories and his thoughts.

Chapter 9

"I have a surprise!" Devon was talking to Sally over their comms.

"What is it?" Her voice had a playful lilt to it. He could imagine her smile as she asked.

"Pack a few things," he said with a smile in his voice, but worry in his heart. His parents had warned him of what needed to be done. "Plan on a few days," he added, hoping he didn't trigger any notice from the computer. He knew Blake was not on duty, but he also knew that he could be close by. He felt a growing anxiety as her answer seemed to take ages in coming.

"That sounds wonderful," she answered to his relief. "I have vacation days coming," she continued. "When would you like for me to ask for them?"

His heart sank. They needed to leave that night. "Oh, I thought you had a few days off already." He forced a laugh.

"I do," she answered. "I thought I would need a few more." She hesitated, "I guess I mistook your..."

He laughed. "Ah, that would be a nice vacation," he said light-heartedly. "Let us leave tonight; as I said, it's a surprise!"

"Okay," she replied. "I will be ready in a bit."

"Meet me in the usual transport," Devon said before she could ask for more details.

"I will! Be there soon."

Devon disconnected the comm and nodded to his parents. He was standing in the middle of their living quarters. They had already packed a limited amount of their things in a few large bags. They had being waiting to hear his news.

"We will go ahead," his father said. "You know the way out."

Devon nodded. "When should I disable the communicator?" he

52

asked quietly. This was his first time to leave without his parents as guides.

"Before you get to the exit. The computer will track you to it if you don't," his father instructed as he handed him a small device. "Good time would be just before you leave the transport."

Devon nodded as he put the device in his pocket then picked up his bag. He had already been to his apartment and packed. He had only what he needed and a few mementos. He looked around his parents' place, his last look. His parents watched him and smiled at him when he looked their way. "It won't look like we left," he observed.

His mother patted his cheek. "That is the point. We will meet you at the nearest village."

He nodded and smiled at her. She gave him a long, tight hug. After she released him, his father hugged him.

"Are you sure?" he whispered to his son.

Devon nodded.

"It will be dangerous," his father added.

Devon pulled away and met his father's eyes. "From what you told me, it is too dangerous for me to stay." He looked from his father to his mother and back. "I know after this I will have to commit to the Travelers." He paused as he organized his thoughts. "But, the last few months, talking about the Path and teaching Sally, I realized I do understand it. More than I thought. I believe in it more."

His father smiled widely and nodded. Turning away, he reached for his wife. He hugged her close, then slipped out the door.

After he left, his mother smiled at him and gave him another long hug. "That is great news, son. I know your dad didn't say it, but it pleased him very much to hear you say that." Devon smiled at her and nodded.

After a few more minutes, his mother gave him a departing smile as she slipped out of the door. Devon knew she was going a different way from his father's route as well as his own. He waited another ten to fifteen minutes, then also left. As he boarded the nearby transport, his senses heightened to alert him to any change in the environment around him. He kept his demeanor calm, acting like it was any other day while he kept his eyes open for any problems but especially watching out for Blake.

He sat relaxed in the seat, letting his thoughts drift as he rode the shuttle. When it arrived at Sally's stop but did not even pause, he knew it was because no one was there waiting for it. He tensed slightly and started to worry that she could've been detained. He was tempted to contact her but didn't want to accidently alert the Society if he couldn't hide the anxiety in his voice. He decided to wait until the next round. If she still wasn't there, then he would look for her.

Thirty minutes later he was nearing her stop again. He was relieved to feel the transport slow to a stop. As soon as the doors opened, she stepped into the shuttle carrying a large bag that was slung over her shoulder.

"Hello!" She smiled brightly. Her face changed slightly as if she sensed something but couldn't place it.

"Hello." He patted the seat beside him. She sat next to him and nestled close. "Are you okay?" she whispered low as the transport started to move to its next destination.

He smiled at her and took her hand. "Yes. I am with you!" He slipped his other arm around her and held her tight.

"You are so sweet!" She smiled as she relaxed into his embrace.

They rode along for several minutes as they talked quietly. When the transport came to a standstill, they stopped talking and looked toward the door, curious as to who would be joining them in the empty shuttle. Devon was barely able to control his reaction as Blake stepped on board.

"Well, hello!" Blake said as he smiled widely. His dark eyes were locked onto Sally. "How are you doing?"

"We are doing well," Devon answered for her. He tightened his arm around her slightly. Sally responded by moving a bit closer to him.

Blake looked at him and around the transport to see no one else was with them. He looked down at the bags. "Where are you two heading?" he asked pointedly.

"Going to one of the off-world colonies for a few days," Devon answered evenly, keeping his voice calm and controlled. He didn't even bother to contact the Watchers. Somehow Blake had slipped through their surveillance again.

"Oh!" Blake was surprised. "I didn't see that Sally had taken time off." Devon felt Sally react to the revelation that this man had been watching her closely.

"She's already off for a few days," Devon answered in a tone and manner that signified he had nothing to hide. "No need for more."

Devon was glad that Sally had quietly been watching the interaction and let him handle this threat. Even though Blake had been around when they were out and he suspected he was watching her as much as he could, Devon never told Sally who he was. He didn't want her fearful or acting differently. It was enough that he could tell that Sally had been disturbed any time Blake had been around. At some instinctive level, she had recognized that he was a potential threat.

"May I escort you to the departure point?" Blake asked, his tone making it sound more like a command than a request.

"Oh," Devon said off-handedly. "We will leave eventually. First we will eat and do some shopping." He smiled at Sally and squeezed her hand.

It took her a split second to catch on to his lead since they hadn't discussed doing anything before their departure. He was relieved when she quickly picked up on the hint. "Oh, yes." She smiled and laughed. "Just the two of us," she said with emphasis as she looked up lovingly at Devon and ignored Blake. Her reaction warmed him as he hoped it was genuine in its intensity and not just for this situation.

As they continued to gaze lovingly at each other, Devon could see in the corner of his eye that Blake watched them suspiciously as his narrowed eyes flicked from him to her and back again several times. As the transport continued on its route, nothing else was said as he glared at them, his expression becoming darker and more serious. When the shuttle stopped, he abruptly stood and stormed out of the opening doors.

After the doors closed, Sally spoke up after a deep breath to steady herself. "He didn't wish us a nice trip."

Devon hugged her closer and smiled at her attempt at levity. When he looked away, he glanced up at the camera. *I wonder if he went back to the control room,* he thought grimly. He noticed that Sally looked from him to the camera and back again. He could see she was suspicious of what was happening while she started to tense up again.

"What's wrong?" she whispered as she glanced at the camera.

Devon kissed her hand to distract her. Smiling, he assured her, "Don't worry. I'll explain everything soon."

As they continued to ride the transport to the launching pads, they held hands as they chatted about insignificant things. But as they got closer to the stop where they had to get off, Devon grew increasingly nervous. Even with every technique to try to mask it, Sally kept looking at him, and he knew she wasn't fooled. It was confirmed when she smiled shyly and leaned forward as if to whisper sweet nothings in his ear.

"Smile like I'm saying something really gushy," she breathed in his ear. "Your nervousness then can be interpreted by the computer as anticipations of something of an intimate nature," she giggled as he blushed. "I don't know exactly what's going on." She continued to breathe huskily. "But I will follow your lead." She kissed his ear and leaned back.

Devon smiled widely at her, an expected reaction after an intimate conversation and pulled her into an embrace. After kissing her soundly, he released her enough to keep an arm around her. She responded by resting her head on his chest.

At the stop before the launching pad, Devon tensed for action not realizing that Sally would pick it up. She immediately was on the alert as she sat up and stared at the doors. When they came open, several masked people stood outside. He felt Sally freeze at the sight; she had no idea of what was going on or whether she was facing friend or foe. "It's okay," he whispered to her. He saw her nod, but didn't look at him.

One of the men shot a device at the camera; another signaled for them to get off the transport. Devon reached in his pocket and waved the device his father had given him over his neck near his right ear. Then he waved it over Sally's neck in the same area. She jumped when she saw the movement in the corner of her eye. "Deactivating the comm, specifically for the Society's frequencies," he whispered to her. She looked up at him, her eyes wide with fear. As she nodded to him, he could see she still wanted to trust him but was getting very scared.

After they got out on the landing, the masked team of seven people surrounded them as a protective escort. Devon took Sally's sweaty, cold hand and held it tight to try to assure her everything would be okay. As they moved down the vacant corridor, everyone stepped lightly, trying to make as little noise as possible. They suddenly stopped to face a random blank area of the white plastic wall. One of the team tapped a complex rhythm on a panel. In response, a section of the wall slid back to reveal a yawning hole that was an entrance to a tunnel that descended downward into darkness.

****

Although she was terrified by the sudden, unexpected chain of events, when the wall panel slid back to reveal an obvious way out of the Complex, Sally's fear was dulled by a sudden intense curiosity. Devon had talked so much about leaving the Complex that she didn't feel totally deceived about the purpose of this sudden trip. She did hope that someone would soon explain what was happening and why so many people were involved to help her get out of the Complex.

As she waited for further direction from her mysterious escort, she took a deep breath and gasped it out quietly at the unfamiliar smell of loamy earth and truly fresh air. A few members of the team started down the steep slope of the tunnel after they gestured for her to follow. As she moved forward, she felt Devon follow closely behind. Before moving away too far from the entrance, she looked back to see that the remaining team members had stayed behind to secure the wall panel in place and make sure their exit left no trace.

As they walked single file along the narrow and absolutely dark, earthy tunnel that seemed to run for miles, she ran her hands along the dirt walls on either side and rubbed her fingers together. She marveled at the new sensation of being truly dirty.

While they continued to move forward in the total darkness, knowing that people were with her only because of their near presence, the muted footfalls, and their breathing, she started thinking through what was happening. She knew she should still be panicked by the unexpected events and marveled that she wasn't.

She remembered that when Devon had suggested the trip and was so set on doing it, she had felt that there was something more going on. She pondered the fact that she still had no idea what would happen next. *It may be a bit scary facing the unknown,* she thought, *but I can't deny that it is also exciting!* She smiled to herself. *Whatever is going to happen, I'm glad Devon is with me.*

Suddenly the earthy texture of the tunnel walls firmed up into stone. A few more minutes into the stone tunnel, she heard the leader speak.

"Devon, you will need to guide Sally. Do you remember the way?"

"Yes," she heard Devon's voice behind her as she felt his hand reaching for hers. "I have her; go on ahead."

In the dark, Sally heard soft shuffling sounds, then suddenly, she couldn't sense the presence of anyone ahead of her. She reached with her free hand in front of her and felt empty air. She stepped forward a bit and stopped as her hand found a stone wall. Before she could ask, Devon spoke.

"Turn to face to your left. Now, without stepping forward, reach out with your hand and you'll feel a metal bar. There is a ladder embedded in the stone wall that you need to climb up."

Still holding Devon's hand with one hand, she searched in front with her other in the absolute dark. After several seconds, her questing hand found the bar as described. "Okay, I found it," she reported.

"Grasp it firmly. Do not let go of my hand until I tell you to. Feel for a rung with your foot. Once you find it, step up firmly on it." Devon continued the instructions, the tone of his voice serious with a hint of urgency and caution.

Sally couldn't help but wonder about the precise instructions but didn't question it as she held onto the metal in the dark. She followed the new directions and found the rung with her foot. "Okay, I got it."

"Are you sure?" Devon asked firmly.

"Yes, I am sure," she shot back, slightly irritated by the whole process. She felt Devon release her hand. With it free, she reached up to find the next rung.

"Now, carefully climb up," Devon said briskly. "They'll help you at the top. I'll be right behind you.

She was still wondering what the big deal was as she cautiously started climbing up. The farther she climbed, the easier it was as the dark started lightening to a deep gray and she could make out the progressive rungs ahead. Soon she could see the top of the ladder and someone looking down at her as he waited for her to get to the top.

When she finally reached the top, all the muscles in her arms and legs were burning from the unfamiliar exertion. She was very grateful when she was helped over the lip that was the end of the metal ladder. As she stood on the rocky floor of a natural cave, she could see light coming in through the entrance several meters away.

Soon Devon was at her side. "Why all the care over a ladder in the dark?" she asked as she turned toward him.

"Because you couldn't see that there was a crack large enough to swallow a person between the floor of the tunnel and the rock wall the ladder was bolted onto."

Sally felt her face blanch with sudden fear, and she felt a bit shaky. "Why didn't you tell me?" her weak voice quavered slightly.

Devon smiled as he hugged her. "We found that people would freeze in fear because they couldn't trust who was guiding them. " He stepped back to study her. "You look better now." He smiled at her. "Are you ready to go on?"

She took a deep breath to calm herself as she shook off the thought of falling into a deep crack in the dark. *After all, it didn't happen*, she thought as she walked with Devon toward the cave entrance. Thinking about what he said about trust, she pondered. *Could I have trusted him enough if I had known about the danger?* But then she mentally shrugged off the question. *Not worth worrying about it now.*

When they emerged from the shadows of the cave, she beheld a vast open sky with a few fluffy clouds that were bright with the rays of the setting sun. Stepping out into a grassy meadow, she looked back and saw a massive building in the distance that extended beyond the horizon. She was puzzled when she noted that it shone gold in the dying light.

"The outside is gold?" she questioned those with her. When she stopped to think, she knew her first question must have seemed odd to them. She didn't ask anything that would've been expected, like who they were or what was going on. It was simply that at that moment she was struck by the oddity, and she couldn't understand why it was that way.

One of the team took off his mask, causing his short, graying hair to stand upright. His face was strong, tanned, and slightly wrinkled. "The creators of this place originally had the outside painted in natural colors to blend it in with the surroundings. As time went on and the purpose of the Complex changed, it was painted gold," he answered in a deep, quiet voice with no hint of thinking her question was weird.

She studied him closely, noting his dark blue eyes and friendly face. "What does it symbolize?"

He smiled at her and winked at Devon. "You have a quick one."

Devon smiled and leaned close to her.

The blue eyes returned to hers. "Do you know the phrase, 'like a bird in a gilded cage?'"

She nodded as she thought. She had seen the phrase in old literature that was in the Society's databanks. Glancing at the gold buildings, she understood. "You have everything. Everything is provided except for freedom." She looked back at the team who had all unmasked. She was surprised to see a few women on the team. She smiled and nodded to them. They returned the gesture. "But there is freedom," she said. "We get what we want, we eat what we want, we do what we want," she spread her hands in front of her. "What more? It's a good life." She felt Devon lean in closer as if he also wanted to hear the response of these people.

Every one of them smiled a knowing smile and waited. The leader spoke. "And are you fulfilled? All your needs are truly met?"

Contemplating how she would answer, Sally stood quietly as the evening light slowly faded into darkness. The air cooled, and the night insects started to sound. She glanced at Devon in the waning light and saw that he was waiting, that he needed to hear her answer.

She looked up to see how the night sky had darkened further to reveal a star-studded sky. She stared at the breathtaking sight for a few minutes then pulled herself away, knowing a response was expected from her. After a deep sigh, she finally answered, "No." She sought each face that was dimly illuminated by the starlight.

"But is living out here the answer?" she questioned herself more than the others.

"It is only a small part," answered the leader. "Follow us," he said as he turned to lead the group into the nearby forest.

Devon linked his arm with hers. "I know the way. Be careful; we can't use much light."

As they traveled through the darkness, with nothing else to distract her senses, Sally was suddenly overwhelmed by the fresh air blowing around her, the sighing of the wind in the limbs of the trees, the crunching of leaves underfoot, the woodsy smell and odor of soil. When she heard the soft skittering of something in the forest, Devon felt her tense. He squeezed her arm in reassurance. "Not to worry," he whispered to her.

The winding trail in the dark led to a quiet village nestled under the trees. With the huts cast into deep, dark shadows by the trees shielding them from starlight, she wondered what they would look like in the light of day. She wasn't even sure how many or how big they were since all she could see were darker patches beneath the trees. She didn't have time to consider much more when she was whisked into one of huts, in which sat someone the leader had said was the Wise Man of the Village.

She barely had time to take in the details of the interior of the hut when she was caught in the steady gaze of the old man. "Hello, Sally." He greeted her as if he knew her and signaled for her to be seated in one of the straight-backed wooden chairs opposite from where he was sitting. She stared at him. Something about him seemed to be familiar.

"Hello, Devon. Good to see you!" he greeted her companion warmly.

Devon simply smiled in response and bowed before he moved toward the group of chairs. "It is good to be back."

Even though the exchange was brief, she could tell they knew each other. As she studied the old man seated behind a wooden table, she still wondered why she felt like she should know him. She was interrupted from her thoughts when Devon guided her to one of the chairs.

As they settled, the old man signaled to someone standing in the doorway. Refreshments were brought in for them. As they ate and drank in silence, Sally could feel the old man's eyes on her as he watched her closely.

As she grew more uncomfortable, she glanced up to meet the deep blue eyes.

She felt awkward; she felt that she was meeting someone whom she should know but couldn't remember his name. Suddenly, she was distracted from his attention and her thoughts as she became aware of the tastes and textures of the food and drink.

She couldn't help but let her surprise show in her expression; her eyes widened as she slowed down to savor the fullness of the flavors, something she had never experienced before. She glanced up at the old man and saw he was smiling. When he saw her looking at him, he gave her a slight nod but stayed silent.

She looked down at her plate to study the food and stare into the cup as she continued to experience nuances of flavor that were totally new to her. She looked up to meet the old man's eyes. "How?" she started, not sure how to express what she was experiencing. "It looks like what is served in the compound." She looked down at the plate and cup again, then up to lock gazes with the old man. "How can it be so different?"

The old man picked up his plate and cup. "This is real." The words were simple and softly spoken but carried weight in Sally's ears.

"Real?" she was confused. "What we eat is real."

"What is provided in the compound is synthesized food. They try to copy real food."

She studied his face, looking for any indication that he was joking and saw none. She didn't want to believe but knew he was telling the truth. The proof was in her mouth. She couldn't say anything further.

"You'll find this food is more sustaining and will make you feel better," the old man added as he set his dishes down and continued to eat.

Sally was suddenly very tired. It was as if her body was working overtime to contemplate all that her senses were taking in ever since she left the compound. Her eyelids grew heavy as they started to close. Through the suddenly descending mental fog, she heard the old man talking to Devon. "This is not the right time to talk."

She barely heard Devon murmur an agreement. She felt his arms wrap around her as he held her, trying to keep her from toppling over onto the floor.

"She will need time to acclimate." The elderly voice echoed in her head. Her own thoughts swirled drunkenly in her mind. *Acclimate or was I drugged?* She felt a tiny stab of fear as she wondered what she had gotten herself into.

"Where can I take her?" She heard Devon ask. His voice sounded hollow and distant to her.

"There is a place prepared," was all she heard of the conversation as she succumbed to the peaceful unconsciousness of sleep.

Chapter 10

She slowly woke up from a very pleasant dream of being in a place of perfect peace. The bed was firmer than usual, but her body felt totally rested. She lazily opened her eyes to look into a light that was clearer and brighter than any of the types of illumination in the Complex. She slowly realized that it was sunshine. The golden rays of dawn shone through a window onto her face. She closed her eyes as she felt the gentle warmth; something the lights in the Complex did not do was waste energy by giving off heat.

When she opened her eyes again, she shielded the direct light with a hand so she could study its complexity better. She noted that the sunlight had more depth, more subtle hues than the artificial lighting of the compound. Her eyes caught minute movements and focused on what was causing it. As she watched, tiny particles danced through the light rays; she wondered what she was looking at.

"Those are dust motes." She heard Devon's voice from the other side of the room. Apparently, he had been watching her. "I thought they were something alive when I first saw them," he continued to explain.

"Dust motes?" she asked as she glanced at him with a furrowed brow. She was still mystified.

"Something we never see in the compound," Devon said as he stood up and stretched. "It's basically small particles of dirt that are airborne."

"Oh." She waved a hand and watched the dust whirl with the eddying wind currents she had caused. As they danced around reflecting the sunshine, she could see how they may look like tiny creatures. A movement in her peripheral vision distracted her.

She looked up to see Devon standing by her with his hand extended down to her. At first, she was surprised by his offer of help and questioned it silently. She was going to ignore him and get out of bed on her own until she looked around and saw that she was on a thick pallet lying on the ground.

"Yeah, it takes some getting used to," Devon said with a smile as he saw her look around at the sleeping mat in dismay. "We're used to a different type of accommodations."

She took his hand as she used her other arm to lever herself off the thick stack of blankets that was filled with something soft. With his help, she was soon standing. She released his hand so she could stretch and bend. "It's harder, but I think I slept better than I ever have."

Devon smiled as he gestured to the door of the small hut they were in. "Wait until you see breakfast."

She stepped through the blanket-covered doorway and stopped. The full sunlight revealed what had been hidden in the dark of the night before. The trees and plants of varying shades of greens throbbed with vibrant life. Splashes of brilliant color, bright reds, oranges, and yellows, peeked out from the foliage in random patterns. As she focused on the bright patches, she saw they were different varieties of flowers and fruits in the trees and on the plants underneath. To her, it was breathtaking seeing in reality what she had only seen in pictures and simulations.

After several minutes, she noticed Devon had slipped around her to exit the hut. He stood alongside her as he waited to lead her into the village. As she glanced at him, she saw he was watching her as she was taking in as much of the surroundings as she could.

Suddenly, she became aware of sounds other than the wind through the trees around them. She heard people talking and laughing along with music. The sounds of a gathering of people didn't grab her full attention as did the various bird songs. She was entranced by the depth of the notes and melodies. It was nothing like the electronically generated bird song she heard at the enclosed parks located in the Complex.

Again she gradually became aware of Devon still standing patiently nearby. She heard his stomach grumbling. "I'm sorry," she said sheepishly. "It's all so overwhelming!"

He nodded at her and grinned widely. "I remember my first time out of the Complex." He looked around as he inhaled a deep breath then exhaled with a satisfied sigh. "There is much to take in."

"Where do we need to go?" she asked as she continued to look around and saw a bright blue sky between the leaves high above them. She felt him gently take her arm to guide her as she started walking with him. They were heading toward the voices and music coming from deeper into the village.

"When was your first time?" she asked curiously. She didn't look at him as she tried to see what was around each hut they passed as they moved through the village.

"Years ago," he answered. "I was very young."

"Weren't you at risk?" she asked as she looked at him in surprise. The teachings of the Society had deeply ingrained into her the dangers of ever leaving the Complex. But it was even more intensely adamant about the young.

He looked over at her and smiled. "Yes, but it was a calculated risk." He waved a hand toward a building nearby. "The lab. They have been working on a vaccine."

"Oh." She stared at the building as they walked. It looked like any of the other huts. "I have heard whispers all my life about someone working on a vaccine for the TEENA virus. But there hasn't been any mention that someone has been successful."

Devon pursed his lips together. "It wasn't totally successful," he said sadly. "I was one of the few."

"Oh," she murmured. She saw the subject bothered him deeply. Even though she was bursting with curiosity, she had no idea what else to say.

As they turned a corner around a thick collection of huts, she saw a large, stone-paved plaza in the middle of the village. The area was filled with people and tables. The surfaces of all the tables were laden with food and stone pitchers of drink.

"Oh, my," was all she could say.

"The meals are communal," he explained as they drew closer. "Helps enhance the feeling of community." He pointed to chairs that were unoccupied. "But, participation is not required. Meals can be taken in the huts if preferred. Most people out here like to eat together."

Sally found her mouth watering as the aroma of the cooked food met her nostrils and the colors of the cut fruits met her eyes.

Devon grabbed a couple of blue and brown stoneware plates from a stack on the end of one of the tables. "Here," he handed her one. "Go get what you want."

Soon they had their plates full and sat down with the others. Sally was about to eat when she noticed the others were sitting and talking with full plates in front of them, but weren't eating. As she looked around wondering what was going on, she noticed a few other people join the group. After they filled their plates, they sat in the remaining empty chairs.

Once they were settled, everyone became silent. All of them looked toward the old man Sally had seen the night before. The white-haired man stood up and raised his hands over the people present. They all closed their eyes with their hands raised, palms upward. Sally was going to ask Devon what was going on. When she turned to look at him, she saw he was doing the same. Not knowing what else to do, she simply stayed silent and watched.

As she looked over the group, she met the eyes of the old man who was watching her. The tanned skin around his bright blue eyes crinkled kindly as he smiled at her. After he nodded at her, he closed his eyes and lifted his face upward. His voice filled the space, strong and steady despite his advanced age. "We gather to share the results of our labors. We congregate to support each other in fellowship. But above all we thank the One on the Path who created all and provides all."

As the words carried over all the people gathered, everyone present sighed deeply together and nodded their heads in silent agreement. Suddenly, Sally felt the presence of a deeply peaceful calm that saturated the place. The feeling intensified until it became almost electric as she felt her nerves tingling and then a warm honey-like sensation that seemed to flood over her.

At first the foreign sensations were pleasant, but then they started to frighten her with their intensity. Goosebumps started to pop up on her arms and legs as her hair stood on end. She didn't understand what was happening. She couldn't see why it was happening. All she knew was that it was a palpable experience and that as she looked at the others present, she could swear they seemed to glow with an inner light. As she looked toward Devon, she could see that his light seemed dimmer than the others, but it was there.

The experience seemed to last a long time to Sally, but in actuality it was a mere minute. Soon the old man clapped his hands and exclaimed, "Blessed be the One and those on the Path!"

The others responded with a single clap of their hands and answered in like, "Blessed be the One and those on the Path!" With that everyone started to smile, talk, and eat.

Sally simply sat for a while, her plate forgotten on the table in front of her. She was still stunned as she thought about what she had experienced as she watched everyone.

"Don't let the food go uneaten," Devon said quietly between mouthfuls. "That is frowned upon. There is no waste out here."

"Oh, um." Sally looked down at her plate. "I'm sorry. I was just thinking." She picked up some fruit and started to chew on it thoughtfully. Leaning toward Devon, she whispered, "That was incredible! What was that?"

Devon looked at her in surprise. "That was the blessing over the food," he said. He chewed on some bread as he studied her face. "What was incredible?"

She picked up some more fruit and chewed on it while she thought of the best response. As soon as she swallowed, she whispered, "There was this powerful presence that I could feel during the blessing. And everyone started to glow, from the inside!"

Devon stopped chewing and looked at her in surprise. The people surrounding them stopped talking to watch her. She saw him look around at the others when they both noticed the quiet spread through the area. Soon everyone was watching and seemed to be waiting for something.

She could see that Devon was confused by their reaction. And that he seemed astounded by what she had said. She saw that he met the eyes of everyone at the table around them, as if he was trying to find some clue as to what was going on. One of them leaned over and whispered something to him. He nodded and turned back to face her. "Can you explain what you experienced?"

As Sally looked around at all the silent people watching her, she started to become frightened. She didn't know if she did something wrong or if she was in danger from some weird cult, like she had read in the old history files. When Devon spoke to her again, she jumped slightly as she turned to him.

"Have I done something wrong?" she asked him. She couldn't bear to see all those people staring at her any longer and dropped her gaze to contemplate her plate.

"No," he assured her. He placed his hand over hers on the table. "You have done nothing wrong." His hand felt abnormally warm to her. She wondered why that was until she realized hers were cold from fear and that she was shaking. "You are not in danger," he stressed to her. He lifted her chin with a finger to look into her eyes. "You are safer with these people than any others."

"Why," she asked, her voice pitched higher with fear. "Why should I be safer here? They don't know me. I don't know anyone but you."

Without either one of them realizing it, the old man had left his seat to move closer to them. "You truly don't know," he stated quietly. The nearness of his voice startled both of them.

Sally looked over her shoulder to meet his bright blue eyes under a shock of white hair. "What?" she was even more confused. "What should I know?"

"Hey," another male voice broke into the silence. "What is going on? Have we missed the blessing?"

Everyone looked to the path leading into the meeting area. A man and woman stood there quietly waiting for explanations.

Devon recognized them immediately. "Mom! Dad!" he shouted as he stood up and ran over to them. "You made it safely!"

After they hugged each other, all the villagers stood up to greet them. They brought out more chairs and made room for them at the table. The old man looked down at Sally once more before he went to greet them. "Don't worry, little one. You will come to know and understand very soon." He patted her shoulder.

His brief touch was like balm to her worried and fearful heart. Her shaking stopped, and she could breathe more easily. Although several of the people still glanced at her curiously, she was released from their intense expectations. Even when she started to eat again, her mind swirled with thoughts of what she might not know about herself. *What could they be wanting from me?* she asked herself over and over.

After his parents were settled, Devon returned to sit by her. "Are you okay?" he asked her gently as he looked her over.

She nodded at him and gave him a small smile. He smiled back and returned to his meal.

As the meal progressed, Sally stayed in her own thoughts as she cleaned her plate. Conversation ebbed and flowed around her. As if they knew, no one asked her any questions. She didn't feel rejected by the inattention and was thankful that they were giving her space.

Her thoughts continued to focus on the Travelers' expectations from her until she became aware that she had lost sight of the experience she had witnessed. As she remembered the powerful presence, she realized that she had buried it with feelings of fear and worry. When she reached out beyond those negative influences, she found that traces of the electric warmth still lingered.

She smiled to herself as she sighed deeply. She didn't know what was going on or what she had gotten herself into, but she suddenly felt that a flash of brilliant color had started to shatter her monochrome existence.

Chapter 11

Blake paced around his living space. He was frustrated and angry. He wanted to know where she was. He wanted to know what she was doing. His jealousy of the other man flared hotly. He had been sent home from his post because of his agitation. He had an appointment with a doctor the next day. He was not acting in accordance with the Society and was going to be treated for it.

All he had wanted to do was to use the Control room's resources to find out which colony Sally had gone to. He was able to access the off-world transport records and found that she had boarded on one of them for the moon colony. But when he contacted the colony, he was told he couldn't talk to her, and they wouldn't give him absolute confirmation she was or wasn't there. He felt that he was being deceived somehow. After he had hit roadblock after roadblock on his quest for information, he hadn't even tried to hide his frustrations and was tagged by the computer.

He also didn't know that he was being watched closely by two occupants in the hidden room.

"He is too volatile," the supervisor was saying nervously to the ancient man in the shadows. "He may need to be terminated."

The old man watched Blake pace the room. *Like a caged tiger,* he thought to himself. His faded blue eyes flicked up to watch the supervisor pace nervously. "You do remember that we choose those with a heightened sense of order and loyalty to be Sentries in the Control room."

The little man quit pacing to face the old man. Beads of sweat still formed on his forehead. He swiped at them nervously with his sleeve. "That is true, sir. But he is making all my crew members nervous. He is constantly in the control room disrupting things."

"Have you asked him why he is acting this way?' the old man asked logically.

"Of course we have," the supervisor said crisply as he stood near him. "He starts to rant and rave about different things and does not answer direct questions clearly."

"Did he say anything about Sally?" he asked quietly.

"The young woman he's been following?" The short man stopped and looked at the old man in surprise.

The silver-haired head nodded slowly. He then sat silently waiting for the answer.

The man stammered a bit as he thought. He finally threw up his hand. "He might have mentioned her a time or two."

"Have you seen the girl recently?" the old man asked quietly.

The small man grew more nervous. He knew the more still and quiet this ancient one was, the angrier he was getting. "I will have our elite team search for her."

"Not just through surveillance," the old man instructed more than asked.

"No, sir!" The supervisor was at attention. "It will be in person."

"Very good." The old man smiled, a feral smile that held no warmth but promised punishment for anyone who failed him.

The superior took that as a dismissal and fairly ran out of the door.

The old man sat back and watched on the large view screen as the supervisor scurried around to talk to certain individuals and whispered instructions to them. They saluted him and started to fan out through the maze of buildings looking for Sally.

The old man continued to watch, pursing his lips as his eyes started to wander away from the screen as he thought. Soon he opened a secret compartment in his chair. From that, he accessed the surveillance system to all the buildings in the Complex. Flicking area after area by on the big screen in his hidden room, he became more and more concerned. *Where is he?* he thought in frustration. "Where did he go," he breathed angrily as screen after screen did not show his quarry. He suddenly had a thought and switched his interest to a new quarry. After not finding the couple he sought, he sat staring at the multiple split-screen views of all the rooms to their apartment. Nothing looked different than any other occupied living space. It looked as if the occupants had simply stepped out to go to work or a brief errand.

He continued to stare at the split screen of the apartment as he tapped the arm of his chair with one finger. The minutes ticked by as he thought; the increasingly hard impact of his fingertip on the padded surface of the arm caused a sharp, staccato sound with each jab.

Suddenly he stopped and toggled his access to the computer mainframe. This was his backdoor to the massive artificial intelligence that he had created and expanded on over the centuries.

After activating his comm, he commanded it to search for the whereabouts of Devon Marshall and his parents, Bruce and Maddie Marshall. After a millisecond, the computer informed him that no person or persons with that name or names existed.

The surprised shock tore through him physically as he stiffened up every muscle, causing his arthritic joints to protest loudly with stabbing pain. He slammed an arm down on the table in front of him, spilling his glass of water all over the table, floor, and himself.

He was so wrapped up in his thoughts that he didn't feel the wetness seeping through his clothes down to his skin. Nor did he register the shock of pain that raced up his arm to his spine. He had suddenly realized that he had been duped and that it could've been going on for centuries.

"Not only did we not eradicate them, we never impacted their strength!" he hissed harshly between clenched teeth. "My brother is behind this," he muttered angrily as he clenched and unclenched his fists, ignoring the resulting spikes of pain. "He is still alive!"

Broin Standhope knew that his brother, Colin, was the only one who could possibly have a backdoor into the system. With this access, he could alter anybody's record, including completely deleting them from the database. He knew it could be done, since he had implanted the ability so he could erase people from the core, thereby from the Society to keep the Society as a whole healthy and happy. This had to be done because of those who, despite the best efforts of the Society reprogramming, were bent on harming others. They were disposed of and completely erased.

Quickly, he asked for the records on Sally Delaine, fearing that they were also deleted. Initially, he felt relief wash over him as it reported that her current location was at the moon base colony. He wanted to believe this information but from what he already found, he had reason to doubt the accuracy. He brought up another split screen showing vast rooms in a secret part of the Complex. This heavily automated area was such a closely guarded secret that only he and the few people that were attendants knew of its existence.

He scanned over banks upon banks of sleeping cylinders in the section labeled 'Moon Colony.' He looked at each of the faces of those who slept but thought they were living, working, or vacationing on the moon. He found one labeled "Sally Delaine" on the small digital display attached to the top. He zeroed in on the face seen through a small glass window inset in the metal container. The woman appeared to be Sally. It was only because of his suspicions being aroused that he stared at her and thought he saw subtle differences. He compared one of Sally's photos from the Society's databanks to the sleeping features.

After several minutes of scrutiny, he sighed in frustration. *If this is a doppelganger, it is a very good one,* he thought as he sat back in his chair. He was hoping she was not. For if she was, then the conspiracy was far deeper and more intricate than he could imagine.

He activated his internal comm to a secret frequency and contacted one of the workers in the sleep room. "Covertly coordinate with health services and do a DNA study on sleeper number..." he zoomed in on the compartment number. "MCC102654. Repeat, do not reveal sample origin." Within seconds, he received confirmation of his orders.

As he rested his chin in his hand with his elbow on the chair arm, he mulled things over in his mind. He had to admit that all he found out in a short time rocked his world. But, as he considered everything, he knew it wouldn't be hugely devastating unless Sally had escaped. *She could bring the whole thing down,* he thought darkly. *I should have destroyed her when she was a child.*

He wiped his face wearily as his anger cooled to a deep disquiet. "But I didn't know for sure. How could anyone?" he muttered aloud into the empty stillness of the hidden room. *I thought she was orphaned after the last Cleansing. So young that the Society could protect and train her. Never knowing what she represented.*

His mind wandered back to when he first met her. Her sea-green eyes, so crystal clear with innocence. Her tousled blonde curls bouncing around her head as she ran to him with chubby arms and hands extended to him.

"Grampapapapa," she had squealed as she hugged him.

He had immediately known that she was of the Standhope lineage. Her features were strongly familial and recognizable, even though he had never known of her existence before then. He quickly surmised that her confusion as to his identity was because she must have been shown images of her ancestor, his brother. "No, dear," he had gently corrected. "I am your great-great-great, too many greats to say, grand uncle."

She had squealed in further delight and hugged him warmly. That long ago encounter had been surprisingly pleasant.

He was brought out of his memories as the computer alerted him that the results were ready. He angrily swept a tear from his cheek. "Sentimental old fool!" he grumbled as he accessed the results.

His mind blocked out anything else as it froze when he saw that the DNA proved the sleeper was not Sally.

Chapter 12

After the morning meal, they all had dispersed to their responsibilities. Since Devon's parents had been slipping out of the Complex for years, they already had their duties. Devon wasn't officially part of the Travelers, so he had no direction to go. He was going to ask some people whom he had known from childhood if he could help them when he was directed to meet with the Wise Man along with Sally.

They were escorted into his simple hut with the small fire in the clay chimney. As they sat down on simple, wooden, but smooth and sturdy chairs, they faced the elderly man.

As soon as they sat down, he studied them in turn and smiled a secret smile. Quickly, his face became stern as he looked down at his interlaced fingers as his hands rested on the rough-hewn table in front of him. He made a decision and looked at Devon first. "Son, where are you on your journey?"

Devon ducked his head as he thought. He knew his answer had to be truthful insofar as he knew without any purposeful deception. He swallowed as he prepared his answer. "Sir, I have been undecided for a long time. And when the Path wouldn't open to me, I felt rejected." He stopped to heave a deep sigh. "But with the encouragement of my parents and the assignment to help Sally understand the Path, I find..." He paused, still seeking the right words. The old man waited patiently as he nodded to encourage him.

Devon had felt Sally draw back away from him as she reacted to the news that she had been an assignment. He wanted to explain right then that it was far from an assignment now. But he couldn't even look at her with the bright blue gaze of the Wise One zeroed in on him. He looked up from his wringing hands. "Sir, I truly want to follow the Path. But it is still closed to me. Will I ever be a Traveler?"

Minutes went by in the complete silence of the hut as the old man continued to study him. Devon couldn't stand the intense gaze and looked back down at his hands. When the old man spoke, what he said surprised him.

"Sally." The Wise One looked at her. Devon saw her jump as she startled to attention. Before that, he had seen how her expression had been downcast and angry. He imagined that she had been drawn out of her thoughts and feelings of betrayal that she had been an assignment. "Yes, sir?" she managed to answer after she swallowed hard as if she had had a lump in her throat.

"Do you see the inner light in Devon?" the Wise Man asked her gently as he watched her with a slight smile on his lips.

Her mouth dropped as she stammered. "Well, yes, I mean, I did there at the blessing." She looked from Devon to the Wise Man. She appeared confused and concerned.

****

Sally was not only confused and concerned, but she was also terrified. She had no idea what was expected of her and was worried whether her answer would help or hurt Devon in the eyes of this ancient one. She had definitely felt the shock of betrayal at hearing that she had been an assignment. But she wanted a chance to talk it over with Devon before she made any judgments about how to react. For the time being, she decided to think of him as only a friend. She had to protect her feelings, especially with all the new experiences she was having. She sighed inwardly and decided that he must have been acting as if he was more than a friend because she was his assignment.

"Do you see it now?" The Wise One asked her quietly. His bright eyes suddenly seemed bluer.

"Well, no. I mean, it was just for a moment. Maybe it was my imagination."

The Wise One smiled patiently at her. "Try to see it again," he firmly suggested.

Sally shifted in her seat slightly and gazed nervously at Devon.

At first she couldn't see the weak inner light she had seen before. She closed her eyes to remember and picture in her mind what she had seen. She wanted not only to will herself to see it, but also to feel the peaceful presence again. As if someone had read her thoughts, she immediately felt a warm, liquid sensation envelop her. Once she felt totally immersed, she relaxed and opened her eyes. There it was. An inner glow – warm and golden.

She looked around the hut and saw that the Wise One fairly blazed with it. There were a few people she hadn't been aware of standing in the shadows of the hut, and their inner light shone strong. When she looked at Devon, he had an inner light. It was not as strong, but it was present and unwavering. Out of curiosity, she looked at herself and saw a flickering light. It was weak and unsteady.

She looked up fearfully into the brilliant blue eyes of the old man again. *Can he see it?* she thought nervously. *What can it mean?* "I can see it now," she answered the Wise One's previous question.

"Tell him what you see," he instructed.

She turned to Devon and met his eyes. She immediately saw the intense worry in his face. She realized that he was worried that she wouldn't see anything. She smiled at him. "Your inner light glows. It is faint but steady."

She saw him gulp once and his eyes brightened with unshed tears. He smiled shakily at her and sighed deeply. "Thank you," he whispered.

"Now," the elderly one spoke to everyone present. "I need to talk to Sally alone." He looked at Devon pointedly. "You can explain how you feel to her later. Right now I need to answer some of her questions."

Devon stood reluctantly and bowed to the old man. Before he left, he reached down to squeeze Sally's hand. "We do need to talk," he whispered. She squeezed his hand back and smiled brightly. As Devon returned the smile, he looked relieved, released her hand, and left the hut.

Before the hut was cleared of everyone except Sally and the old man, the Wise One called for refreshments. Two stone mugs were brought in promptly, and then they were left alone. After Sally took her mug, she looked at it suspiciously.

The old one watched her with a smile. "Yes, it is the same drink as last night. And no, it is not drugged."

"Why did I fall asleep so quickly?' she asked bluntly. "That is not something I usually do."

"It is because you knew instinctively that you were home," the Wise One said quietly.

"What?" Sally was stunned. The word slipped out of her mouth before she realized it. She gulped and looked around the hut. *Home?* she thought, her mind in shock. *How could this be home?*

Her mind suddenly freed itself from its frozen state to whirl in confusion. Childhood memories surfaced in flashcard fashion. Most of them were images of being in the compound but, at random intervals, she saw other people and places she had never remembered seeing before. She looked at the drink in her hand. Had she been drugged?

"You haven't taken a drink yet," the old man's voice had a lilt to it as if he was trying to keep from laughing.

She placed the cup on a nearby table to hold her head in both hands. "What is happening to me?" she whispered hoarsely, not really expecting an answer.

"Realization," the aged voice of the Wise One stated clearly, cutting through her confusion.

She dropped her hands to stare at him. "Realization of what?" she asked, her voice quavering with fright. She wasn't sure if she wanted to hear the answer, but she realized that it could be part of what she had been feeling lately. Something missing.

The Wise One cleared his throat as he sat back in his chair. He took a drink while he seemed to contemplate what to tell her. "Sally," he started as he leaned forward to rest his elbows and hands on the table. "You are a child of this world."

Sally wrinkled her brow in frustrated confusion as she stared at him. She sat back hard against the chair back. "Of course I'm of this world. I am not an alien." She put her hand over her mouth after she realized how snarky that sounded. She couldn't believe she had let down her guard so quickly since she had left the compound.

The white-haired head shook slightly at her mortification. "We do want discipline. But we do encourage true expression."

Sally looked at her hands after she had dropped them to her lap.

She took deep breaths as she composed herself more. She finally felt that she could continue. She met the blue gaze again. "What is it that you mean when you say I am of this world?" she asked quietly, blind to the violent wringing of her hands as she waited for his response.

"You were born out here."

Her eyes widened with shock as they locked eyes. Hers were stormy seas while his were calm skies. "No! That is impossible!"

The lined face smiled at her gently. "So we thought as well. Until you were born and thrived despite the threat of the virus."

Her hands flew to her open mouth as she thought of all the implications. Then questions started to flood her mind. With everything she wanted to say, all she could ask was, "How?"

"You were born with a natural immunity," he said matter-of-factly as he shrugged. "It happens in time as a response to most viruses. But it seemed to never happen with this particular one. Until you," he pointed at her. He dropped his hand as his gaze dropped to the floor. "And there have been no others."

"But hasn't a vaccine been developed?" she asked quickly. "Devon has been coming out of the compound for years. It seems like he was able to come out earlier than ever expected."

The white-haired head nodded as she talked. "Yes, the vaccine worked on him but no others. We didn't risk more young lives when it was clear that his response was a fluke."

Sally sat back and stared at him. "Okay, we are unique," Sally admitted. "How come I was raised in the compound? To be indoctrinated by the Society?" She was surprised how much inner anger flared as she asked.

The Wise One waved aged hands around as he answered. "There are no children out here. You needed those your age to be properly socialized."

Sally couldn't say anything more since that is what she had been taught in child development studies. She nodded that she understood.

"Do you have any further specific questions?" The elderly one asked as he searched her face.

Sally looked away as she tried to sift through many trails of thoughts. She did not know where to start. She looked up to see an interest, an expectation on his face. Suddenly she realized she had a very important question. Why did he look familiar? The feeling was fleeting as her mind couldn't connect why she felt that way, and she felt that she would embarrass herself by asking.

Finally, she shook her head. "I don't know where to start." She thought further. "If I was born out here, how did my parents integrate into Society without problems? Without being found out?"

"That is a very good question," he answered. "The short answer is that they didn't. You were placed in the care of foster parents."

Sally's mouth dropped. She was aghast. She knew she had had parents. She remembered them in the Complex. She remembered when she was a pre-teen, they gone on vacation to one of the off-world colonies and had died in an accident.

"Um," she stammered. She was not sure what to say. "I, I really don't understand." She tugged at a lock of hair that had fallen in her face. She felt as if the ground shifted under her feet. Her reality, as she had known it all her life, was cracking more and threatening to shatter.

The old man's voice, low and gentle, interrupted her thoughts. "I think we have covered enough ground today."

She bolted upright to meet his gaze again. She held the seat of the chair with both hands to steady herself. "No," she managed to croak though a tightened and dry throat. She grabbed her cup and drank deeply. The sweet flavor soothed her dry throat and calmed her nerves. "Please, before we stop, can you tell me who my parents are? Are they alive?"

****

Colin smiled broadly. He was glad and relieved that they could take care of this particular hurdle sooner rather than later. "Yes, they are alive. They are in another village. They have been contacted and are making their way here."

"Really?!" Sally exclaimed, not realizing her voice sounded much like a small girl. The Wise One watched and knew that she couldn't believe her ears with this news. He saw her expressions that mirrored her thoughts as she contemplated all the lonely years with no family and thinking she had only the Society to be her guide in life. He could see that she was excited and apprehensive that she had family but they were unknown to her.

He waited in silence and knew that at some point the anger would rear up. It wasn't long when he saw the conflicting expressions of anger and sorrow. He knew her questions about why didn't they reach out to her to comfort her when she thought her parents had died.

"They wanted to contact you," he said into the deep silence of the hut. "But the danger was too great."

"What danger?" Sally spat out with venom. She suddenly had a focus for her anger. "The Society takes care of everything. What possible danger could there have been?" Her hands let go of her chair to ball into fists that she held in her lap.

"The danger is the Society itself," Colin murmured. He saw that she had tried to shut him out, not wanting explanations that could dissipate her feelings of betrayal and give her reasons to wallow in self-pity. He knew she had heard him as her face fell in astonishment. He saw his chance to explain. "The Society hunts Travelers and executes them." He saw disbelief flash in her eyes. "They killed your foster parents," he stated firmly, bluntly.

Suddenly, to his shocked surprise, she yelled out and grabbed her head. He shouted out for help as he tried to get around the table to get to her. He wasn't fast enough to prevent her from slumping to the floor.

Several people rushed into the hut. "What happened?" they asked anxiously as they talked over each other.

"Get a light," he ordered urgently. One was brought in. He saw that she was translucent pale, while her pupils were fully dilated. She was sweating as she shivered, and her pulse and breathing were rapid and shallow.

Another person arrived. "What is going on?"

Colin looked up into the eyes of Devon and Trevor standing near him. He noticed other villagers hugging the walls, giving them room. "My brother is what's going on. He placed a memory lock on her. It's trying to kill her!"

"What can we do?" Devon's voice shook as he picked her up in his arms to hold her close. "She's so cold!" he exclaimed as he grabbed nearby blankets to wrap around her. He was trying to warm her as best he could. As he looked anxiously at her face, Colin knew he wanted her to revive and see that he was there for her.

"Put her on the pallet over near the wall," Colin ordered. He turned to Trevor. "We need to have her enter the Path. She needs power from the One to battle this."

Trevor shook his head. "I don't know who could reach her to lead her. From what I've been told, she hasn't had any experience of trying to access the Path, just the basic knowledge."

"She's more powerful than you think," Colin interjected forcefully. "She saw the inner light! Who sees that?"

Trevor nodded. "Not everyone. It is a very rare ability."

"She needs someone she can trust. Someone she can recognize and follow," Colin said as he pulled another warm, roughly woven blanket over her.

"What about Bruce?" Trevor interjected. "He was her instructor."

"Maybe. Maybe," Colin muttered as he thought furiously, *We cannot lose her!* "How fast can we get him here?" He looked down to see Sally was fading fast. "We don't have time."

As he was about to grab her hands to see if he could connect with her, to escort her to the Path himself, he saw Devon clearly since her collapse. He was holding tightly onto her hands as his head bent over her. Colin moved away slightly as he felt the barest sensations of the Path opening.

Trevor was about to step out of the hut. "Wait, Trevor," he whispered loudly enough for him to hear but not enough to disturb Devon.

Trevor walked over to stand by him as they both watched. Colin's eyes grew misty. Devon was finally joining the Path. All he had needed was a reason beyond himself.

Chapter 13

Devon had no idea what he was doing. His horror at seeing Sally lying on the floor nearly dead brought out a fierce, protective instinct in him. When he heard the Wise One proclaim what had happened and what needed to be done, he had a new determination to try to join the Path. He was still afraid of failing and losing her, but he hoped he could help while they got his father.

As he physically held her hands, he accessed the part of his being that he had been told could enter and experience the Path. Soon he stood at the door to the Path, the one that had never opened for him on his past attempts.

As he waited by the door, he hoped that he had taught her enough to get to this point, the area the Travelers had named the 'The Seeker's Spot.' It was the point anyone could achieve if they had even heard the name 'Path of Totality' and attempted to find it.

He didn't know what to call the form or describe the state that those who sought or traveled the Path took. To him, he looked like he was made up of a version of pure energy. It was shaped like his body but seemed less confining than his physical form.

After a while, he fretted over the delay and wondered how he could find Sally in this different realm. As he turned his back to the door, he continued to cast his mind out to find her. He felt enormous relief when he finally saw a female energy form approach him.

He knew it was Sally even though the energy form was pale and frail. His worry intensified as she drew closer. She looked worn and tired as she weakly stumbled to him. He ran to her as she fell short of the door. When he gathered her into his arms, he knew he was rapidly running out of time, her energy was spiking and unstable. He rushed back to the door as he hugged her close.

Grimly, he faced the door again. To him it always seemed to be more like a dark energy barrier than a typical door. He shifted Sally so he could knock on the surface and call out for admittance. He used the same words and phrases he had always used, the ones that he had been taught to use, the ones that had never worked for him before. This time, he uttered them with a forceful purpose and urgency that he had never felt before. He had also added a heartfelt appeal to the One for a life that was failing.

The barrier immediately dropped. He stood for a moment in amazement that the way was open. As he clutched Sally closer to him, he stepped through the portal onto an energy path that alternated color as it stretched into the distance. As he strode forward, he kept glancing down at Sally and hoped he could find the One quickly.

As he moved along the path, he saw other paths, like his, all around him that alternated colors but were never the same color at the same time. He also noticed that all of them drew closer together as they extended into the distance. As he walked farther along, he could see ahead where all the paths joined a single path, one that was made up of pure, blinding white light.

He quickened his pace and broke into a trot as he tried to look further ahead to find the One he sought, but he couldn't see anything past the blazing light. He wasn't sure what the One looked like, but he had been told he would know him once he saw him.

When he reached the white path, he stopped, still trying to see ahead. He didn't wait too long as he felt he had to trust that the One was there, close by. He hugged Sally as he stepped blindly onto the Path.

Immediately, he felt electric energy flow through him and into Sally. With it came an enveloping peace, indescribable joy, and incredible calm. He looked at Sally and saw that she seemed a bit stronger. He continued to move forward with more confidence. He trusted that the One would guide his feet to Him.

Once he decided on fearless trust, he immediately saw a tall, golden figure approach him. He appeared to be living, molten gold. Devon didn't have to ask; he knew…this was the One.

Chapter 14

Broin Standhope shook off the shock caused by the revelation that Sally had escaped. *Apparently she is planning on coming back,* he contemplated, *since her records are still intact and they had slipped a double in her place.*

Broin pondered his next move as he sifted through the new information. As he thought, he stared unseeing at the screen showing the control room. His eyes slowly focused on it as the activity of the personnel within the area became agitated. He quickly pinpointed the problem: Blake was there and causing problems. His eyes widened in interest as he sat up to watch the situation more closely.

They were about to escort Blake out of Control and to the mental health department when Broin toggled his personal comm. "Put Blake in my office," he ordered. "I want to talk to him." As he watched, he saw his orders being followed when the security team wrestled the agitated young man out of the room and into the hall. Sitting back as he contemplated the new development, the barest seed of an idea formed. As it began to take root and grow, the old man smiled in his sinister way. He had just figured out how to take care of two problems.

He slowly stood up from his chair and walked with the care of the very aged. As he made his cautious way out of the secret room and down the hall, he muttered, "Should have made sure this long life was without the aches, pains, and problems of the old."

When he entered into his office, he found a very angry Blake along with two security officers who had to continue to restrain the struggling man. Broin studied the young man as he passed by him to make his way to his chair behind the massive, black plastic desk. He could see the fanatical look in Blake that he had seen in many of the youths of late. His deep sigh was masked by a soft puff of air as his deeply cushioned chair adjusted to his weight as he sat down.

As he continued to inspect Blake's body language, he steepled his fingers in front of him and tapped his chin as he thought. He could see that there was danger using this youth for his plan, but he didn't want to risk anyone else.

He gestured to the guards. They forced Blake to a straight-backed metal chair and planted him in it. The young man loudly protested the treatment and fought hard against the guards as he refused to stay in the chair.

"Either sit quietly so we can talk like adults, or I will have you bound to the chair," Broin said calmly. His ice-cold tones affected the young man as he expected it would.

Blake stopped struggling and met his steady, penetrating gaze. Whatever he saw made him blanch with fear and start to tremble. He opened his mouth to say something, but stopped when Broin raised his hand for silence.

"Do you know who I am?" Broin started his interview.

Blake swallowed hard and nodded. "You are the Ancient One. You are the creator of this Complex and the Society."

"That is true." Broin signaled the guards to leave. They immediately turned to march out of the room. The door shut firmly behind them.

Broin watched as Blake glanced around him and saw they were gone. He found it interesting that instead of relaxing, the young man tensed up even more.

"Why were you causing a disturbance in Control?" Broin asked as he continued to study him.

Blake gulped and furrowed his brow. Broin could see he was trying to formulate an acceptable answer. He banged his fist on the desk. The youth startled and stared at him. "I want honest answers without thought!" His voice rose as he firmly instructed him.

At first, Blake looked confused then he nodded. He swallowed hard then offered, "I will endeavor to try." His voice was high pitched with stress. In response, the computer tried to interject counsel.

"Oh shut up!" Broin shouted at the Society. "Cease operations in this room immediately!" he ordered. The computer acknowledged the orders and became silent. He looked around to see that all the indicator lights on the surveillance devices were dark.

"Now, we can talk," he said as he turned back to Blake.

Blake was looking around the room in astonishment. His mouth gaped open as his wide eyes studied the room and the man in front of him. "I have never seen anyone who could do that," he ventured to say cautiously.

Broin grunted as he settled back into his chair and steepled his fingers again. "No one can," he said softly, "but me."

Blake nodded once. His eyes shone with respect and near worship of the man in front of him.

Broin saw it and sighed. He would tolerate this as long as he could use this youth to his purposes. As soon as the task was complete, he would have to have this one eliminated. If he wasn't destroyed on the mission he had in mind.

His mind drifted to think of the disturbing data on how higher percentages of the youth population became unstable with each subsequent generation since the development of the Society. He couldn't understand why it was happening. And those he had researching it either had unacceptable answers or couldn't find the cause at all.

His focus snapped back onto Blake. He needed to see if this deluded young man would cooperate even though he was showing advanced symptoms of instability.

"Back to my question," he said as he pointed at Blake. "Why were you causing problems in the Control Room?"

Blake met his gaze steadily. "I was trying to find someone. She had disappeared."

"And who was this someone?"

"Sally Delaine. She works with the elderly."

Broin nodded solemnly. "And why is it important to find her?"

Blake looked away for a moment as he blinked rapidly. He looked down at the floor. "I am interested in her."

"For what purpose?"

"I think I love her," the young man muttered as he continued to look at the floor. He blushed as he fidgeted in the hard chair.

Broin tapped the desk with his fingers. *He really thinks he loves her,* he thought analytically. *Ah, well, it will suit my purpose.* He made a show of activating his keyboard that rose from a hidden compartment from his desk top. He tapped the keys even though he knew what he would find. "The computer shows that she is at our moon colony."

"I know that!" Blake answered angrily. "But I don't understand why I can't talk to her and the man she went with is no longer showing in our system!" His red face became even more red as he scowled in anger. His fists clenched at his sides.

My, my, he is jealous, Broin thought. *Interesting.* "Who is she supposed to be with?"

"A Devon Marshall," Blake snapped the name out as if he wanted to bite the man.

Broin keyed in the name. He knew it wouldn't come up with anything. "The Society doesn't have a record of such a man."

"I know!" Blake pounded his thighs with his fists. "It is wrong. It is wrong!" He met Broin's eyes with a bleak expression. "Why is it incorrect? The Society can't be wrong! The Society is perfect! It must be! It has to be protected!" He looked wildly around the room. "You must see! You have control over the Society so you must see how it must be perfect!"

Broin sat back to ponder the intensity of the young man's devotion. He weighed the importance of the task he had in mind against the potential of it backfiring if this young man's loyalty and complete trust in the Society was shattered. *It could happen,* he thought guardedly, *if he were to stumble onto more of the Society's secrets.*

He made a decision. He would have to move forward to get Sally back. He would have to hope Blake didn't discover any other discrepancies with the Society.

"Blake," he started to say as he met the young man's eyes. "I have an important mission for you. It is to save the Society." He saw the young man stiffen to attention as he sat, his tirade forgotten in an instant. His eyes widened and started to glow with purpose and dedication.

"Yes sir!" Blake responded quickly and forcefully. "I am the man for the job!"

Broin forced himself to smile favorably at him. "Yes, I think you are." He tapped the desk as he laid out the plans he had in mind. "We need to find those that are against Society and want to destroy it."

"Yes, sir!" Blake responded. "Do we have intel on who they are?"

"We do," Broin confirmed. "There are some amongst us, but there are many outside the Complex."

"Outside?" Blake's eyes were wide and staring. "How can they exist outside?"

Broin sighed inwardly. The programming of the Society to not want to seek outside of the Complex was strong. "They have found ways. There are means to protect anyone we send out there."

Blake nodded. "I see. The Society protects its own."

"Yes." Broin was fascinated by the complete trust Blake showed. "Yes, it does."

"When do I start and what exactly are the mission objectives?"

"You start immediately. Mission objectives are to destroy anyone that is outside of the Complex."

"I see." Broin could see Blake thinking hard about how to go about the mission. "Am I to have backup?"

"Not at this time,' Broin said. "The fewer sent out, the faster the recon and the element of surprise will stay intact."

"So, I am to recon first?" Blake asked, his brow furrowed in confusion.

Broin belatedly realized that the inconsistency in his orders was going to make Blake suspicious. He quickly recovered. "Yes, find out all their locations and report back. From your report we will determine the best course of action. If you find the one that is missing from the records, kill him immediately. There will be no need to wait to eliminate him."

Blake's eyes glowed at the prospect of destroying his rival. "Yes, sir!"

"And, if Sally is with them instead of at the moon colony, bring her back."

When Blake's face went absolutely still, Broin held his breath. He knew he had taken a risk and had no idea what reaction Blake would have to this request. The idea the computer was wrong about her location could shatter his faith.

"So, these dissidents may have altered records in the system?" he asked urgently, his expression intense.

"That may be. Look at what you may have uncovered." Broin stated with enough lightness in his voice to sound congratulatory.

Blake puffed out his chest in pride and nodded. "You believe me," he stated with satisfaction.

Broin wanted to heave a great sigh and roll his eyes in reaction to the ignorant devotion. But instead, he said, "I do." He nodded approvingly at the young man. "We must move to save the Society."

"Yes," Blake agreed heartily. "We must save the Society."

"You will be provided with equipment and protection for the outside. You will be escorted to a secret exit point."

"There is an exit?" the young man was surprised.

Broin felt like shouting at Blake's stupidity that of course there was an exit! They had to have gotten into the Complex at the beginning somehow. Apparently the Travelers were getting out! Before he got distracted in wondering how they were doing that, he said, "It was how the original inhabitants came into the Complex. It still exists but has been closed for centuries."

"I see." Blake looked pleased that he would be allowed to know an ancient secret. "You can trust me!"

"Yes, I know." Broin grew weary of the youthful exuberance of one who would be sacrificed for his own aims. He needed to end this exchange. "I will let the appropriate people know of this mission. Tell no one else."

"Yes, sir."

Broin pushed a button on his desk. The guards that waited outside came in. "Take Blake to the supervisor." They nodded as Blake sprang out of the chair with his head held high and followed them out with a strutting gait.

After they left, Broin used his keyboard to send a coded message to the supervisor about what to equip Blake with and the orders that he was to be escorted outside. He didn't fill him in on the full plans. Those he would keep to himself and dole it out in portions to a select few so they wouldn't realize what was happening.

After that was done, he wearily rose from his desk and moved through a hidden portal in the wall into his living space.

As he lay down, the dark voice came again to him. "Time to destroy all of the light!" He could hear it with his ears as it threaded like a tentacle through his mind.

Grimly, he turned on his side and closed his eyes. He had thought he had destroyed the light, but it had still remained. How could he snuff it out forever? He pondered this dark purpose as he tried to rest.

Several hours passed, and he was restless and very weary. As he rolled to his other side, he realized he hadn't rested well in centuries. Not since the plan had been put into place to completely control mankind. He felt as if he had been promoted to a god-like status with this purpose. But somehow he had been driven to make decisions he never thought he would have to make. *Like who lives and who dies,* he thought without remorse or any feelings.

Rolling onto his back, he reached over to the control panel on the wall. "Rest formula 154," he ordered. A small vial appeared in the compartment underneath the panel. Snapping it open he dropped the contents on his tongue. Placing the used vial back in the compartment for recycle, he lay back and allowed the combination of drugs to induce a dreamless sleep.

Chapter 15

Slowly, Devon became aware of his surroundings as he felt the physical weight of Sally in his arms. He wasn't sure when he had scooped her up to hold her tightly, but it didn't matter; he was in no hurry to let her go. After he opened his eyes, he looked down at her to see her sleeping peacefully. He smiled in response because he knew she was out of danger.

As he sniffed the air, he looked around in the dimly lit hut. The atmosphere was thick with the sweet aroma of multiple prayer candles. After blinking several times, the shadows around him slowly came into focus. He was able to make out many faces reflecting light from the flickering flames of the candles they held. It was obvious to him that the small hut was packed with people. *Solidarity of the Traveler community,* he thought as he nodded and smiled as he deeply inhaled the calming fragrance and sighed.

He winced slightly as his arm and leg muscles started to spasm. Reluctantly, he had to admit that he needed to let Sally go and move around. After gently placing her on the thick pallet, he sat back on his heels and wiped his face with a sleeve. He was exhausted but in a good way. He glanced at her to be sure she was comfortable and smiled again. He knew she would be okay. All she needed now was to sleep. A natural, healing sleep.

He looked up and around at all the people again. This time they all had their eyes open and were watching him expectantly. "She will be okay." He kept his voice low, not wanting to bother Sally's slumber. "The One removed the lock on her memory."

He looked around, seeking a particular face: the Wise One. He had been tasked with giving him information that was for his ears only. He needed to speak to him privately and wanted to do so as soon as possible. He was so disturbed by his thoughts of the news he had to relate to the old man that he hadn't noticed a couple sigh in relief at his announcement that the One had helped Sally.

Belatedly, he was aware of their presence as people around them hugged them and murmured encouragements before they filed out. Soon all that remained were the Wise One, his parents, and the two he assumed were Sally's birth parents.

The Wise One spoke first. "Son, let Sally's parents attend to her. It is their right and privilege." Devon nodded at them and stood up. He had never seen them before but allowed the tall man and the shorter woman to hug him tightly. They both whispered a heartfelt thank you to him before they released him to go sit with their daughter.

After he moved away to give them room and privacy, the Wise One said, "Now, let your parents attend to you." The old man smiled and patted his shoulders. "Welcome Traveler!"

Devon smiled as realization and peace washed over him. He had been accepted and now was on the Path. As he turned into the arms of his parents, he could see tears in their eyes as they joyfully embraced him.

As he embraced his mom, he looked over her shoulder to meet the Wise One's eyes. In response, he nodded that he knew they needed to talk. With a gesture to the doorway with a wave of his arms, the old man indicated he was to celebrate with his parents.

Devon nodded at him slightly as his mother released him so that his father could hug him. He knew that he had to wait until the Wise One was ready to hear what he had found out. He left the hut with his arms linked with his parents' as they stepped out into a beautiful day with the sun blazing in a cloudless sky and bird song filling the air.

****

Within the hut, Colin watched Sally's parents sit on either side of their daughter as she lay on the thick pallet. Each one of them held a hand as they waited for her to wake up. He could see they were heartbroken by what their daughter had gone through. He also knew from talking with them that from the day they made the hardest decision of their lives and sent her into the Complex as a toddler, they worried about how she would respond to them after all the silent years.

He sat cross-legged on the ground as he settled beside Sally, near her feet. Closing his eyes, he petitioned the One for Sally's complete recovery and a peaceful reunion with her birth parents.

****

Trevor had wanted to stay in the hut, to give his support in prayer. But he had been urgently summoned to the Watchers' room by a nervous messenger. He ran to the room nestled inside a grassy hill and entered the electronically illuminated dark. He watched the screens for a moment, noting one was dark.

"Aaron, what is happening?" he asked urgently. "Your messenger didn't tell me much but that I needed to be here."

The older Traveler was on duty. He swiveled partially around in his chair. "No good, I assure you."

"Show me the recordings," Trevor ordered as his throat tightened up. Not much bothered this particular Watcher. The few words Aaron had uttered were uncharacteristically strained.

Trevor watched the unfolding scenes with growing unease. He watched the scene with Blake in the control room; the subsequent sequence of events in the secret room as he saw Broin access computer files and show images on his view screen.

When he saw the sleepers, intense horror flooded through his being. His thoughts bogged down with the realization that they did not know of this dark secret of the Society. His throat clenched up further as he barked an order, "Find this secret Complex. We must get Pat out!"

He was dimly aware of the scrambled activity behind him as the door to the Watchers' room rapidly opened and closed.

He watched the scene in Broin's office, another area they recently were able to access through the existing surveillance system. He watched tensely with clenched fists until the screen went dark. Broin had stopped surveillance in his office. "What are they talking about?" he muttered between clenched teeth to no one in particular.

Aaron looked up as Trevor leaned over his shoulder. "Sir, if I may state points to consider." Trevor nodded for him to continue.

The Watcher tapped in commands on his keyboard. All the screens were activated to show scenes of interest. He intoned a narrative as he highlighted the scenes. "Blake's interest in Sally unraveled things," he said as the control room scene played out. "This drew the attention of Broin, Colin's brother who, until recently, we didn't know still pulled the strings in the Complex."

He keyed the computer to zoom in and highlight Broin's recent computer searches. "Here is where Colin's brother discovers that Bruce, Maddie, and Devon are missing and Sally has been substituted."

Aaron swiveled in his chair to fully face Trevor and meet his eyes. "He is not stupid. He knows from these revelations that we have deeply infiltrated the Complex and have had access to the computer." Trevor nodded for him to continue.

"In addition, we find that those who think they are living or visiting off-world are not." He flashed the video of the sleeper room on the screen. "We have sent people to the colonies," he growled lowly. "Obviously, they have not gotten off world. Are they part of the sleepers or have they been disposed of?"

Trevor nodded tightly at him, feeling the other man's agitation and knowing it was because he had friends and family that were supposed to be off world, just as he did. "We have revealed a dark secret in the Society that no one knew about," Trevor said to all the Watchers in the room. "Although this is extremely upsetting and it looks like our operations have been exposed, we have to extract those people out of the sleeper units as soon as possible."

He stared at the video feed of the secret Complex as he thought more about what they learned. "I do have a question. Why the need for this deception?" he asked as he looked around the dark room to see that everyone was watching him. Their faces glowed faintly blue from the lights of the control panels. "What happened to the colonies?"

A gasp of realization swept through everyone in the room. He saw the reactions as many turned to look at each other. Some muttered quietly amongst themselves. He knew that questions had surfaced in everyone's minds about how, when, what, why…

"Could the virus have affected them?" one of the Watchers asked in the hubbub of frantic whispering. "Being a contained society in their bio-domes, with no escape, could everyone have died?"

Trevor rubbed his brow as he thought. His head was beginning to ache with the building tension of the situation. "As soon as we realized the TEENA virus had been released, all travel to the colonies was stopped. Once it was deemed safe for those in the Complex to travel, it was resumed and nothing amiss had been reported."

"Could that have been when it happened?" another Watcher asked.

"Or," Aaron spoke up. "Did the off-world colonies cut off access to them because of the virus and later the Society took advantage of it by using their existence as a deception, another illusion of freedom?"

Trevor looked at him intently as he nodded. "That is possible." He started rubbing the back of his neck. "We would have to try to contact them to see what the true situation is."

Everyone in the room became silent after he spoke. After a few minutes, one Watcher pointed out, "How? We thought we were in contact with the colonies through our people."

Another interjected, "Only when they got back did they report. No one reported anything while they were there. It was deemed more secure to wait until they got back."

Trevor nodded as he listened. He started to rub his forehead as the pain increased. He felt everyone was starting to see that the deception could have been going on for centuries. He dropped his hand to his side as he sighed heavily, suddenly feeling weary. "I must report this to the Wise One," he said as he looked around at everyone in the room. "I still want that secret sleeper room found and a plan for how to extract our people." He looked up at the screens that still showed scenes from the Complex except one. "And I want to know what plans Broin has for Blake."

The room was silent once again as they all returned to their regular duties, doing whatever they could to gain information needed for the tasks that were laid before them.

Aaron swiveled in his chair to face Trevor again. "I wouldn't doubt that Broin would use Blake's fascination with Sally to find us so he could destroy us," he stated in clipped, concise tones.

Trevor dropped his hands to clench them at his sides. He ground his teeth as he thought of what the Watcher had said. "You speak truth, Brother Traveler. After all, it is his fault all this has happened." He brusquely turned to leave. "He would have absolutely no qualms about using a misdirected boy to do his dirty work," he muttered angrily as he left the room to go find Colin.

Chapter 16

It was the dead of night. Everyone in the village was asleep. All except the Watchers doing their duty in the room full of glowing monitors and the three men who sat in the Wise One's hut illuminated by the small fire in the clay fireplace. Colin, Trevor, and Devon sat in a small circle on the packed dirt floor. A single, honey-scented candle stood unlit in the middle.

"I have summoned you two here," Colin spoke, his aged voice full of authority and wisdom even when quietly uttered, "to discuss your respective revelations." He looked to Trevor. "I am sorry to have put off your important news earlier, but too many people could have heard." He held a hand up when he saw Trevor open his mouth to say something. "No. My intent is not to keep secrets. I simply need to be informed and have time to develop a plan, and then all will be revealed." He emphasized the word 'all.'

He looked from one to the other as he waited to see who would speak first. Devon looked to Trevor. He could see that Trevor looked stressed and worried. He felt his news could wait.

Trevor took the silence as an invitation to speak. "The Watchers have revealed a series of events that have led to the revelation of more of the Society's dark secrets." He paused as he looked up at Colin, his eyes full of misery and fear. "Your brother will move against us very soon, and our people in the Complex and off world are in danger."

Colin nodded at the pronouncement. "Details," he stated calmly.

Trevor revealed bit by bit how he came to the revelations. He described Broin's interaction with Blake and the subsequent disappearance of the young man from all the monitors. He also revealed the sleepers in the secret part of the Complex.

Devon watched and listened with horror as Trevor continued. He first worried for Sally then it grew to encompass them all as the scope of the danger grew wider and wider.

When Trevor was done, Colin sat hunched over as he stared at the unlit candle, fingers interlaced and resting against his lips as he thought. Great sadness emanated from him as he absorbed the news quietly and concentrated on the next step.

After a while, he looked at Devon. "Your news, young man."

Devon cleared his throat. "After hearing all this," he said, gesturing to Trevor, "my news seems trivial."

"It is news, nonetheless. A little bit of news or fact does not mean it is insignificant," Colin instructed him.

"Yes, Wise One," Devon hung his head. After a few moments to organize his thoughts, he looked up into Colin's blue eyes. "While I was on the Path, the One told me to tell you that your brother travels in the darkest black." He looked down at the dirt floor embarrassed. "It seemed so important at the time. Now that I say it, it seems hardly worth bothering you." He lifted his eyes enough to stare at the candle and didn't see Colin's reaction. But Trevor did.

"Colin, what is wrong?" he asked quietly.

Colin was sitting ramrod straight while his eyes focused on a faraway point. He hands were clenched in his lap as he started to rock slightly back and forth.

Devon and Trevor watched him for a few moments. When they glanced at each other, Devon could see that the other man was as worried as he was and wondered what it could mean.

Soon the old man snapped out of it. Looking at Devon, he said, "My son, your news confirms the first and is the direst of all."

Devon looked at Trevor then back at Colin. "What does it mean?"

Colin spread his hands over the prayer candle, a flame immediately blossomed from the wick. Devon's jaw dropped. He didn't know such power existed.

The old man ignored his reaction and started to speak in a low voice. "Ever since the days of Creation, there have been two paths for humanity to choose from." He waved a hand. Sparking from the candle flame and streaming overhead were brightly colored strands. These strands converged and melded into a single, brilliant white strand.

Devon stared wide-eyed as his mouth gaped open. "That's the Path! That's what I saw!"

Colin and Trevor smiled indulgently at him. "Yes, once we all pass the door, this is where we are."

Devon had to ask, "Why does the One place a door to block access to the Path?"

Colin shook his head while Trevor looked down and stifled a sigh. "Devon, why would the One, who wants good for all His Creation, want to block us from Him?"

Devon stared at them in confusion and shrugged. He had no answer.

Trevor spoke up. "The door of disbelief is not placed by the One; it is created by ourselves."

Devon looked from one to the other in open-mouthed astonishment. "I was keeping myself from joining the Path?"

They both nodded at him.

"When someone else's life was on the line," Colin offered, "you broke through your disbelief to take her to the One."

Devon leaned back on his arms in thunderstruck wonder. Then he smiled. "So she doesn't have to find her way now."

Colin shook his head as he moved his hands again. As he spread his hands from the lighted paths outward, it was as if he removed a veil from the area around the white path and the ones of bright colors. "She will have to find her own way. No one can enter the Path on the basis of someone else's belief or faith."

Devon heard his words and nodded that he understood while he watched with fascination as the scope of the revelation expanded. He saw the emergence of other lines that were darker, duller, going from grey to dark grey then black until the darkest of all – obsidian. There were many obsidian paths that veered sharply away from the white path until they faded into oblivion.

"Behold, this is the entirety of the spiritual continuum," Colin said as he raised both hands as if he could hold it all in his palms. "This is a representation of the spiritual world that we mortals can understand and interact with. It is granted and allowed by the One." He placed his hands in his lap as he looked from Devon to Trevor. After a few moments, he looked up again at the spiritual continuum. "This revelation came after much seeking for divine help and understanding in the days following the destructive effects of the virus and the resulting war."

Devon stared at the darker paths. He gulped heavily as he felt a deep foreboding. "What are those darker paths?" he asked quietly, frightened of the answer.

"Those are any other paths that are not the One True Path." Colin placed his hands in his lap as he looked from the spiritual continuum to Devon. "The two choices for humanity are to follow the true Path, the path of light. Or to not follow the true Path; that is to follow anything other than the light, which would be one of the dark paths."

"There are so many," Devon stated, feeling overwhelmed with what he saw. Suddenly, understanding took hold. "I was on one of those, wasn't I?" he asked as he looked to Colin and Trevor. They nodded solemnly.

"So are many in the Complex," Colin said sadly. "Because they are not aware of anything else."

Trevor shifted uncomfortably. "Why are you showing him this?" he asked sternly. "Very few of the Travelers ever see the full scope of what is going on."

Colin met his eyes and nodded. "True. But the message was given to him. Therefore it was his right to know and understand the importance of what he was entrusted with."

The other man nodded his understanding and bowed his head. Devon thought he acted as if he was not fit enough to see the revelation.

Colin smiled at Devon. "This is the first he's seen of the entirety of the spiritual continuum." His face grew serious as his voice dropped to continue quietly. "It is a heavy responsibility. There a very few who can be exposed to the knowledge of the dark paths and not be tainted by it. Knowledge brings temptation, which can be a hook the dark one uses to trap human souls."

Devon nodded as he contemplated what the Wise One said and took the warning to heart. When he thought about the message he had been given by the One again, it dawned on him what it meant. "Your brother is on an obsidian path?"

The unshed tears in Colin's eyes sparkled in the candle light. "Yes. He has totally immersed himself in ways contrary to the One."

He sighed heavily then wiped away the image of all the paths with a wave of his hand. All that remained was the single flame of the prayer candle to light their faces. "And that is why he is the pawn of the dark one to deal so wrongly with his fellow man."

Devon looked around uneasily. He was suddenly aware of a great sense of wrongness. He almost could feel something lurking in the dark corners. A cold shiver crept up his spine.

Trevor noticed his uneasiness. "Revelation of the dark paths can cause attention from those things that inhabit those paths," he said quietly. "I may never have seen the dark paths before, but I knew they existed and what travels on them."

Devon looked to Colin, who had closed his eyes with his hands resting on his knees. He leaned toward Trevor. "So there is something there? It's not my imagination?"

Trevor nodded as he also looked uneasily into the dark corners. "That's why looking into the dark paths is forbidden for those of the true Path."

"What do we do?" Devon was growing increasingly fearful. Trevor shook his head.

"We know we are stronger through the One," Colin interrupted their fretful whisperings. "And we learn to fight them." He started to glow with intense light as he raised his arms. "And this is the core of the matter and why you both are here. If you do not know of the danger, how do you know to fight?" He raised his hands further as a strong wind started to blow through the hut. "And if you don't know you can fight, how do you learn?" He hadn't expected them to answer as they sat staring in awe of the blaze of power emanating from the ancient man.

Suddenly, his voice rang out with authority, "Be gone!" A blinding flash exploded from him and spread through the hut and beyond.

As their vision cleared, Devon and Trevor saw Colin sitting on the floor with his head bowed and hands clasped in prayer. The only thing that had changed was that every candle in the hut was lit and burning bright.

Devon saw Trevor look around and relax. When he stared into all the now brightly lit corners and no longer sensed anything creeping around them, he also relaxed. He was quick to realize that the sense of fear had vanished. He began to wonder if the fear had been his reaction or something generated by the presence of whatever came from the dark paths.

As the fragrance of all the prayer candles intensified in the hut, Devon and Trevor looked at each other and then at Colin. Colin's bright blue eyes were open and watching them. "And now you know the enemy and the power of the One."

Devon was momentarily confused and dazzled by what he had just witnessed. "Are you the One?" he asked timidly.

Colin shook his head. "No, I am not. What I am is what everyone on the Path can be. A tool for the One to use." As he bowed his head again, all the candles went out except the one in the middle of the circle. He looked up and met Devon's and Trevor's eyes. "Retire for the night," he instructed them. "I will commune with the One on behalf of my brother."

He looked down as they stood up and brushed the dirt from their loose fitting pants. As they approached the doorway of the hut, Colin had additional instructions for them. "Trevor, set the guard. Devon, visit with Sally tomorrow. She will need a face she knows."

"She is awake?" Devon asked quickly.

Colin nodded as he smiled gently. "She is awake and whole. She is getting to know her parents. Do not intrude too heavily on her time. Be there as she adjusts to her new reality." His face grew serious as his gaze intensified. "Teach her of what you have seen tonight. She needs to be aware of the dark one and the dark paths."

"Should she have been here to see this?" Devon questioned.

Colin shook his head. "She is still recovering from her near death experience. She needs more time to be able to properly handle viewing the continuum. She can learn all she needs to know from you. But do not forget, she needs to be forewarned of these dark paths."

Devon nodded back solemnly. "Yes, Wise One, I will tell her of this," he promised as he bowed. "I will not forget," he emphasized.

Devon and Trevor nodded to Colin, then stepped through the doorway. They didn't speak to each other as they went their separate ways. Each of them had his mission and was deep in his own thoughts as they considered what they just saw and heard.

In the hut, Colin stared into the steady flame of the candle, breathing in the soothing, honeyed fragrance. "A three-stranded cord is not easily broken," he whispered to himself. "But adding the fourth strand will make it stronger."

He thought of the threads intertwining into a rope strong enough to defeat the dark one and the dark purpose of the Society. The One on the Path, the experienced Travelers, the young Travelers, and those in the Complex who would come to believe.

He could sense that events would shortly be in full motion that would end the centuries of waiting for action. "The fate of humanity will soon be in the balance," he whispered into the silence of his hut. Closing his eyes as he relaxed his body with his hands clasped in his lap, he joined the Path and communed with the One.

Chapter 17

Blake was frozen in absolute terror. After his interview with the ancient one of the Complex, he was quickly bundled up by the members of an elite security force he never knew existed in the Society. They thrust him in body armor and gave him ancient percussive weapons that he had used in his early days of training for sentry duty but hadn't seen since.

After the quick gearing up and even quicker verification of his mission objectives, he was ushered at a quick march to the oldest part of the Complex that was no longer in use. After making their way through the dimly lit hallways that were slowly decaying and collapsing in on themselves, Blake was placed in front of a rusted metal door.

"Stand there!" ordered a mechanized voice uttered from the face mask of the leader of the squad. The few men who escorted him this far were outfitted in environmental suits with their own oxygen supply. He looked around and wondered where his was.

"Don't I get an environmental suit?" he asked, mystified by the rush of it all.

"You have been deemed safe to go outside." The disembodied voice answered impatiently.

Blake stepped away from the door. He was getting angry. "How could I have been deemed safe? No tests have been run. There has been no time!"

Thickly gloved hands roughly positioned him back in front of the door. "There is no question. It is safe for you."

Before he could respond, the door started sliding upward. The screaming and grating of an ancient mechanism pulled the metal, breaking rusted joints and areas that had melded together over the long span of time since it was last opened. As the door first cleared the floor, opening up a small gap, a quick rush of air expelled, as if the building sighed hugely and released a long pent-up breath of air.

Blake bent over to look outside before the door was fully opened. What he saw amazed him and caught his full attention until he was unceremoniously pushed out. Unable to keep his balance, he hit the grassy dirt outside the Complex and rolled down a small hill until he landed in a small, burbling stream.

Angrily, he jumped back up and faced uphill, spotting the doorway that was already closing. Before it fully locked him out of the only world he'd known, a last message came over his comm, "Contact us when you have found them, not before."

Before he had a chance to reply, he could hear the comm being shut down. His link with the Society had been severed. As he turned slowly around to take in his surroundings, the impact of all the sudden changes filled him with uncertainty and overwhelming panic.

On one side, the massive metal wall shot straight up to the sky, its grey surface covered with flaking gold paint. On the other side was a wide world with no walls. The wind blew his hair and made his eyes water. The sound of the breeze in the nearby trees and the water that still flowed by his booted feet met his ears. He saw no one. Not a soul was around. He felt as if he were the only human outside.

Once he calmed down, he stepped out of the water to stand on the grassy bank. He was thankful he hadn't made a fool of himself by running up to the door and banging on it to demand that they let him back in. After he took a deep breath, he decided he needed to take stock of what he had. In the backpack they had slung on him in the rush, he found rations of food, water, and a hand-held device. When he figured out how to turn it on, having buttons and not being voice activated, he found that a screen activated that showed a geometric shape and a single red dot that blinked. He watched it as he moved around and found that he was the dot and the geometric shape was the Complex.

Glancing up at the imposing façade of the Complex, he smiled. "They are still with me", he muttered to himself. "They are tracking me and will come get me if I get into trouble." With that doubt eliminated from his mind, he repacked his supplies, stuck the tracker in one of the many pockets on his pants leg and struck out away from the metal building.

Hours went by as he wandered aimlessly through forests and fields. As he irritably batted away the tall grass and plants as he walked, he thought how horribly disorganized the outside world was. The bird song and buzzing of insects started to annoy him. He had always kept his living quarters silent, preferring the quiet so he could concentrate on his own thoughts. He felt on edge in the alien environment.

When he noticed that the previously bright daylight was starting to dim, he stopped to stare up at the sky. He watched in baffled amazement as the bright orb in the sky slowly dropped to the horizon and disappeared in a blaze of colored light.

As the dark started to become complete, he was again surprised when supplemental safety lights hadn't appeared. Having lived his entire life in an artificial environment, he hadn't ever experienced complete darkness with no safety functions in place to prevent missteps or falls.

As he started walking again, he tripped over unseen stones. After falling several times, scraping hands and knees on the uneven ground, he sat on a boulder to consider what to do.

As he sat and pondered his situation while trying to ignore the sighing night winds and the utter darkness, his eyes slowly started to pick out pricks of light. They were not at his feet, like the familiar safety lights, but high above him. As he looked up, his mouth fell open as he was totally and utterly entranced by the smattering of starlight across the heavens.

Wrapping his arms around to hug himself tightly, he felt suddenly very small. The revelation of a world and space much larger and grander than he had even known or imagined engulfed him.

His attention was abruptly yanked away when he heard sounds in the surrounding forest that he couldn't identify. As his heartbeat raced and sweat poured from his face and palms, he listened as footsteps of something large came closer to him.

He fumbled for his weapon and the light source he had found in his gear. As his hands shook violently with fear, he turned on the light and swung it around as he tried to focus on his night visitor. As the beam of light caused bright reflections to glow high off the ground that were framed by a dark shape, he zeroed in on it. When he made out that the reflected lights were eerily glowing eyes in a long beastly face that sprouted spindly, branched horns from between its ears on top of its head, Blake screamed and ran.

He darted frantically through the forest without any sense of direction as tree limbs and thorny bushes grabbed at his clothes while the uneven ground and scattered stones caused him to stumble and fall. As his terror subsided and sudden weariness took hold, he crawled into a tight clump of bushes. Feeling safe within the small place, he rolled up into a tight ball as utter exhaustion forced sleep upon him.

The young buck that had startled Blake had easily kept pace with the terrified man as he followed him. When he sniffed out where the strange human was hiding, he started grazing in the area. He was in no hurry to move on.

****

"You almost feel sorry for the guy," one of the Watchers in the room commented as he reviewed the video feed from their deer guard.

Trevor had been summoned to the Watchers room as soon as the buck had spotted Blake outside the Complex. He shook his head as he watched the review. *They took no time to prepare him*, he thought quietly as he tried to puzzle out this strange event. "Why did they send out one young man who is so ill prepared outside the Complex?"

"Is he the one that is supposed to track us all down and kill us?" one of the Watchers asked. He looked slightly amused at the thought.

Trevor shrugged and shook his head. He had been right that Broin was using the lad but couldn't quite figure out the mechanics of his mission.

"Keep an eye on him. I would switch out the guards so he will not suspect their purpose. He is armed, and I do not want any of them being hurt by him, even accidently."

"Yes, sir," they all responded.

Still shaking his head, mystified by the ultimate goal of Blake's mission, Trevor left the room and made his way to talk to Colin.

He arrived at the hut and found Colin still awake. He was sitting in his usual spot behind the table. Trevor sat in one of the many chairs that faced the Wise One. As the small fire in the clay oven illuminated their faces, Colin wordlessly nodded for Trevor to make his report. After he was done with relating what he had seen in the Watchers' room, he patiently waited and watched as Colin thought about what he had been told, his hands clasped calmly on the wooden table in front of him.

After several moments, Colin moved slightly as if he were coming out of a light nap. Trevor knew better as he sat forward expectantly. "What do you think?" he asked quietly.

Colin looked at him, his blue eyes slightly clouded. "I can see several possibilities," he answered solemnly.

"I have thought of a few myself," Trevor offered. Colin nodded to him to share his theories. "He could be a diversion. Send a bumbling idiot out, and while we're watching him, Broin sends out the true forces and surprises us." Colin nodded for him to continue; he didn't offer any comments or change expressions.

Trevor continued, "Or, Blake is to act like he wants to join us. He infiltrates us and then betrays all of us." He watched Colin expectantly for a reaction. The Wise One simply nodded for him to continue.

Trevor sat back with a sigh. "He could be booby trapped in some way. Maybe what we are seeing is simply an act. Maybe we're supposed to feel sorry for him, then when we help, something happens to destroy us." He looked away as that was the last thing he could think of. He looked around the hut while he was trying to formulate any other theories. When he couldn't think of anything further, his eyes rested back on Colin. He saw that the Wise One watched him patiently with his hands unclasped as they lay palms down on the table.

"Which of these seem to you the most likely?" Colin asked quietly as he met Trevor's eyes.

Trevor looked at the ground as he considered. Finally, he looked up to answer. "I really don't know. I don't know your brother personally. You would be the best to judge this."

Colin looked away as he seemed to search for something outside the walls of the hut. After shutting his eyes for a few minutes, he turned back to Trevor. "Unfortunately, I don't know if I know my brother anymore." He met the other man's eyes. "Since he follows the obsidian path, I cannot truly predict his actions or inactions."

It was Trevor that looked away this time. What was revealed to him that one night still made him uncomfortable. He looked down at his clenched fists, then willed them to relax and open in his lap. He sighed, then looked up to meet Colin's eyes again. "From what little I know of the dark ways, they are contrary to the ways of light and will magnify the negative, the bad in a person." Colin nodded. "From that and your brother's past behaviors, can you extrapolate possibilities?"

The white, shaggy-haired head nodded slightly. Colin drew a deep breath and released it in a sigh. "And that is what I fear the most. Broin always took the quickest, easiest path. That is why the age-extending virus turned deadly. He didn't want to do all the hard work for full development. He also didn't want to wait for full testing and approval."

Trevor nodded as he turned away. He couldn't stand to see the pain in Colin's face, the despair in his eyes, or the broad shoulders that slumped in mourning for all the sorrows his brother had caused. "That is why he released the virus..."

He heard Colin choke back a sob on a memory that was now ancient but was still a fresh wound in his thoughts and soul. "I tried to stop him," he murmured sadly, not for the first time. "I was too late."

Trevor jumped out of his seat and walked to him. Clasping the old man's cold hands in his own, he bent to look into his sorrow-ridden eyes. "We know that you tried to stop him," he said firmly as he got the old man's attention. "We know you did everything you could." He studied the lined face again in concern; he couldn't let their strongest leader get lost in the past. "You were the one who saved future generations. You were the one who built the Complex and the computers to run it. You were the one who found a way to circumvent the virus that still persists to destroy our young."

"But then he used my creations to entrap humanity," Colin looked up. "Once they reach full maturity, anyone can leave the Complex.

It was meant only for the young!" He hit a fist against the table in anger. "But he hijacked the computer AI, named it the Society, and brainwashed generation upon generation into believing that they couldn't leave the Complex. He wanted to rule them completely. Control every nuance of their lives, as if they were in a zoo for his entertainment."

Trevor nodded. "And he sterilized anything spiritual out of mankind. To keep everyone on a materialistic level."

Colin's anger sparked again. "By doing that, he leads them down a spiritual void that will eventually entrap the unsuspecting onto the obsidian path." He clutched his hands into fists that shook with the intensity of his emotions. "The spiritual is as much of mankind as the physical! Even more so, because that is the only part that truly lives on forever." He bowed his head as he murmured darkly, "And those that walk the dark paths are doomed to eternal death."

Trevor gulped at the mention of the dark paths and looked around tensely. When he saw no shadows and felt no sharp pangs of terror, he smiled and nodded. "And you have helped many become Travelers and meet the One. You have served the One to save the spiritual part of mankind."

"For those who will believe." The whisper was barely heard as the old man bowed his head further, as if a great weight pushed him to rest his forehead on his hands. All Trevor could do was rest his hands on the slumped shoulders, trying to give the older man strength.

After a moment, Colin looked up and nodded. "Trevor, I appreciate your encouragement. But I know." He sat back in his chair to meet Trevor's eyes. "I know that if I could have stopped him in the beginning, before he developed the virus, none of this, none of this would have happened." He rubbed a hand over his eyes. After letting his hand fall back to the tabletop, he spoke as he remembered the past. "There was so much fervor and competition over who would be known to produce the first anti-aging vaccine. He wanted his name in history!"

Trevor hugged him over the table, then took his seat again. He couldn't change the past. He couldn't change the events or the memories formed from those events. All he could do was to try to encourage the bright outlook for the future. "Colin," he spoke to the old man conversationally, but firmly. "Colin," he repeated when the old man didn't respond. When the blue eyes met his, he continued. "Don't we now have a tool against the virus?"

Colin nodded as he sat up straighter and squared his shoulders. "Yes," his voice became stronger and more in control. "We actually have two."

Trevor looked at him in surprise. "I know about Sally. Who is the other?"

Colin smiled as his eyes sparkled, looking more like himself. "Devon."

Trevor searched the old man's face for answers. "How?"

"Devon started coming out of the Complex when he was a small boy. You were helping with the outlying villages at that time."

"How is that possible?" Trevor was confused. "Did one of the vaccines work?" he asked with sudden revelation.

Colin smiled, "It did! But," he raised a hand when Trevor opened his mouth. "Only with him. We still don't know why."

"Oh," Trevor sat back with the new knowledge. He was thinking of the future. "So..."

"Yes!" The wrinkled face looked young as he smiled broadly, "We believe if those two marry, their offspring will be immune."

Trevor smiled as great joy filled him. "A new Adam and a new Eve! They could be the start of a new humanity!"

Colin nodded his head as he smiled. "Yes, if it works out. We cannot force them together." He looked down at the table. "If we did, we would be no better than my brother." He thought a few moments, then met Trevor's eyes again. "Now for the current problem, whose name is Blake. I believe his purpose may be a combination of everything you mentioned."

"Combination?" Trevor's thoughts were scrambling to keep up with the elder's agile thinking.

"Broin purposely pushes Blake out into a world where he has no idea of what to expect to elicit our sympathy. We take him in, and he either has a memory lock that releases and he becomes a killing machine, or he is booby-trapped with some weapon of mass destruction, or some part of his gear is booby-trapped."

"Oh, I see," Trevor nodded as he could see how Broin's plan could be anything but simple. He wondered if there were other factors they weren't aware of to make it even more convoluted. "So what do we do?"

"We instigate a plan of our own." Colin smiled mysteriously. "Let Sally and Devon know we need to meet them tonight."

"Yes, sir," Trevor responded. He was curious about what Colin was thinking. He waited a few minutes to see if the older man would say anything else. When nothing else was added as Colin sat staring at his hands on the table, he realized he had been dismissed.

After he stood up quietly, not wanting to disturb the Wise One's thoughts, he stepped softly toward the door. As he was about to leave the hut, Colin spoke. "All will be revealed tonight. I don't like explaining things more than once." He smiled and nodded as he gestured for the other man to leave with a wave of a hand.

Before he stepped through the doorway, Trevor turned to look over his shoulder to respond with a nod and smile. He was relieved to see Colin back to his usual demeanor that exuded faith and hope. As he walked out of the hut into the bright day, he pondered how even the most seasoned and strongest Travelers still needed support and an encouraging word at times.

Chapter 18

At the crack of dawn, Blake had awakened with a violent start. As he pushed off the hard, cold ground, his body complained of the overnight abuse as his stiff muscles burned and his joints ached. Once he managed to sit up, he tried to brush the dirt and leaves from his chest armor. He stopped and looked around as he heard the trill of bird call in the cool, crisp morning breeze. It still irritated him, these noises of this outside world.

Forgetting his soiled body armor, he studiously peered through the woven branches of the group of bushes he had used as refuge. As he watched, dark sky slowly morphed through the grays then brilliant yellows until the blue sky emerged. When he painfully crawled out from his hiding place, he saw a few clouds floating high overhead as the blazing ball of fire lit the sky.

After retrieving his gear, he stood up and stretched to relax the kinks in his body and to settle the body armor in place. He made a mental note that it wasn't wise to sleep in the armor and to make sure to take it off next time. After shouldering the backpack and the rifle, he stood and looked around. He had no idea where to go and was aggravated that the Society had given him no specific direction to take. He felt he wasted time the day before.

As he stood gazing around, he sought for any hint or clue where he should look for his quarry. But just like the day before, he saw no trails or any indications of any humans in the area. As he thought about his next moves, he became aware of skittering sounds in the woods near him.

Fearfully, he gripped his weapon and stalked toward the noise. As he got closer, he could make out a small furry creature that was rooting around in the leaves. He was trying to figure out what it was when he heard a piercing cry overhead. He stepped out into a clearing to look up in the sky. As he shaded his eyes from the bright sunshine, he saw a huge bird that circled high overhead.

When he heard more strange sounds to his left, then his right, he became even more nervous and started to sweat profusely. Feeling threatened, he looked around wildly with fear-dilated eyes as he tried to see from what direction the danger was coming. Not seeing anything to defend himself against, he thrashed around wildly. His sudden, reactive movements sent him blundering into a stand of trees to crash around in the undergrowth.

The dense underbrush quickly slowed him down to a stop. Feeling trapped, he was forced to stand still, allowing himself to calm down so he could reassess the situation logically. As he took deep, slow breaths, he looked around. While he intently listened to all the small sounds, his eyes picked up flashes of color in the surrounding tapestry of greens and browns. When the breeze turned to a mild wind that whispered through the branches overhead, causing the soft rustling of the leaves, it gently lifted his hair to playfully rearrange it on his head. He sniffed the air, picking up the fragrances of the rich, earthy smell of the soil and the delicate perfume of flowers.

In his heightened state of anxiety, along with the sudden overloading of all his senses, he had an epiphany. The outside world was not uninviting. Something in him, something that he never knew existed, awoke, and he was mesmerized by the natural environment that surrounded him.

His trance was broken by a voice in his head. His comm had activated abruptly. "Blake! Blake!" It demanded his attention.

Blake nodded to himself. He knew he hadn't been alone. The sense of awe he had experienced evaporated as he toggled his comm open and spoke, "Yes, sir."

"Don't forget your mission," the authoritative voice ordered.

"No, sir." He looked around again. The world was again a foreign and foreboding place. "What direction should I go?"

"Choose a direction and travel a day. Use a grid search." It paused. "Use your scanner."

Blake reached in one of his pants pockets to pull out the device. He could see more detail on the screen. There were symbols indicating streams, forests, hills, and mountains. As he scrolled it around, he could see there was a vast amount of land that needed to be covered. Pursing his lips, he looked around. *I could be out here for months,* he thought to himself. Knowing that the Society was still with him, the thought of being outside for a long period didn't bother him anymore. Shouldering his rifle, he decided what to do and started walking forward.

****

"You're just going to let him wander around aimlessly?" the captain of the Society's elite team asked gruffly. He was looking over Broin's shoulder at the big screen in the secret room.

Broin shifted uncomfortably in his chair so he could look up at the hulking man standing over him. "He is our key for this Cleansing to work."

The big, shaggy head shook with disbelief as the man ran fingers through a full beard. "I don't see how. He's not been trained for the outside. Look." He pointed at the screen as Blake dodged a fluttering butterfly. "He's not equipped at all!"

Broin tapped the table in front of him impatiently with a finger. "I know, Karl. You and your team have been specifically trained for missions in the outside." He watched Blake march determinedly through a field of flowers as he flinched at every insect that passed by. "He has other motives. Other driving forces that we can use. He is our distraction."

Karl crossed beefy arms over his broad chest and groaned. "He is an embarrassment to masculinity."

Broin looked up again at the captain, his eyes sharp and angry. This may have caused anyone else in the Complex to back off, but Karl and his team knew the dark secrets of the Society. In other words, they knew where the skeletons were hidden and could bring the whole thing down. Karl met his eyes steadily.

"Your version of masculinity has been carefully bred for over the centuries," he barked at the bigger man. "You and your team have been trained since childhood to protect the Society from all dangers."

The dark, shaggy head nodded in affirmation of his statements. But his face still registered disdain for the man shown on the screen.

Broin shifted his body to watch the screen. "All I need is loyalty, not necessarily strength."

Karl stifled a sigh. He had had the loyalty speech drilled into him from birth. He didn't doubt that he and his men had mental triggers that would kill them if they were ever disloyal in any action. He knew that technology existed, for he and his team were the ones who escorted people to the secret medical team that installed them.

"Maybe if I knew the plan and the purpose he plays, it would make more sense," Karl stated logically.

Broin continued to watch the screen, his finger still tapping irritably at the hard surface of the table. "Need to know, Karl. Need to know. You don't need to know. Just have your team ready for action at a moment's notice."

"Yes, sir," Karl saluted, even though Broin wasn't looking. He stalked out of the room, knowing he had been dismissed.

Broin studied the screen, then using his secret control panel in his chair, he toggled it to show multiple views from all the cameras placed around the outside of the Complex. He was watching and looking for movement. He was sure that the Travelers knew that Blake was out and about in their world, and he waited for them to contact him.

While he continued to watch all the video feeds, he triggered another panel and sent out a dozen drones to fly over the land surrounding the Complex. Once he activated their infrared sensors, he sent them in a sweeping search pattern starting from the Complex outward to the outermost regions of the continent.

As he watched another display showing the readings from the drones, he thought, *Never thought I'd need to use these again after the last Cleansing. Chances are everyone else had forgotten about them.* He frowned deeply. *Except for my brother.* He interlaced his fingers and tapped his chin. *I wonder if they can still hide from my seeking technology. The fact they survived after the last Cleansing, shows they have a way. But does it still exist after so long? And will the element of surprise keep them from deploying whatever shields them?*

After several days of Blake's wandering around without any contact and Broin seeking from the Complex without results, he started to wonder if he had imagined a threat that was not there. Suddenly, one of the drones picked up heat signatures from the far edge of the continent. As it zeroed in on the area, Broin sat forward to watch in startled amazement as the signatures expanded from a few points to multiple as the drone drew closer. He realized he was seeing a populated area of hundreds. "This can't be," he muttered. "There is no way any one could have built up a population like that. The Society hasn't lost that many people..." He looked down at his desk screen. "Or have we?"

He toggled his internal comm on, "Karl, get your team ready. I have coordinates."

"Yes, sir," came the happy reply.

Chapter 19

The Watchers alerted Trevor. Trevor informed Colin. "Broin has located the coast colony."

Colin looked up in surprise. "Did they not get the message? We informed them that he had the seekers out."

Trevor shook his head. "I don't know if they didn't heed it, thinking they were too far out to be found. But they did verify they got the word."

"Send them warning that they have been found," Colin ordered brusquely. "I hope they heed this warning."

"Should they evacuate or try to disappear?"

"Either way, they are now in danger." Colin shook his head sadly. "It would've been better if they had not been detected at all."

Trevor sent a message back to the Watchers to send the warning. He hoped their coastal colony would take it seriously and be able to get to safety. He shook his head as he thought of their carelessness in thinking that they were safe because they were the farthest from the Complex. He quickly sent up a prayer to the One for their protection.

Meanwhile, Colin sent out a messenger to pass word around to the rest of the villagers to pray for the safety and well-being of the coast colony. As he folded his hands in preparation to join the Path, he shook his head at their thoughtlessness. "There's a price to pay for foolishness," he muttered as he feared for their lives.

****

"Maybe I should go back in..." Sally murmured fretfully when she found out about the Society seeking out the Travelers and launching an attack on the seacoast colony. She knew that everyone outside the Complex was in danger. "If this is all because of me...I don't want to be responsible for people dying."

Bruce shook his head. "No," he said quietly, then louder, "No! This is happening because he found out that the Travelers still exist."

"But that was because of me," Sally stated firmly as she met the eyes of each person seated around the table with her.

After her near-death experience, she had spent several days recovering with her parents constantly at her side. She had no memory of what had happened. All she remembered was talking with Colin, then waking up with him sitting cross-legged and head bowed at her feet. She had been confused even further about what happened when she became aware of a man and woman holding her hands as they also sat on the floor beside her with their heads bowed. When they saw she had awakened, she saw joy spark in their eyes. She then became wary as Colin introduced them to her as her birth parents.

The revelation that her birth parents were still alive at first shocked then angered her. After they were able to talk heart to heart, she could see how much they loved and had missed her. Her anger had eventually subsided and was replaced by curiosity. She recognized that they could help and were willing to help her navigate in this new world, a world she quickly found gave her new life and a happiness she had never experienced until then. Now, her joy had dimmed as she heard about what was happening.

Sally and her parents were sharing a meal with Devon and his parents in their hut. After playing catch-up for the lost years, Sally wanted them to meet Devon. Although Devon's parents had known Sally's parents, Devon had never met them before and was happy that Sally wanted them to meet.

"What is going to happen now?" Dan, Sally's father, asked Bruce. His tall, lean frame was folded up in the wooden chair like a jackknife. His narrow, clean-shaven face framed large, intelligent green-gold eyes. He exuded openness and honesty.

"Hopefully, the other colonies are hidden," Bruce said as he refilled everyone's glasses with one of the fruit juices their village made. "Those from the coast colony that can escape should disperse to the other colonies for safety." He saw confusion in the faces of Devon and Sally. "There are shields in place that each colony can activate. It camouflages everything in its range to look like the surrounding environment. It also hides heat signatures." He placed the earthenware jug on the table. "They should be safe unless the seeking technology has been upgraded."

"What if the other colonies are compromised?" asked Cindy, Sally's mother. Her short, honey blonde hair crowned her head with a halo of curls. Her blue-green eyes were wide with concern.

Maddie, Devon's mother, placed a hand over the other woman's hand on the table. "All we can do is join the Path and beseech the One."

Devon and Sally were watching their parents and listening to their responses. Finally Devon had to speak up. "Isn't there more that can be done?"

Bruce turned to look at his son with a puzzled expression. "Like what?"

"Aren't there weapons or something that we can use to fight them?" Devon looked around the table, meeting each one of their eyes. "Won't we all be hunted down and killed?"

Bruce shook his head while he draped an arm over his son's shoulders. "The Society is not wasteful," he said quietly. The older adults nodded in agreement. "They will round up everyone they can find and pull them back into the Complex."

"They won't kill them?" Sally asked quietly. She wanted to feel relieved, but she sensed that there was something deeper going on.

Bruce shook his head. "No. They won't kill the body, not immediately anyway. They simply try to kill the spirit."

Sally glanced at Devon and saw that he looked as confused as she felt. He glanced at her, then leaned forward suddenly. "What are you saying?" he asked quickly.

Sally could tell that Dan tried to hide deep emotions when he shook his head slightly as he talked. "The Society wants more people to control. The fact that there are people outside of its realm whom it is not controlling is upsetting its system. Once people are caught, they are brainwashed. It is a very intense mental and psychological torture that very few can overcome."

Bruce looked at Dan, meeting his eyes. "I don't know if you heard yet. I heard recently that Broin is still alive and remains in active control of the Society and Complex."

Dan and Cindy looked shocked. They looked at each other, then back at Bruce and Maddie. "How can that be?" Cindy cried. "I thought years ago, word went around that he had passed on and that the threat against us had dissipated."

Dan interjected, "I thought everything that is happening now was the Society's doings!"

"We only recently found out that he is still alive," Bruce muttered as he looked at his stone plate on the blocky wooden table in front of him. The remnants of their first course, the fruit, were ready for the compost pile. "The most recent events have started to unfold while you were getting to know your daughter." He raised his eyes to smile at Sally and her parents.

After studying everyone around the table, he pushed back his chair and stood up. "Anyone ready for the meat?" he asked as he forced a cheerful tone and brightened his smile. Sally could sense that he was trying to break the cloud of tension that had thickly enveloped their personal dinner gathering.

Sally and Devon looked at each other in confusion as he walked outside. They felt that there was more going on than they were aware of. They heard Bruce make a comment over his shoulder. "Might as well enjoy it; it is already prepared."

Bruce walked back in carrying a large, hot cast iron skillet. While he served the sizzling, golden brown fish that had been cooked over the open fire outside, Sally saw him look at her father and meet his eyes. "We need to tell them the real story of what happened. They need to know the truth."

She saw Dan glance at Cindy then at Maddie. An intense look passed between the parents, and an unspoken decision was made as they nodded slightly to each other. Sally and Devon looked at each of them, then at each other. *Everyone looked so grim,* Sally thought. She wondered and feared what information she would hear.

Bruce sat down and started eating the fish. The blessing had already been given earlier over the entire meal. He gestured to the others to do the same. As everyone ate in suspenseful silence, they soon relaxed as the texture and flavor of the well-prepared and seasoned fish pleased their palates as well as warmed their bellies.

Once they were done, they sat back satisfied with the meal. Sally watched her father as she wondered what was going to happen next.

Soon she saw him look around at each person at the table, making sure everyone was ready. When he saw they were watching him, he pushed his plate toward the center of the table. After he placed his elbows on the empty spot, he leaned on the wooden surface as he sat forward. His expression was serious.

As he began, his voice had a storyteller quality to it; the tone reverberated with an intensity that Devon and Sally had never heard. They began to realize that the intensity was because it was the spoken truth. "It is said, but we know that the Society was born out of need. It was to protect humanity's young from the dreadful disease that was released upon it. Not many knew the genesis of the illness that killed our babies and our children. Not many knew that it came out of one man's quest for fame and a place in history. That it came out of a need to control what should only be determined by the One."

Dan sat back and took a drink of fruit juice. Sally could tell that he knew he had their complete attention. As he sat more relaxed, his voice continued to weave the story around them. "Two brothers, Broin and Colin, twins, were born in a world much different than ours. A world that teemed with billions of people of different nations, races, customs, and languages. As mankind sought for colonization of the stars, one brother worked to defeat aging and ultimately death. He tried to achieve eternal life, a physical immortality."

"The other brother loved mankind, but saw the danger of people living an extremely extended life. He saw the danger of playing God and tried to stop his brother. But he did not know the deep darkness of his brother's heart. Broin deceived his brother, Colin. He acted as if he abandoned his quest for eternal life of the flesh, even though he continued to pursue it with his entire being."

"When he thought he had the answer, he didn't heed protocols or rules. He felt that he was wiser than any man. He chose to release it, as he thought he could alter what God had created. He thought he could be God."

"When the babies started dying and the prepubescent children followed soon after, the world was thrown into terrible turmoil. The effect was catastrophic as nations blamed nations and went to war. Most of those adults destroyed each other."

"Ultimately, the few survivors around the world were able to band together for survival. When they found that the virus persisted and babies would not survive past their mother's womb, a solution had to be found. For despite the possibility of an extended life, humanity was destined to eventually die."

"Colin mastered the idea of a place of safety for children to be born and raised until they achieved the age at which they could join the world safely. Since there were so few people at first, he built the computer to run the Complex at its most effective peak. Over the centuries, the original structure was expanded and more buildings were built on until it became what it is now, the massive Complex that spans over most of what was known as the Americas."

"Broin volunteered to stay in the Complex, saying he was penitent about his misdeeds and wanted to assure the survival of mankind. Colin stayed on the outside to work on a cure or vaccine so that eventually babies could be born and raised in the natural world."

"Colin did not know that Broin was deceiving him again. Soon, Broin had reprogrammed the computer to create the Society. With this new AI in control, he controlled all humanity and twisted the purpose of the Complex from a safe haven to a cage. He refused to follow even the remnants of the original plan by not allowing anyone outside, even if it was safe for them to leave."

He saw Sally's expression of sudden clarity. "Yes, Sally. Anyone past puberty can come outside of the Complex. Although all mammals are carriers for the TEENA virus, non-humans do not have an extended life but are also not afflicted with life-threatening illness. For some people, it does still grant an extended life."

Dan returned back to pick up the threads of the verbal history. "By the time Colin realized what his brother was doing, he was not able to reenter the Complex to correct the wrong, for he was permanently locked out."

"Many dark years went by, and Colin found the Path. He told the others who had stayed outside with him about it, and they also found and followed the Path. The One enabled him to contact his brother to share news of the Path. At first, his brother agreed to listen. He came out of the Complex and met with Colin. He heard about the Path and experienced it for a split second. Instead of making him hunger for communion with the One, he hated the

Path, what it represented, and all who followed it. His heart turned black, because he wanted to play God."

"After this encounter, he shut himself back into the Complex and talked to his brother no more. This was when he removed any reference to the spirit of man, any religion, or any deity, especially God, from the Complex and from the databanks of the Society. He made sure everyone had everything else. He made sure they enjoyed the freedom of doing anything that would support and enrich the Society. Everything except the most important thing, the nourishment of the human spirit."

"The impact of this spiritual sterility in humanity took a few generations to show problems. Soon the Society had to deal with a plethora of psychological disorders that not only disrupted the orderly nature of Society, but were dangerous to others who were around those afflicted. The Society first tried to treat these people. When it found they could not be cured or controlled with technology or medicines, they were simply removed and destroyed. The Society tags them as genetic mutations and cleanses them from the gene pool. It never considers that a person with no eternal purpose, no hope, and dark with no spirit has no goodness."

"Instead of turning from the damage his path had caused, Broin chose to blame the Travelers, as those of the Path had been named. With that, he instigated the first Cleansing. It was at that time he found that utter slaughter did no good since it made martyrs out of the fallen. When those in the Complex found out about it, many people sought the Path and found it. After that, any Cleansing was done secretly as he would gather people of the Path and try to reprogram them."

Dan leaned forward and held up four fingers. "One of four outcomes was seen with each person as the Society worked to turn them from the Path. They wouldn't be reprogrammed and were eventually killed." He flexed one finger to hold tight to his palm as he continued to hold up the other three. "They would reprogram and join the Society, forever lost to the Path." He moved another finger. "They would reprogram and be so empty that, in their torment and confusion, they would end their own lives. Or," he now held up one finger, "their belief would survive, but they were able to hide it from the Society. These were the ones who stayed to help those in the Complex to find the Path and develop ways of getting them out." He dropped his hand to grasp his cup again.

While he raised it to his lips to take another sip, Devon asked, "When was the last Cleansing?"

"About twenty years ago," spoke a deep voice from the doorway. Everyone at the table turned to look to see who it was. Trevor stood just inside the doorway, leaning against the wall.

"How long have you been there?" Devon asked, his voice brisk with surprise.

"Long enough to hear a well-told truth," he said as he left the doorway and walked toward them. "Don't look so nervous, Devon; it is no secret out here. We don't hide things from each other." He looked to Bruce. "I'm sorry, Bruce; we need your help." Then he nodded at Sally and Devon. "Colin wants to meet with you two tonight." They nodded back that they understood.

"Anything I can help with?" Dan asked quietly.

"Not at this time, Dan." Trevor smiled at him as he gave him a slight nod. "But we may need your skills soon."

He met Bruce's eyes again. "Bruce, we think we have found the sleepers' room. Colin feels this is the right time to release all who are in its clutches. Those are Colin's words," he smiled. "The time does seem right while Broin is busy trying to find us out here."

"Where is it?" Bruce asked as he pushed his chair away from the table and turned to face Trevor.

"Once we started looking, we found an unusual power signature coming from one of the mountain ranges." Trevor was speaking to Bruce but looked around the table to meet everyone's eyes. "That is where we think it is."

Bruce nodded, then stood up.

"Do you still have your gear?" Trevor asked.

Bruce grinned and walked out of the hut.

Devon looked from his mother to Trevor. He was confused about how his father could help. "What are you expecting him to do? And what gear are you talking about?"

Maddie smiled sadly at her son. "Devon, your father was trained as a member of the Elite security force in the Society."

Devon's mouth fell open. He knew the elite team was not generally known to everyone in the Complex, but he had been taught about this group by his parents so he could be aware and watch for them. He knew the members of the elite force were the toughest, most ruthless men ever born.

His father came back in wearing the black protective gear of the security force. Devon stared hard as he nervously wondered if the black-clad figure was his father or if the Society had found them. When Bruce raised the face shield, Devon expelled a pent-up breath in a relieved gasp. "Man, I thought they found us."

Bruce grinned at his son. "Don't worry, son, I won't revert back to the old ways."

Maddie stood up and walked over to her husband. Hugging him tightly despite the carbon fiber armor, she reached up to kiss him lightly, then let him go. "Be safe. Seek the Path and the One."

He kissed her back and nodded to Devon in farewell. No words were exchanged as Trevor and Bruce left to go on their mission. Devon sat stunned as he stared at the doorway after they were gone. Soon he sought his mother's eyes. "What happened?"

His mother sat down next to Cindy as her eyes turned from the empty doorway. "Your father was part of the last Cleansing. He saw something in the people he rounded up and wanted to know more. They told him of the Path. He heard and believed. Because of this, he tried to save as many as he could from the reprogramming and was able to deceive the computer to think they had been destroyed. But he was found out and labeled a traitor. His reprogramming was even more fierce than the typical, because of his betrayal."

"He saved us," Cindy said as she took Maddie's hand and placed a hand on her husband's arm.

Maddie patted her hand and smiled at Cindy. She turned back to her son. "He was one of the few who survived. He was able to convince the Society that he no longer followed the Path although he never left it. He was repurposed as an instructor. With that position, he was able to watch out for people who were candidates for the Path."

Devon sat in shock, his mouth still gaping open. He shut it with a snap then said, "He was part of the brutal elite security team?" he pushed both hands through his hair as he tried to absorb the information. "Wow!"

"He has been instrumental over the past twenty years in

establishing more secure routes in and out of the Complex. There were some before, but they were fraught with dangers of cave-ins and of being discovered," Dan added.

"Those out here wanted children," Cindy picked up the story. "So when we were found to be pregnant, we were smuggled in and slipped into the Society to have and raise our children."

"But," Sally, who had been silently trying to digest everything that was said, spoke up, "how would they be integrated? How could they be in the computer?"

Dan smiled at his daughter shyly. "Colin had told me that he had found a weak spot in the program, a backdoor to the database. He gave me the information to establish a link through the old Complex into the mainframe. With that, we have an undetectable way to add or take out people in the computer. This way we can enter or leave the Society."

Sally nodded but was still confused. "Isn't there a danger of people from the outside going into the Complex? I mean taking the TEENA virus in and infecting the young?"

The adults nodded at her. "Yes, that has always been a concern." Maddie spoke for them. "In humans, once we are exposed and antibodies are produced, we are not carriers. But we do have to be careful of our clothing. The virus cannot live on inanimate objects very long and usually is dead in less than twenty-four hours. We simply avoid anyone younger than prepubescent age during that time. Since the Society has the children segregated most of the day away from the adults, it is not hard to do."

"We have never had an incident in all the years this has been going on," Cindy interjected. "Those who go into the Complex know the dangers and are very careful. That is the last thing any of us would ever want to happen."

"Another thing you have to keep in mind," Dan started to speak, "is that an occurrence of someone slipping into the Complex is rare. When it is deemed necessary, there are many things that have to be done in preparation for the event."

Sally looked at her parents, then down at her hands. Her thoughts were in turmoil. The initial thoughts she had after meeting them of being abandoned had returned and strengthened with this new information. *Why did they have to abandon me if they could've just manipulated the computer and joined me in the Complex?*

She looked up to meet their eyes. She could see that they sadly contemplated her. They seemed to sense that she was in turmoil. "Why?" she had to ask, her voice high pitched as her throat tightened. "Why couldn't you have joined me?"

Cindy moved closer to her daughter and reached for her hand. Sally pulled back; she wanted answers, not comfort. Her mother got the message and simply sat near her. As she spoke quietly, she met Sally's eyes with a sadly gentle gaze. "We could not go in. No manner of computer manipulation could hide us from the Society."

Sally's brow furrowed in angry confusion. *Why?* she wondered. *Why couldn't they?*

Dan cleared his throat. "You see, Sally, we are direct descendants from Colin. Broin is part of our family. He would know us on sight and knew that we were Travelers. Even when we thought he was dead, we couldn't risk that he didn't program the Society to destroy us."

It was Sally's turn to look shocked. Her anger evaporated with the new revelations. "You mean Colin is my great-great-great..."

Cindy laughed quietly. "There are so many greats in front that we just call him granddad."

Sally looked at her, still stunned. "So that makes Broin..."

Cindy looked down at her hands. "Him, we would call your great-uncle."

"Ah," is all Sally could manage to say. She sat back in her chair to stare off into the distance. She had to have time to think. Too much was happening all at once.

She suddenly had a flashback to when she was small and her foster mother was still alive. They were walking down a corridor in the Complex and saw an old man. She had run toward him, calling him "Papa." She remembered how the old man looked shocked and corrected her.

She straightened up and looked at her parents. "Broin has known about me all along! I remember now that I had seen him in the corridor when I was really small." Placing her elbows on the table, nearly putting them in her plate, she buried her face in her hands. "What has been going on? If I'm out here, and he knows it, what is his plan?"

She kept her face buried in her hands as they continued to talk amongst themselves. To her, it sounded like a muted murmuring as she wallowed in her thoughts and private fears. She was terrified about what her presence, her existence could mean for those around her. *Why did he never move to harm me or to try to influence my judgment?* she wondered. When she heard her name being called, she looked up to see Devon talking to her.

"Sally, we are aware he knew about you. He had that memory lock placed. Remember? I told you about it. The one that activated when you were talking with Colin the day after you got here. Its intent was to destroy you if you ever started remembering certain things." Devon held her hand and was intently looking into her eyes. She nodded that she understood what he was saying. Even though she couldn't remember exactly what had happened that day, during her recovery he had told her what caused her collapse and near death. "I really think we should talk to Colin," he was saying. "He could help."

She closed her eyes, and took a deep breath, and let it out slowly. This simple action allowed her thoughts to calm down. After a few moments, she opened her eyes and nodded at Devon. "He wants to meet with us anyway. We should go ahead and go earlier."

She stood up with Devon. Turning to Maddie, she bowed. "Thank you for the excellent meal." She looked to her parents and saw they remained seated. They both waved her to go without them.

"We'll meet up later," her mother said as she smiled. She appeared tense and withdrawn. She glanced at her father and saw he also seemed the same way. She could see they were worried about how she felt about them with what she had learned today.

Sally met their worried gaze and smiled at them fondly. "Yes," she said as she bowed at both of them. "We will." She was glad they both looked relieved when they returned her smile. As she turned toward Devon, who was waiting by the door, she felt that she truly understood the scope of why they had to do what they did.

Chapter 20

After they left the hut, they walked side by side through the village to Colin's hut. Neither one of them said a word. They were deep in their own thoughts about what had been revealed to them. Once they reached the Wise One's hut, they knocked on the doorframe. Immediately, they heard Colin welcome them in.

When they stepped in through the blanket-covered doorway, they were surprised to see Bruce and Trevor standing in front of the Wise One. Colin turned toward them to gesture for them to have a seat on the nearby chairs until he was done with his current business.

"Are you sure?" Colin asked, responding to something said before they entered the room.

Both Trevor and Bruce nodded once in affirmation. Colin sat and contemplated with his hands resting on the table in front of him. After a while, he looked up to meet Trevor's and then Bruce's eyes. He nodded once. "Then, so be it," he stated and dismissed them with a wave of his hand.

After they were gone, he turned to Sally and Devon. Sally stifled a gasp as he tilted his face a certain way. In that glimpse, she recognized the familiar features she had seen long ago in her brief encounter with Broin.

Colin smiled at them and asked, "You have news for me?"

After a few moments of silence while Sally organized her thoughts, she told him what she remembered. After she was done, she sat tensely in the wooden chair waiting for his reaction.

She saw Colin close his eyes wearily with the news and briefly bow his head. The attitude of contemplation didn't last long as he looked up, his bright blue eyes studying her closely. "You do know that the current action against the Travelers is not your fault." His voice a whisper but firm. "But this does explain how he knew about you. And why he had taken action to install the memory lock."

She looked away as she swallowed. Tears had been lingering below the surface since she remembered that long ago encounter. "I am the reason all this is happening," she said sadly, her voice hoarse with emotion. She felt Devon lean in toward her and put an arm around her.

"No, it is not," Colin repeated louder with more authority. "We knew there was a risk when we took you into the Complex. You were a child and had no idea of what was going on."

Sally took a deep breath, straightened up, and met his eyes. "I should go back in. Maybe all this will stop," she said bravely, although she felt scared of what might happen back in the Complex.

Colin shook his head gently. "This will not stop, my child," he said quietly. "My brother will not quit. He has been our enemy for a very long time, and he will not stop for one person."

"Is there anything I can do?" Sally asked as she spread her hands in front of her beseechingly. "I feel powerless!" She felt Devon tighten his arm around her.

"Colin," Devon spoke quietly from beside her, "I would like to do something as well."

Colin looked from one to the other. He thought for a while then stood from his chair and slowly made his way around the table. "I wanted to talk with you two tonight; might as well have that conversation now." Waving them over to the empty space on the floor in the middle of his hut, he slowly sat down on the hard-packed dirt surface and crossed his legs. Devon and Sally did the same.

"Sally," Colin said as he reached into the large patch pocket on his woven, loose-fitting tunic. "I have something for you. It is very old. It is older than the Complex. It was made before the devastation created by the TEENA virus."

Sally felt an excited thrill run through her to have something entrusted to her that was so old. She watched with curiosity as he held out his closed hand. Reaching over the small space between them, she held out her hand to receive whatever it was.

"Keep it with you always," Colin said seriously as he met her eyes. "You never know if it could be a help." He opened his hand to allow whatever it was to fall into hers.

Her eyes broke free of his intense gaze to look at what rested in her hand. It was a necklace made of a long, continuous, gold cord constructed of multiple fine chains interwoven together with an attached pendant. She picked up the elongated, slender pendant and looked at the etched figure on it. It looked a like a man, arms in front of the body with his hands clasped loosely. The wider top of it appeared to be made up of upward-swept wings that came from the back of the figure. She looked up to see Colin's bright blue eyes on her. She smiled happily, then she wondered why he was giving her an obviously precious gift. "Why me? I don't deserve something so valuable as this relic."

Colin pursed his lips in thought, then smiled. "Consider it a family heirloom."

"What is he?"

"That is a depiction of an angel." Colin winked as he smiled even wider. "Jessie Daring told me that you asked about angels. In fact, that was the first thing you had wanted to know."

"Oh!" she exclaimed softly. She was even more excited about the gift. "So that's what they look like."

Devon leaned over to look at it and nodded. "It is what artists think they look like. I don't know of anyone who has actually seen one."

Colin nodded and smiled but made no comment on the matter.

Sally stroked the surface of the pendant, feeling the contours of the figure and the fine and intricate etchings. "No matter. It is beautiful." As she placed the chain around her neck and settled the pendant under her tunic, she smiled at Colin. "Thank you. I am honored." She bowed her head to him, feeling humbled by the gift. When she lifted her head to meet his eyes, she said, "I will never take it off."

He simply nodded in return, his expression unreadable in the dim light of the hut. He looked as if he wanted to say more but changed his mind as he started to study both of them in turn. It was obvious to Sally that he was getting down to business.

"Devon, you have made it to the Path because of your concern for another." He looked at Sally. "Sally, you were taken to the Path but need to know your own way."

They both nodded that they understood.

"For either one of you to be helpful to the One on the Path, you must know Him and the Way before you can help others." Colin peered severely at Devon then Sally. "This is very serious and not to be taken lightly. It is not for wealth or status. It is not for pride or to claim great humility. It simply is."

Sally allowed his words, his warnings, to sink deeply into her mind and soul. When she turned her head to look at Devon, she could see he understood as well. She noted that his inner light seemed to burn a bit brighter. Nervously, she looked within herself. She saw her light, still very dim but steady and not sputtering. She took a deep breath and let it out slowly. She felt ready. When she looked up, she saw Colin nodding at both of them.

He gestured to Devon. "Although a prayer candle is not absolutely necessary to join the Path, they sure smell nice!"

Devon smiled as he jumped up to retrieve a candle from one of the many that were scattered around the hut. He placed it in the middle of their small circle and sat back down on the floor, rearranging his legs to sit cross-legged.

Sally watched him and waited for him to light the candle from the small lamp on the table. When it didn't happen, she looked from Devon to Colin in confusion.

Colin had his eyes shut and head bowed. Once the candle was in place, he lifted his hands over it. Instantly, a flame blazed on the wick.

Sally watched in fascination, then closed her mouth, which had gaped open in reaction. When she looked to Devon he too had his eyes shut and head bowed. Copying them, she shut her eyes, bowed her head and then ... had no idea what to do next.

As she sat in the silence of the hut, she wondered if it was some sort of instinct to find the Path. As her ears started to pick up the smallest sounds, she could hear the flame burning the scented wax and the candle wick. She could hear the breeze around the hut. She could hear the villagers move about in fearful silence around the area. Her mind turned inwardly as she thought of her feelings of being monochrome and how hearing of the Path quickened something in her.

She followed that thought of being curious and wanting to learn more. She wanted to fill the deep void she sensed within her. She started to think of what she knew and had been told about the Path, about the One. The One she had not met on her own yet, but who had saved her life.

Slowly, she realized that she was feeling herself drift into an unfamiliar state of heightened awareness. It was not only of everything physical around her, but also all that within her and beyond. Suddenly, she found herself in front of a door.

She studied the door closely as it was so familiar but at the same time so unusual in the setting of ethereal dimness of self. She reached out with a hand and could feel its solidness. She reached for the handle but couldn't turn it. It was locked. She pulled the handle; it would not open. She pushed on the door; it would not budge. It blocked her.

Then she remembered Devon telling her of his experiences of trying to get to the Path, of how he had been blocked by a door. It wasn't until he had gotten through the barrier that he found out that it was his own disbelief that had formed the door.

Drawing from that memory, she restructured her thoughts and pleaded to the One to help her disbelief, to allow her to have faith so she could truly join the Path. She knew she could not do it on her own, that she needed the power of the One to achieve this privilege.

She stood at the door waiting for something to happen. Suddenly, she felt a presence of someone near and heard a familiar voice.

"Sally, how can I help?"

She turned suddenly to see a bright energy form near her. She knew that it was Colin. "I'm trying to believe," she answered him. "What must I do to believe?"

Colin looked from her to the door then back at her. "To access the Path is a privilege," he said quietly. "But it is one that anyone can have, if they believe and receive the gift."

"The gift?" Sally asked with curiosity.

Colin nodded at her. "It is the gift that the One can offer because He loved and died for all of humanity's sins. And because He defeated death and evil and rose again."

"This gift allows me to join the Path?" Sally was confused. "No one had told me about the gift."

Colin smiled and nodded at her. "This gift is the Path," he answered. "It is a purpose in life and life after death."

"Ah." She smiled. "What do I do to get the gift?"

"Simply believe in the One."

"I know He is powerful. I know now that He sacrificed Himself for us," Sally replied. "Is there anything else?"

"Know that He is God. He created all things and controls all things. Only He is the One that should be worshipped, no other." Colin paused for a moment then continued. "When you follow the Path, you are to trust in the One, no matter what."

Sally thought about what she had been told. She thought of her life of emptiness even though Society gave her everything. She thought of what she had learned about humanity and the mess that had been made of it by one man. She knew humans had no reason to be worshipped. She knew technology could be controlled by humans, and therefore it couldn't be worshipped. As she thought, a question and doubt started to grow. "If He controls all things, why did all this happen?" she said as she thought of the virus unleashed, the resulting war and destruction, and the young having to be enclosed in an artificial environment.

She could feel a great sadness wash over her from a powerful presence that suddenly joined them. She heard Colin reply, "Because humanity was given free will. With that free will each person could make a choice. There is a power in free choice that overwhelms and dims choices that are reluctant or forced. But it is a power that can be misused and can go contrary to the perfect will of the One. When that happens it is allowed for a time, so that others can experience the consequences of that poor choice, then it is diverted by His Power into something good for all humanity."

Sally thought for a while and could see what Colin was telling her. She nodded to herself that she could follow and worship such a wise entity.

As soon as her mind settled on that thought, it grew like a sudden blazing light. She reached for the door handle again, and it easily opened. As she walked through the doorway onto a brightly colored path, she felt the powerful presence flood her with joy and peace. As Colin slowly disappeared, she heard him say, "Welcome, Traveler, to your gift. You have joined the Path."

She looked around her in amazement as she slowly walked the neon-bright path in front of her. She noted the other paths around her, converging ahead. When she saw the shifting bright colors on each path, she wondered about their significance. Walking farther, she got to a point that she could see where all the paths joined into a single, bright white path ahead.

Suddenly, she was running in anticipation of what she would find on the bright white path. As soon as her path joined the white one, a white mist enshrouded her. She stopped and closed her eyes for a moment. She could sense the power of the One who had been talking to her through Colin, who had helped her understand the final steps she needed to take to join Him. Opening her eyes again she ran to Him and was embraced by the One. Instantly, all the years of loneliness and emptiness were completely swept away as she accepted His Love and Peace.

With that encounter, the One told her of her mission. Now that she had an authority and power she could fully trust and a purpose, she felt that she was empowered and she mattered.

Chapter 21

Sally opened her eyes and looked around the hut. Her senses and awareness were now sharper, more finely tuned to all that was around her. She looked up at Colin standing with Devon and another man. They were talking intently in hushed tones.

She couldn't hear their words but could tell the subject was of great concern. Before she engaged in the conversation, she studied Devon and smiled. She knew he had walked the Path again and was confirmed as a full Traveler. His inner light shone like the sun.

She stood up and brushed the dirt from her loosely fit, homespun, woven pants and adjusted her peasant top made of the same fabric. "What is the news?" she asked as stepped slowly toward them.

All three men looked at her in surprise. The first to speak was Colin.

"I hope we didn't disturb you," he said apologetically.

She shook her head. "No," she said quietly. "I was not aware of anything until I was..." She wasn't sure how to phrase her current state of being. She wasn't truly off the Path, for she would travel it from now to eternity. She had never left her body, so she couldn't say that she was back to this existence. As she hesitated to finish her spoken thought, Colin smiled.

"Yes," he said gently. "It is hard to define once you've joined the Path. What is this existence?" He spread his arms wide with hands open. "It is called many things, depending on the Traveler. I'm sure whatever term you decide to use will be understood by another Traveler."

Sally smiled and nodded her head, not bothering to finish her sentence. They understood.

The small group of men stood slightly apart to allow her to come closer to see what they were looking at.

The third man held a tablet. On its screen was a graphic representation of a land mass showing mountains and forests. There were also symbols that she took for the locations of the other villages and a large, blocky outline that she knew was the Complex. Bright dots of different colors moved throughout the land that hadn't been swallowed up by the Complex.

The man started to point at the screen. "The dark blue and black dots are the forces the Society has sent against us. Some are airborne technology; most are ground forces," his deep, sad voice explained. "The other dots, the red, orange, yellow, green, depict the villagers from the different colonies."

Sally saw how the dark dots fanned across the land and seemed to be driving the bright dots toward the Complex, toward their colony. "What is this?" she asked as she pointed out a lone purple dot. It looked as if it may have started at the Complex and was making its way to the village she was in.

"That," Colin spoke up, "Is Blake."

Sally was stunned. She knew that name. His face came unbidden to her mind. "The stalker? I heard that the Society had sent out forces, but I hadn't heard anything about him!"

She had felt Devon react as she did. "What is he doing?" he asked, his voice tense and angry.

"He has been sent out by my brother to find us," Colin said quietly.

Sally glanced at the screen, then at Devon. His surprise and confusion matched her own. "But he has found us." She pointed at the activity on the screen.

The third man shook his head. "He has not found this village. I doubt he is aware of the other activity." He pointed out the line of dark dots, "These are the hounds." Then he pointed out the scattered bright dots, "These are the prey." Then he pointed at the dot representing Blake. "He is the hunter."

Sally furrowed her brow in confusion. That explanation further muddied things in her mind. "I thought the Society was capturing Travelers to take back to the Complex." She pointed at the black dots and then at the Complex.

The man nodded, "That is only part of his plan." He pointed at the purple dot. "We believe Broin is using Blake's obsession with you to find this colony so he can destroy us."

"I thought the Society wanted to reabsorb anyone it could," Devon stated as he looked at the display.

"That's been true in recent Cleansings," the man started to say. "But this time we feel that Broin has another goal."

"He wants to destroy any remnants of his family," Colin said sadly. "And he doesn't care how many other people he kills in the process." He pointed at the purple dot. "I believe the Society knows nothing about Blake's purpose: otherwise, it would have tried to stop him."

"Why is this colony so important?" Devon asked. When a sudden silence greeted his question, Sally looked at each of the men. She saw Devon look up from the screen and do the same. Their eyes met as they wondered what they were going to learn next.

Colin looked at him and then at the other man before he answered. "Devon, most members of this colony are direct descendants of mine."

Sally kept looking from one to the other. She knew there was something she was not catching when the information didn't ease Devon's tenseness but seemed to amplify it into a horrific surprise. This tenseness was eased when Colin spoke again.

"Don't worry, Devon, your parents are transplants into this colony. Once Bruce joined the Path, he met and married your mother, who was from the Complex. When she learned of the Path and became a Traveler, they started slipping out of the Complex. This is how they tested different routes and established the safest ones. With their regular visits to this village, they became a part of it, although they still had a life inside the Complex."

Sally still was mystified as to why this detail about his family had been important to Devon when she heard him release a pent-up breath in a relieved sigh. She furrowed her brow and looked back and forth at everyone. She was about to ask for clarification when Colin interrupted her thoughts.

"What did you learn on the Path?" he asked firmly. She turned to him and met his eyes. She could swear they twinkled mischievously.

She frowned slightly as she switched her mental gears to what she had been told by the One.

"Um," she started as she stood straight with her hands clasped loosely in front of her, subconsciously enacting her early training for speaking before authority figures. "The One said I was to go back into the Society." She ignored Devon's reaction as she continued. "He had told me to take the wolf back into his cage. Now that I know about Blake, I am sure that was a reference to him. He also said that the wolf is dangerous in ways he isn't aware. My interpretation is that I am to draw Blake away and get him back into the Complex. He is carrying a dangerous weapon." She looked at the others, then thought further what her instructions were. "I am also to submit blood to your lab." She looked at Devon, "You are as well." She met Colin's eyes. "By using both of our blood samples, a vaccine can be made to safeguard any individual, no matter the age, from the TEENA virus."

She saw Colin's eyebrows twitch upwards in reaction. He looked away slightly as he thought, as if viewing something in the distance. Soon he looked over at Devon. "Do you agree to this?"

She saw Devon jump in surprise as the question pulled him out of his thoughts. He scowled at the ground before he answered. "I don't think she should go meet Blake alone."

Colin stopped him with a shake of his head. "That was not what I was referring to, Devon. I was asking about submitting blood to the lab."

Devon looked from Colin to her. "I guess. But hasn't a vaccine from our blood been tried and failed?" he asked quietly.

Colin nodded. "That is true, but something we never ventured on was the different qualities of the immunity each one of you has. The ratio of humoral immunity and cell-mediated immunity could certainly be different. We have never thought about producing a vaccine from both of your blood samples." He thought longer, then nodded his head. "Yes, that must be the key. That could be why it has not worked better than it has in the past."

Sally felt goosebumps popping up on her arms. Originally, she had thought the idea sounded odd. In fact, so odd that she wondered if she would have sounded stupid even saying it. But she had been sure of what the One had told her, or she thought she had been sure. The experience of her encounter with the One on the Path was fading in intensity, so she was becoming a bit uncertain that she was remembering everything exactly.

As she heard Colin's reaction to the idea, she was relieved and excited to be a part of the plan to help humanity break free of the virus and the need to have and raise children in the compound. Her thoughts were diverted from her internal contemplations as the man who had been standing quietly near them spoke.

"It is a message from the One, so it must work," he said, his deep voice in hushed tones. "But how will we get it into the compound? The Society will do everything it can to prevent its distribution."

Colin moved around the table while he thought. He sat in his chair, propping his elbows on the wooden surface as he leaned forward to face the others. After several minutes, he spoke, "I believe right now we need to develop the vaccine. After that we will consider how to distribute it to those inside." His brow furrowed as he continued to consider the problem. His eyes became slightly unfocused as he thought deeply. Suddenly they sharpened, "Aaron, escort them to the lab. Tell the scientists the plan. That is enough for them to consider at this stage." He looked at Sally and Devon in turn. "When you are done there, return to me."

All three nodded to him, then turned to leave. They knew they had been dismissed as Colin's bright blue eyes closed as he prepared to join the Path.

Chapter 22

Broin watched the action with growing excitement. He was pleased with the results from stirring the pot and felt that he was reaping rich rewards. His hunters were chasing the Travelers from all parts of the continent toward the Complex. He watched as those escaping capture ran to other colonies previously unknown to him before. The number of people that could be caught and re-assimilated into the Society was rising. "Yes," he muttered happily as he rubbed his arthritic hands together in glee. "This will wipe out their sect! They will have to obey me!" His grin twisted into a sardonic smile. "They can worship me!!"

He snapped out a command for the computer to provide food and drink. A glass of water and a plastic bowl of thick stew immediately appeared on the table beside him in his secret office. Settling back into his chair, he made himself comfortable as he began to eat and drink without moving his eyes from the action on the large screen. To him it was like a glorious movie.

As he watched, he suddenly realized that the dark voices in his head were silent. When he found the huge breach in his control of the Complex, the voices had tortured his thoughts with images of doom, failure, and eternal torment. As his plan unfolded before him and was working smoothly, like a well-oiled machine, the dark voices were quiet. He smiled as he chewed his food, continuing to celebrate his victory throughout the night.

After twenty-four hours of no sleep as he watched the action, Broin began to wonder what was going on with his killer. In his mind, he thought of Blake as his wolf that he had sent out to slay the sheep. He triggered his spying devices to scan the countryside for the lone man.

He finally found him bumbling around the rough landscape, looking like a lost, forlorn puppy in an unfamiliar world. *Good,* he thought to himself, *he looks wretched enough. Their soft hearts will take him right in! A wolf in sheep's clothing. They have no sense of the danger that he is!*

As he watched, his expression of victory changed to one of confusion. For out of a belt of thick trees came forth a figure that walked right up to Blake and hugged him. As he toggled in closer to see who this newcomer was, he was shocked to see it was Sally. As he watched, he held his breath as he waited to see her bring Blake into the fold of Travelers. He quickly became dismayed and then angry as she led him back toward the Complex.

"No!" he shouted at the monitor. "No, that is not the plan, you idiot!" He banged a withered fist against the metal surface of the table. He felt the cracking of frail bones and the fiery trail of pain that shot up his nerves. Along with the sparks of pain, his internal demons awoke to restart their accusations against him as they spouted off his failures and inadequacies.

Meanwhile, the screen showed Blake, with an attitude of absolute devotion, following Sally back toward the Complex. He never looked backward, not realizing how very close he had been to the village he was to destroy.

****

Devon watched the interaction between Sally and Blake via their spies' feed into the Watchers' room. A rabbit was following the pair through a field of tall grass, while a hawk watched from the skies overhead.

His fists clenched and unclenched. He still felt it was too risky and unfair that Sally was sent out alone to meet Blake. As the pair moved into the trees, the spies in the forest took over watch as the feedback to the Watchers' room continued seamlessly but from different angles.

"She will be okay," a deep voice came from the person sitting in the chair in front of him. The chair swiveled to face him as Devon looked down. There sat the mysterious man he had met in the hut with Colin. The dark brown eyes met his from a nut brown face, framed by black hair on his head and full beard and mustache. "Relax."

"Aaron, I know you are used to this sort of stuff, but I am not," Devon retorted sharply. He was quickly sorry for his tone and was going to apologize, when Aaron lifted a hand to stop him.

"So, Colin finally filled you in on me?" he asked, his eyes twinkling a bit.

"Yes," Devon looked down at him again, tearing his eyes from the screen. "How did you remain hidden from me? Although I didn't know my father had been an Elite Security Force Team member, I just found out that as I was growing up, those of his team who became Travelers had been around as family friends. All but you."

Aaron smiled and shook his head. "I am a loner." He shrugged a shoulder. "I've always been that way. If the team needs me, they know I am here." He swiveled the chair back around to face the screens. "Out of the Complex, I'm either sleeping or in here watching."

"Or out doing secret missions?" Devon added. Over the top of the chair he saw the dark, shaggy head nod slightly. "Why aren't you with dad right now helping with the raid?"

Aaron looked up and over his shoulder at Devon. "Colin is wise to use the people under his command according to their skills. Although the operation is suited to my talents, Trevor has greater ability. Another fact: ultimate command of the Watchers' unit is split between us. Both of us are not to be absent from the Watchers' room or out of the village at the same time."

"Oh. That makes sense," Devon responded and turned his full attention back to the screen. He knew it would take days of walking for Sally and Blake to get back to the Complex. The route was purposely convoluted to keep Blake unsure where the colony might be.

"Devon, it is unlikely there is going to be anything to watch except for two people walking over the land," Aaron said reasonably. "Why don't you get some rest or visit your mom? You know she's going to be worried about your dad and would appreciate your presence."

Devon clenched his fists again in frustration that he couldn't be with Sally. As he thought about what Aaron said, he relaxed his hands by his side. He knew the older man spoke the truth and started to feel guilty that he hadn't thought about what his mom may be going through with his dad on mission. "Will you contact me if anything happens?"

Aaron looked over his shoulder again and met Devon's eyes. "I will. But I want you to consider something."

"What's that?"

"If anything does happen, what are you going to do?"

Devon stood undecided for a moment. Then he smiled as he met those serious dark eyes straight on. "Whatever I must."

Aaron nodded in approval, then faced the screen. Devon watched the tranquil scene of a couple walking through a field of flowers. Still wishing it was himself with Sally instead of his rival, he turned and walked out into a bright day.

As he walked the grassy pathway to the village, he thought about how events led to this. They had dutifully reported back to Colin after they had their blood drawn by a scientist in the lab. Once they were both settled in the ever-present wooden chairs opposite the Wise One, Colin had laid out the plan.

"Devon and Sally." Colin had sat forward with arms on the table that was always in front of his chair. "You two are very important to this endgame."

"Endgame?" Devon asked

"The events that are in motion will be the end of either the Travelers or the Society."

"What is the plan?" Sally asked quietly.

"The first part is already underway. For any plan to free the inhabitants of the Complex to work, the TEENA virus must be defeated. We will know in a few days if we are successful. If so, we can instigate the second part."

Colin had stopped to study each one in turn, then took a sip of water from the stone mug nearby. "We will then breach the Complex and destroy the Society."

"What about your brother?" Sally asked quietly. "Devon told me about the spiritual continuum and the dark paths. He also told me how Broin walks the obsidian path, and because of that, he continues to be a danger."

Colin sadly nodded and looked down at his hands. When he

looked up at them, unshed tears shone in his eyes. "I will confront him. He will have one more chance."

Devon's blood started to boil. "A chance! After all he has done to humanity!"

Colin calmly watched the youth fume, then raised a hand. "Be at peace. You are a young Traveler and do not know all the ways of the Path of Totality. You will learn. Right now, know this: the One gives repeated opportunities to everyone to join the Path of Totality, the path of light. This only stops after death."

"Can you and Broin die?" Sally asked quietly. "Since life has been extended, is there death anymore?"

Colin smiled gently at her. "Yes, even with the extreme extension of our lives, death still comes. If not by violence or illness, it will still come." He lifted his arms and spread them wide to include all things. "In this creation, all things die. We are to die so we can reunite with the One, as long as that Path has been chosen in life."

Devon and Sally had nodded at him that they understood. When Colin met their eyes again, they could see that his expression was grim.

"Sally, you will be going back into the Complex." When he saw Devon reacting to the news, he raised a hand to calm him. "It must be this way. Sally has been told and I have confirmed." He put his hand back down and sat back. "While I was communing with the One on the Path, it was revealed to me that Blake is carrying a deadly weapon." He met Sally's eyes. "Another confirmation of what you had been told earlier. But there is more."

He sat back to contemplate his hands that rested on the table. "Broin's intention is to wipe out this colony. However, it has been revealed to me that what he did not consider is that his weapon would wipe out all humanity, even in the Complex. We cannot take the risk of his deploying the weapon."

He looked at Sally again. "Blake has no idea he is carrying this deadly weapon. The only reason he was willing to do this mission, and the only reason he was chosen, is because he is smitten with you."

Sally's face fell as she pressed her lips into a thin line. Devon could see she feared what he was going to say next. He was secretly glad she was reacting with displeasure to the news but was hot with anger about what he saw was coming.

"I'm sorry, Sally," Colin was saying. "But you and only you," he said as he glanced at Devon with a warning look, "need to go out and greet him. Once you have him with you, you need to lead him back to the Complex."

Devon saw Sally grow pale as she clenched her fists. "I was hoping Devon could go with me," she whispered hoarsely. "I didn't want to do this alone." Devon wanted to reach over to hug her but was stopped by a warning look from Colin.

She closed her eyes for a few moments, then relaxed as she pursed her lips in thought. After she took a deep breath and opened her eyes to meet Colin's gaze, she asked, "How do I convince him of the reasons I am outside the Complex? I am supposed to be at the moon colony."

Colin nodded and smiled gently at Sally with approval. "We need to work on a plausible reason. Maybe a shuttle crash on the planet?"

"And say that everyone on it had been killed except for her?" Devon offered, trying to be as calm as Sally seemed to be. He also received an approving look from Colin.

"That would please him, would it not?" Colin asked.

"Yes." Devon thought about it. "He'd be glad to think I was dead."

Sally looked from one to the other. "Yes. By the way he has acted before, that would please him and lead him to think I was available for his affections. I think that would create a feeling of trust." She thought awhile. Her face fell as something started to bother her.

"What is wrong, Sally?" Colin asked her gently.

"This is so wrong," she said firmly. "Broin is using him, and now we are planning to do the same!"

Devon stared at her in shock. "You care about him? I thought he bothered you with his attentions!" he blurted out as jealousy reared its ugly head.

"Devon." Colin's voice was firm and warned him to be quiet in one word. "Sally, can you explain why you feel this?"

"It's...it's..." She looked at each of them with frustration. "I have no feelings for the man. He is creepy and irritating. But he is a human.

He has feelings, and he is so misled. I really feel he is the way he is because he knows nothing about the Path!" she blurted out.

When she explained her position, Devon felt himself relax. She was being a true Traveler, concerned about her fellow man. He felt guilty about not feeling the same way. He had known better, being raised with knowledge of the Path. Meeting Colin's eyes, he nodded, knowing the Wise One knew his defect and that he would work on improving.

"When does this need to happen?" Devon asked, wanting the planning to move forward so it could all be over with.

"As soon as possible," Colin stated as he watched Sally. "He is getting close to us."

Sally nodded that she heard. Standing up, she smoothed out the homespun loose tunic and pants she had been wearing since leaving the Complex. "I need to find the clothes I came out with. It will be very suspicious if I met him in these." She sighed as she looked down at her outfit. "Even though I prefer this attire. It is so comfortable!"

Colin smiled at her comments on her attire preference. "I believe your parents have your other clothes." He nodded at her. "Changing back into them would be very wise. Go ahead and prepare while I talk with Devon."

She nodded and bowed to Colin, then turned slightly to smile at Devon. "Talk to you soon," she said to him, then walked out of the hut before he could respond.

Colin watched silently until she was gone. Then he turned his bright blue eyes on Devon. Devon stared back, not knowing what to expect. He sat slouched in his chair, expecting a lecture.

"Devon, I've known you since you were a boy," Colin started. "Even though you have grown up with the knowledge of the Path, you have to relearn now that you are actually on the Path."

Devon nodded that he understood.

"Experiencing something is different than actually knowing about something." Colin studied him closely. "Do you understand the difference?"

"I think so," Devon said carefully. "It's like walking the Path and communing with the One gives clarity and insight to what was so one dimensional before. It's like taking something one dimensional and converting it to 3D."

Colin nodded as he thought about what he said. "Yes. Yes, that is a good way to put it." He smiled at the young man in approval. "I am glad you understand and are open to the teaching."

Devon smiled and nodded at the older man. His face fell into serious contemplation as he wondered what he was going to do. "What is my part of the plan except for giving blood?"

"I expect you will be going into the Complex with the team that will be breaching it." Colin leaned forward again. "It has not escaped my attention that you have been trained to maintain and fix the components of the Complex."

"Yeah, for the off-world colonies," Devon grumbled as he thought about those colonies that may or may not exist.

Colin cleared his throat to get Devon's attention. When he looked up to meet the bright blue eyes, Colin spoke. "With the knowledge of the existence of the sleeper room, my guess is that if you had been sent there, you would've gained experience in the virtual environment. With that working knowledge of the equipment and its function rounding out your education, you would have then been 'transferred' back to maintain the Complex."

"Deceptive," Devon stated.

"Yes, but clever," Colin observed. "You would have never known it was all still training and would've reacted accordingly."

"So, my life's purpose may still be of use?" Devon asked hopefully as he felt a bit lighter to know that all that hard work and studying might still be helpful, at least for a time.

"Everything is for a purpose when we walk the Path," Colin stated wisely.

Devon looked at him curiously. "Even before we actually join the Path?"

Colin smiled mysteriously at the young Traveler. "Not all is revealed to us. The One knows all, whether it be past, present, or future."

Devon pondered that point. As he thought, he realized the deep depths of what was said and the potential revelations that would be too much for human thought. "That is a lot to keep track of," he muttered.

"And that," Colin stated firmly, "Is why He is God."

Devon's memories were wrenched back to reality as he heard an unfamiliar buzz. When he looked through the branches of the trees overhead, he saw a drone flying above. Panic shot through him as he spun around and ran back to the Watchers' room, making sure to keep under the trees.

He burst into the room to find that the Watchers were already aware of the intrusion. Aaron was in control and was in contact with the team that was in the sleeper room in the mountain. Devon watched another screen showing black-armored men rapidly waking up the occupants in the vast secret Complex.

"What do you want us to do?" Devon recognized his father's voice over the comm.

"We need a diversion to get the forces away from our doors. We have drones overhead."

"Do we have enough influence over the spies to have them act?" Trevor's voice came over the speakers.

"Nothing like that has ever been tried," Aaron replied. "They have consented to allow us to fit them out with surveillance equipment and go where we direct them. But we never intended for them to go into danger."

"Ask them," Bruce urged as he helped another group that had just awakened from their pods to leave the Complex. "Our hands are filled. We will not be able to destroy the sleeper rooms for hours yet. There are so many people here!"

"Do you need more help?" Aaron asked.

"The additional teams you already sent should be about here," Trevor stated.

"Okay," Aaron said as his fingers rapidly inputted commands on a keyboard that he had pulled in front of him. "I will see if I can get the spies to help."

Devon looked up at one of the monitors when he noticed the video feed had abruptly changed. On it he saw a high-level view of the forest above them with a single drone flying low over the trees. He realized he was seeing the feed from one of the eagle spies. As he watched, he saw the video abruptly dive into a plunge. Suddenly, cruel talons flashed into view as they grasped and crushed the drone. The video started to tilt up to show the sky as the eagle swooped up from the dive, and a brief glimpse of the talons was seen as they opened to release bits of useless technology into the air.

The Watchers' room erupted into cheers as the passive spy became an active combatant. Devon joined the cheering team as he watched Aaron key in a thanks to the eagle through their animal communication technology. He saw the reply on the small screen by the keyboard. The eagle seemed to have enjoyed getting rid of the irritating machine. He smiled to himself as he suddenly felt as if they had a chance to not only survive but also be successful in righting a longstanding wrong.

Chapter 23

Sally was running out of things to talk about. After a few days of walking with Blake, she was ready to get back to the Complex. The man still creeped her out, but she tried to give him the benefit of the doubt that maybe he could be changed. She had tried several times to steer the conversation around to talking about the Path, but he seemed to avoid it as if the subject hurt. He only wanted to talk about himself and kept alluding to their life together.

She was so glad that she wasn't completely alone with him. When the Travelers had reactivated her comm so that she could reconnect to the Society once she was back in the Complex, they had also programmed in their specific frequency that hadn't been detected by the Society. Through this link, the Watchers helped her deal with Blake, kept her informed of what was going on, and assisted her to lead Blake on a convoluted path toward the Complex. She felt more secure knowing they were watching and directing her to prevent them from aimless wandering and getting lost. She did not want to risk being with Blake any longer than necessary.

One day, when they were about to come into sight of the Complex, the Watchers had contacted her about what she needed to do. The delay in their getting back to the Complex gave the Watchers time to analyze the samples of what Blake had with him. By using their animal spies, they had taken small samples of his clothes, the backpack, and its contents back to the lab. Most of it had been done at night by mice, and Sally helped when she could when Blake was asleep. With the analysis completed, they found the source of the danger.

"Sally." Her comm came to life as she lay half asleep under the stars. Blake was awake as his voice droned on and on about his accomplishments. "Um," she subvocalized to let them know she was awake, barely.

"You need to have Blake leave his backpack in the airlock as you reenter the building," the voice instructed.

"Okay," she responded in a whisper to let them know that she understood. She was fully awake now, and she wished they could've given her more information. *What is it?* she thought. *What will it do?* She glanced nervously at the backpack in the faint light of the stars. The danger suddenly became more real to her.

At the break of dawn, she was ready to move. After she urged Blake to hurry to start their day's travel, they began to climb to the top of a nearby high hill. Once they got to the top, she saw the walls of the Complex suddenly rise from a nearby plateau and reach high into the sky. "Look," she exclaimed, feigning brightness at the sight. "We're home!"

"Yes," Blake stated as he looked at the imposing structure. His response had been flat, unemotional. Sally glanced at him, uncertain what was going on.

"Aren't you happy to be home?" she asked as she tried to sound more curious than concerned.

"Yes," he said carefully, then turned to study her. "Why did you not ask why I was outside the Complex?"

"I thought you were looking for me," she answered truthfully.

He seemed to think about her answer. "Why was I told you were with our enemy and I was to find them and destroy them?" he seemed to ask himself more than her as he looked around at his surroundings, then stopped to stare at the Complex.

"I'm not sure I can answer that," she again answered truthfully. "Why are you wondering about these things now?" she asked. She had a suspicion that the Society was talking with him through his comm. *Or was it Broin?* she wondered.

She quickly grew more concerned as his actions grew more fidgety and agitated. She held her breath as he kept constantly turning to glare at everything around him. Frequently, he would glance at her as if to make sure she was still there. Suddenly, he stopped and stood rigidly as he stared at the Complex.

"Blake," she called to him, speaking in the soft, caring voice that she used on aggressive children. It usually helped to soothe them.

"What is wrong?" She paused as she noticed his hands repeatedly clench and unclench rapidly. "Aren't you glad to be back home?"

He forcefully swung around to face her. In the blink of an eye, her quick reflexes took her out of range of his flailing fists. "You are an illusion!" he screamed in her face. His face was stretched and twisted into a mask of fury and hate. He suddenly looked like a feral animal, a wolf. She stepped further back as her body started to quiver with fear.

He was unaffected by her stiff shock as her rounded eyes watched his every move. She couldn't even subvocalize her terror to the team that was anxiously trying to find out what was going on. She closed her eyes briefly, uncertain if he would maul her in that split second, but she had to break contact with those maniacal eyes. In that brief blink, she sent a quick prayer to the One.

Immediately, she felt a peace that was not her own. She relaxed and was able to look upon the beastly man face. "Blake, I don't know what you think is going on," she crooned to him, "but I am real." She slowly approached him to gently touch his arm to try to reassure him. He flinched back as if her touch burned him.

"The Society can produce such illusions!" he growled at her. He stepped away from her without taking his eyes from her face. "They are real to those it wants to torture. It sees what is in their heads and hearts! I have seen it!" he yelled as turned away from her.

She was shocked to see tears forming in his eyes as he turned to face away from her. She had a sudden thought that there was more to hear of his life's story. "Blake," she whispered gently to him. She dared not get closer to him. He was near enough that she knew he could hear her.

"Blake?" she repeated louder. He brought his head up but didn't look at her. "Tell me," she pleaded. "What happened? How do you know this?"

Blake glanced at her, then back away to stare at the Complex. "I know of the Path," he started, his voice choking on the words as he forced them through an emotion-tightened throat. "My parents were Travelers." He lifted a hand and wiped his hidden face. "They were caught and subjected to Society's reprogramming." His shoulders slumped forward more as he seemed to crumple in on himself.

"They left me!" he suddenly keened into the quiet air. "They left me to it..."

After she heard him, Sally had to shake off her surprised shock to contact the Watchers. "What do we know of Blake's parents?" she subvocalized into her comm.

After a long silence, she heard Devon answer. "We don't know who Blake's parents were. He is labeled as an orphan."

"Blake, what can you tell me?" Sally urged Blake gently. "We are out here. The Society is in there. We can talk without fear."

"We are being watched," Blake growled as he started to get more agitated again. "I feel eyes on me. I know it is watching us." He started to pace fretfully. His head jerked around in sudden quick movements as he kept looking around him.

Sally clamped her lips shut before she divulged that they were not being watched by Society but by the Travelers. She suddenly wondered if all this was a ploy for her to reveal the others. She thought about it as she studied him. *No,* she thought to herself, *he seems genuinely convinced he is in some illusion.*

"Will it help to talk about it more?" She tried a different tact.

He wheeled around on her again, doubt etched on his every feature and pose. "Ah, so that's it, a psychological program! Forget it! That is what killed my parents! When they were so confused by the reprogramming, they sought help from the Society. When it couldn't help them, they killed themselves!!" He suddenly whirled around to face the Complex and shouldered his rifle and aimed at it. Rapid-fired shots rang out as he shot at the building in the distance.

Sally stayed on her feet but crumpled up to hold her ears as the sharp report of the old-style percussion weapon tore away the silence of the world. She was greatly relieved when he ran out of ammo and all she could hear was the click of the rifle as he continued to try to fire. She walked up to him and turned to face him. "It is empty. It did no good." She pointed at the building, standing as it did before.

He grunted as he threw the weapon down. "An illusion shooting an illusion," he muttered darkly. "Time to leave the illusion," he said as he started running toward the Complex.

Sally started after him, not sure what he was going to do. As she chased him along the top of the hill to a connecting piece of land that skirted around the ravine and slope upward to connect to the plateau, she watched the backpack, still hanging on his shoulder but bouncing around on one loose strap. She gulped nervously as it nearly slipped off until Blake readjusted it with a hasty hand.

She tried to update the Watchers while they ran, but she was soon too winded to give them a report. When Blake stopped at an old, hatch-like door set in the splotchy gold metal wall of the imposing building, she stopped and bent over to catch her breath.

"Blake, what are you doing?" She gasped out the words.

He started to pound on the door with his fists and shouted, "I am going back in. The mission was a lie. My life is a lie. I need to get out so I know I am not in an illusion. From there I don't know what to do."

Suddenly, he stopped and stood still. He seemed to be listening to something. He started to pound at the door with another fit of anger. "I know this is not where I came out!" he shouted. "Let me in! I know that you are lying to me! You didn't need me at all! I am not playing any more mind games!"

Suddenly, he stopped again. "They are coming," he said with a sudden, tense calm.

"Blake, I'm going in with you," she said as she walked up to him.

"No," he said firmly as he stared at her over his shoulder. "You are an illusion; you cannot come out of this place!" He suddenly seemed to remember the backpack. Shrugging it off, he handed it to her. "This can stay here with you." Once he did that, he studied the equipment he had with him. Eventually, he discarded everything he considered part of the illusion, except his clothes. When they heard a sound from the door, like a lock being thrown, Blake barged his way in, pushing whoever was on the other side out of his way.

Thinking fast, Sally threw the backpack through the doorway seconds before it slammed shut with a sharp, metallic clang. She flattened herself against the corroded metal wall nearby, hoping the backpack had landed safely in the airlock without detonating the weapon.

After everything became quiet, she listened intently for any signs that someone from the Complex was coming out to find her. She glanced around to see if there were cameras and didn't see any. She thought about her situation for a while. Should she allow herself to be caught to complete her mission or hide and make her way back to the village?

She contacted the Watchers. "Do you have eyes on me?" Immediately, she heard a response, "Roger." Before she could ask what she should do, she heard the comm activate again. "You are to abort the mission and take cover."

Skittering along the wall, she found a thicket of bushes that grew near the building. She dove into it as fast as she could while trying to protect herself from its thorns and small, clawing branches. She kept going until she crawled deep into the core of the twisted branches where she felt safe. There she decided to wait until nightfall. When she saw no activity outside the massive Complex, she relaxed a bit more and knew it was time to contact the Watchers again. As she lay curled up in the cool still of darkening shadows, she gave her full report on what had happened.

"What do I do now?" she asked wearily after she finished filling in the details of what had happened up to the point Blake had pushed his way into the Complex. The stress of being with him and lack of sleep over the last few nights was catching up with her rapidly.

"We will come and get you," Aaron said. "Don't worry."

"I wasn't able to fulfill my mission," she answered, her voice dripping with disappointment.

"In a way, you did," he replied in his no-nonsense way. "You kept everyone safe."

"But I didn't get back into the Complex for the next phase of the plan," she retorted.

"Ah, no matter," the deep voice replied. "We have other ways. The plan is basically going to be the same with a few modifications."

Sally shrugged to herself. She was still disappointed by how things turned out. She started to think again how quickly things turned sour once Blake saw the Complex. She wondered if he had a mental lock that brought the memory of his parents out. *A punishment for his failure?* she thought to herself. She wondered what he was doing in the Complex and what was happening. Again, she worried if the backpack impacting the ground had released the deadly weapon.

"Sally?" It was Devon. Sally smiled; hearing his voice cheered her. "We have developments happening here that are very positive."

She could hear the excitement in his voice. "One of them is that Broin has pulled back his forces. The Cleansing is over! We will be coming to get you very soon!"

****

"Oh, mighty leader." The mocking voice woke Broin up as he felt someone shaking him.

His mind refused to engage completely as the newest drug combination was still in his system. He grew angry that his blissful unconsciousness had been interrupted. He opened one eye to see the bulk of Karl hanging over him. "What do you want?" he growled in irritation. He scowl grew deeper as the dark voices he had tried to escape from with the new drug started to torment him again. They had restarted their tirade with a vengeance when his plan started to go awry with the distraction of Blake.

The large man straightened up and crossed his arms in front of his massive chest. "Well, besides my idiot son playing hide and seek with me throughout the Complex, your wolf is back. He's foaming at the mouth."

Broin groggily sat up. "Blake is back? Did he bring Sally with him?" *They came back to the Complex?* he wondered as he fought the mental haze of drugs and mental torture. *Why?*

The dark, shaggy head shook jerkily. "No, that boy is as crazy as they come. If he were a wolf, he'd be considered rabid and needing to be put down."

"Where is Sally?" The old man clutched his blankets around him. He couldn't trust his legs to hold him up yet.

Karl shrugged roughly. "Don't know. Didn't see her. Blake is convinced he was in a simulation and she was an illusion."

Broin shook his head violently, then regretted it as the room started to spin. He felt nauseous. "He was with her, the idiot. He didn't get anything done right." When he didn't hear a response from the Elite Forces leader, he glared at him.

The smug expression on the man's face said it all. Broin knew he was thinking *I told you so.* "I know what you're thinking," Broin spat at him. "Quit it!"

The man simply smiled and nodded.

"Where are our forces? Did we find all the Travelers?" Broin continued as he tried to catch up with what had happened while he rested.

"We've got quite a few," Karl started slowly. "Whether we got them all, it's hard to say. We had to pull back..."

"You pulled them back!" Broin barked at him. "Why? Without my orders?"

"We couldn't wake you, oh mighty leader." Broin bristled at the sarcastic tone but let the man speak so he could hear what else had happened. Karl continued, "We found out about your secret sleeper complex."

Broin glared at the other man's flat eyes. "How did that happen?"

"When it blew up and we went to investigate." Karl glared back at Broin.

Broin could see that he was intensely angry about not knowing about this certain secret of Society. He decided to move off that subject quickly. "So you decided to regroup the forces at the Complex."

"That sums it up," Karl stated flatly.

Broin suddenly remembered something. It made him jerk upright, causing spasms of pain down his back and legs. "What happened to the backpack Blake had?"

Karl furrowed his brow as his eyes turned away to think. "I don't know." He thought further. "It was sent out with him, but it wasn't on him when he barged back into the Complex."

Broin decided to risk standing up. His legs were still a bit wobbly as he took a few steps, but after a while, the movement helped and he felt strength returning as his mind cleared further. Along with that, the dark voices grew louder and more insistent. He shook his head to ward them off. "Meet me in the secret room in twenty minutes," he ordered the commander. "We need to make more plans."

"Yes, sir." Karl snapped a salute, then left the room.

Broin stood looking at the doorway. He worried that his Elite Forces leader might become disloyal with the revelation of the sleepers. He shook his head again as he belatedly wondered if everyone in the secret facility had died in the explosion. Shrugging his shoulders, he started to change his clothes and prepare for the meeting.

Chapter 24

They came to get her in the dark of the moonless night. Sally had just heard the footsteps and seen the lights of the Society's forces that were searching for her when she heard rustling of the bushes near her. At first, she tensed at the thought that they had found her. Then her thoughts turned to what would happen if she were captured and taken into the Complex – could she still fulfill her mission? She closed her eyes and gulped, dampening down the rising fear. No, she knew too much. She was sure Broin would have her disposed of, especially because of his intent to destroy any and all of his family.

She thought of how the original plan was for her to gain access into the Complex with Blake and then slip away with help from the Travelers inside. From there, she was to spread the word of the Path to those ready to hear it by using her ability to see their inner light. They knew that doing this would not only help others decide their own destinies by having a choice but also that it would create multiple distractions for the Society. While the computer and security forces were busy with trying to control this, a coordinated effort to assault the Complex from those inside as well as the Travelers on the outside would be instigated. Huddled in the brush listening for any sounds of someone drawing near to her hiding place, she wondered how much of the original plan they would use since this one had to be aborted.

When the black-armored search team moved farther away from her, she heard her name quietly called from behind her. Relief flooded through her as she recognized Devon's voice. Looking back once more at the foreboding Complex, its shattered gold glowing dull in the starlight, she knew she would still be able to do her part of the mission, somehow.

Devon helped her out of the clump of bushes and led her to the group that had come for her. At first glance, they looked exactly like the Society's forces with their dark amor, deep black silhouettes standing in the starlit night. But she knew they weren't. Not because of Devon's presence, but because she could see their inner light and knew they were of the Path.

As soon as they got to the village, they went to Colin's hut. Once they were inside, the team leader took off his helmet and smiled at Sally. "Hope we didn't scare you. That patrol was very close to you."

She smiled. "At first, your team's appearance startled me. But I could tell you were the good guys."

"Good," Trevor said as he nodded to her.

"Yes, very good," Colin said. He was in his usual place, seated behind his table. "You are uniquely equipped for your part of the mission. As we knew you would be."

Sally frowned slightly as she replied, "But it was a failure."

Colin smiled gently at her. "It was not a failure because you weren't able to begin that phase of the plan. The time was not yet right."

Sally pursed her lips as she thought about what he said and what Aaron had stated earlier about keeping everyone safe. She nodded as she smiled at him, deciding not to dwell on what she felt was a failure but they did not. She turned to Trevor. "So, your mission was successful?" she asked with a tinge of worry in her voice.

Trevor nodded. "Yes, we got all the sleepers out." He looked at Colin. "Broin had dedicated all his forces to the Cleansing. There was no one of consequence to keep us from our task."

"Are the sleeper rooms destroyed?" Colin asked quietly.

"Yes," Trevor answered as he stood at attention. Sally could see he needed to make his full report.

As she moved away, Devon signaled that they should sit and wait. All of them needed to hear the report.

Colin nodded to Trevor to continue.

"When we found the secret sleeper Complex and infiltrated it, we found it was primarily run by automatons. There were a few human attendants there, but did not resist us." He looked at the door of the hut, to where his team was waiting for him outside. "In fact, they seemed relieved." He looked back at Colin. "To them, it was a type of solitary confinement."

Colin sat with elbows on the table, his tented fingers tapping his chin slowly as he listened. After a brief silence as Trevor waited, he nodded for him to continue.

"We are moving everyone from there to the far side of the continent. Away from everything else that is going on."

"Who is helping with them?" Colin asked. "There must be thousands."

Trevor squared up his shoulders and stood even more erect. He glanced at Bruce, who had slipped into the hut to join them. "Actually, Colin," he started, then stopped. The silence grew heavy and somber as Trevor couldn't seem to continue. Bruce stepped out of the shadows.

"If I may," he said quietly. Colin looked from Trevor then to Bruce and nodded.

"Society has been systematically exterminating the sleepers," he reported grimly. Sally stifled a gasp as her surprise morphed into shock. She heard Devon echo her reaction. Apparently, he hadn't heard this part of the news yet.

Colin's eyes widened as he took in the disturbing information. He looked back at Trevor with sympathy. "Your children?"

Trevor nodded as he tried to control his emotions.

Bruce shifted slightly. Sally could tell he had more to report. "This has been going on for centuries," he said after Colin nodded toward to him to proceed. "There's a boneyard in one of the caverns. Some are so old they are turning to dust." He placed a tablet on Colin's desk. "Here is the rest of the report. There are more details you need to know." His voice was tinged with sorrow and exhaustion.

Sally looked at Devon as he shifted in his chair. He looked very disturbed. "Were there ever any colonies?" Devon asked everyone in the room. She looked around to see how everyone was reacting to the question. She saw Colin reading the tablet. His face was set like flint and unreadable.

She saw Trevor and Bruce share a look. Then Bruce looked at his son and answered him. "Yes, Devon. I had no reason to question when you said you were going to be stationed on one of the off-world colonies. There were colonies established before the TEENA virus and the World Viral War. We truly thought we still were in contact with them through the Travelers that went off world."

"I could've been one of those sleepers," Devon said matter-of-factly. Even though his voice was calm, Sally could feel him tremble through his hand that she held.

Bruce nodded, then glanced at Trevor and then Colin. "I think I state the truth that it was the One who interceded and kept you from that fate."

Sally looked from one to the other. She was confused about what they were talking about. This was the first she had heard about Devon being scheduled to go off world.

Devon looked at her and saw her confusion. He leaned toward her to explain. "Before I met you, I was to be transported to one of the colonies. At the last minute, my orders were changed. No one knew why. No one had answers about what happened. In fact, it all was totally lost in the system. I literally fell through the cracks, which was fortunate since it was time for me to leave the Complex for good."

Sally looked from one person to the other. "So no one out here tampered with the computer?" Everyone shook his head. "Other than altering the databanks for those slipping in and out?"

Again, everyone shook his head. "It would be too risky to interfere with a transfer," Colin interjected. "There are redundant entries for a transfer. Too many people who view the paperwork. Having someone disappear during this process would definitely draw attention from someone. The way everything was lost without drawing any attention was a miracle."

Sally nodded slightly, as the explanation made perfect sense. Thinking more about what she had been told about their access to the Society, another thought hit her. "So, has anyone ever considered simply shutting down the computer?"

Colin smiled slightly and barely shook his head. "The computer is needed to secure the environment and coordinate the vast number of automatons that service the Complex and its inhabitants." As he studied her intently, his face reflected deep contemplation, as if he were considering or weighing something. When he didn't add anything more, she looked away to think.

Having lived most of her life in the Complex, she could see how everything depended on the computer. What he had pointed out made perfect sense. Devon's voice brought her out of her thoughts.

"What is the next step from this point?" He was asking not only Colin but also Trevor and his father.

"While Sally was distracting Blake," Colin started as he looked from Sally to Devon, "and you as well, Devon." He smiled at the young man's awkward reaction and blush. "The lab has developed a vaccine."

Sally at first was distracted by what Colin said about Devon and what he meant by it, but then she heard the word vaccine.

"Does it work?" she asked in excited expectation.

Colin smiled at her. "In the lab it does. But lab conditions don't always relate to conditions in living things."

"So," she asked, looking at everyone in the hut, "how is it going to be tested?"

"One of the young in the Complex has volunteered. He is the son of a Traveler," Colin answered.

"How will he get out?" Devon asked quietly. "Aren't things pretty intense right now? Won't the Society be harder to fool?"

"The situation is even more complicated than that," Colin sat back as he met everyone's eyes. "His mother is a Traveler; his father is not. She has been able to teach her son the ways of the Path because the father is away most of the time on duty."

Sally was quick to notice that Bruce and Trevor reacted to the words 'on duty' and wondered what it meant to them.

"Who is the father?" Trevor asked, his voice tense in anticipation of the answer.

"Karl," Colin replied calmly.

Both Bruce and Trevor reacted. "What!" "Are you kidding?" "Isn't there someone else besides his son?"

Colin raised a hand to quiet them. "He has his father's skills of elusiveness and sense of duty. He also has his mother's faith."

"Who is going in after him?" Devon asked quietly. Sally glanced at him, wondering if he knew why his father and Trevor had reacted so strongly to the information.

"No one," Colin stated firmly. "He will come out on his own. He didn't wish to put anyone in danger. He considers it a part of the risk that he will be taking in helping us." He stopped as a thought hit him. "Actually, he will serve to help all humanity."

Sally's thoughts were drawn away from wondering who the father was as she quietly contemplated Colin's words. As she thought of the unnamed youth's bravery, she worried for his safety. "As long as it works."

Colin met her eyes. "Even if it doesn't, Joshua will be remembered for taking the risk. But there is an excellent chance it will work. After all, the idea was given to you by the One."

"But what if I misinterpreted it?" Sally started to worry even more because she would be responsible if the youth died. "What if I thought that's what the One told me, and there was something else that I missed?"

Colin smiled as he shook his head. "I doubt you heard wrong. When the idea was passed on to the scientists, they were very excited. That particular method of developing the vaccine never occurred to them and struck them as the missing key to their being successful."

"When will we know?" Devon asked as he sat forward in his seat watching the conversation closely.

"He will be with us soon. The vaccine has already been delivered to him. We didn't want him exposed to the virus before he had the vaccine in his system."

"So this plan is already being implemented?" Bruce asked quietly. His and Trevor's face and body language radiated tenseness and unease.

Colin sat back to look at him. "Yes. As soon as we had a working vaccine, we moved up the time table to implement it while everyone else was busy with the other things going on."

Sally looked at Colin suspiciously. "How was the vaccine delivered?"

Colin smiled as he met her eyes. "While the contents in Blake's backpack were being investigated, we had one of our mice spies place it in there."

Sally's mouth flew open. "It was in his backpack!" she exclaimed suddenly. "What if I hadn't been able to get it back into the Complex?"

"We would've found another way," Colin replied calmly.

"So the backpack didn't explode or whatever when I threw it into the airlock?"

"No," Colin shook his head. "When the vaccine was retrieved, he checked on the contents and secured it so it would stay in the airlock."

Sally sat back and sighed heavily. She brought her hands up to her face briefly to wipe sudden tears of relief from her eyes. "I am so glad to hear that I didn't activate the whatever it was when I threw it into the airlock." She looked at Colin again. "I was so worried that I had killed everyone in the Complex!"

Colin shook his head slightly. "Everyone is still alive. And you were able to deliver the vaccine to our test subject."

"When will he slip out?" Bruce asked as he glanced at Trevor. Sally could tell they were still worried because of the father.

"Should we meet him?" Trevor followed through with the thought.

Colin shook his head. "His comm is keyed into our frequencies. He is being directed to the village by the Watchers. Once he gets here, he will be staying in the lab. Once the usual time of incubation and symptoms appearing are passed, the scientist will let us know the results."

"What should we do until then?" Bruce asked. Sally could see he was still tense and worried about the situation.

"Place extra guards on every known exit outside the Complex. The Watchers have already placed all our spies on high alert." He gave Trevor and Bruce a hard look as he stated, "I am not a fool. I know who we are dealing with. Yes, our volunteer's father is the commander of the Society's elite forces. And, yes, it is likely he will come looking for him."

He placed his hands firmly on the table as he leaned forward toward them. "Our volunteer is the perfect candidate. He's young enough to not have developed a natural resistance and would definitely need the vaccine to survive. And he is old enough to make this choice on his own with the support of his mother."

"His father may not be a Traveler, but the boy's instincts have been inherited from his father. The Travelers in his mother's core group report him to be excellent in subterfuge and has a strong sense of duty." He looked from Trevor to Bruce and back again as they stood in rigid attention. "Do I need to repeat anything else again? Are there any other concerns?"

Both of the men snapped out a quick, "No, Sir!"

Colin sighed deeply and sat back in his chair. "I understand your concerns; do not doubt that. If I have missed anything else we should be doing, please inform me."

Trevor and Bruce relaxed slightly as they considered the situation in light of the facts they knew. Trevor spoke for both of them after he shared a look with Bruce. "No, Colin. Not at this time."

Colin nodded to them and gave them a tense smile. "Go, attend to your men. Coordinate with the Watchers and the spies."

"Yes, Colin." Both men bowed to him and left the hut.

Colin sighed as he looked down at his hands as they lay on the table. "I am glad that is over with. I do hate secrets." He looked up at Devon and Sally as they quietly waited. "Suffice it to say that some secrets are needed, but only for short durations of time. We do not believe in covering up secrets and creating conspiracies."

"I, for one," Sally spoke up, "am glad I did not know about the vaccine in the backpack. I was already stressed enough knowing there was something deadly in there."

Colin smiled at her and nodded. "That is also why we didn't reveal all we knew about what Blake was carrying."

Devon's hand tightened around Sally's as she asked, "What was in there? It sounded deadly." She glanced at Devon to see he was watching her anxiously. "You know, don't you?"

As he nodded, Colin spoke up. "It was a brutal mixture of chemical and biological warfare." He shook his head as he looked down at his hands again. "My brother never contemplated that the chemicals used would have eventually interacted with the seals on the Complex's outer walls, causing penetrating holes into the compound. Not only would everyone be exposed to the TEENA virus but also to the deadly chemical and the biological agent."

"It would have killed all life on earth," Devon added quietly as Sally looked from one to the other in shocked silence.

After a few minutes, her numbed brain was able to start thinking. "How could he have not known about that collateral damage?" she asked in disbelief. "He's a scientist, right?"

Colin met her eyes, his reflecting great sorrow and grief. "He never looked at the big picture. That's why he never completed all the safety testing on the TEENA virus before he released it. His narrow-minded focus saw what he wanted to see and didn't investigate it fully."

All Sally could do was shake her head in suppressed anger as she thought, *After all these centuries, he still hasn't learned. He almost wiped out mankind again!*

Colin seemed to understand what she was thinking as he nodded to her. "It has been and ever will be a great shame to our family," he said gently.

Sally nodded in silent agreement then looked at Devon. After they shared a glance, she turned back to Colin. "What do we do now?"

"The mission is on hold until we know the vaccine is a viable solution. I suggest you both rest and strengthen yourselves for the task ahead. Visit with your families and commune with the One on the Path."

The thought of resting brought up another thing Sally wanted to ask Colin. "What of the sleepers?"

"They are given a choice," Colin started to answer. "Those already of the Path are being escorted to their villages. Those that are not of the Path are being introduced to it. If they seem receptive to it, they will be placed in a village to mentor them."

"If there is someone who won't consider the Path, then what?" Devon asked.

"They will be detained so as not to get in the way. Once our plan is enacted, they can do whatever they wish."

Sally nodded and understood the information he was giving them. Then she had a sudden thought. "How are the children being protected?"

Colin sat back as he laid his hands on his lap and he seemed to contemplate what to say. "According to the complete report," he gestured to the tablet on the table, "there were no children." He looked up to meet her eyes. "That is a good thing, for we could not have protected them from the virus."

Sally's mouth dropped open. "But many of the villagers have talked about their extended families based on off-world colonies!" She was shocked. "How did they get that idea?"

"Your father," Colin started as he leaned forward on the table, "thinks the Society's program for the sleepers put them in a virtual world where they lived their lives, including having children. He is looking through the sleepers' database to see what he can find."

Sally thought of what Blake had told her about his parents and the reprogramming he had witnessed. She raised a hand to her open mouth in astonished revelation. "Blake told me something about illusions created by the Society that seemed to be reality itself. In fact, it confused him because while he was outside the Complex, he started to think he was in some artificially created world."

"I wonder if they were living lives so real that they thought they were having children and raising families," she muttered out loud. She met Colin's eyes, "Then if they were transferred back, how would it be explained that those children did not exist?"

Colin shrugged his shoulders as he sat back. "Perhaps they weren't transferred back until their children were grown. Or would they have died in that virtual world?" He pursed his lips as he thought.

She glanced at Devon and saw he was following the conversation and thinking about what was being said. She looked back at Colin. "It has to be devastating to learn that they have lived spans of time that are not real. That they've had children that never existed…" She hastily brushed tears from her face. The thought of such deep deception and the impact of the revelation on the affected people's thoughts and psyche overwhelmed her.

Colin watched her as he thought about what she said. "You are correct, Sally. They very well could go through severe psychological stress when it is revealed how deeply they have been deceived.The impact can run deep and take a long time to overcome."

He waved at the tablet on his table again. "Plans are being made to help them. Teams that are being assembled will need to be prepared to deal with these issues along with many others," he said quietly. "Of course, we hope that they will join the Path and allow the One to heal the deepest wounds, the ones of their spirit." He brought a hand up to rub his eyes briefly. Sally could see he was tired and worried as he dropped his hand to stare off into space.

Devon and Sally shared a look as they waited quietly, not knowing if they had been dismissed or not. When Colin sat back and looked at them, he smiled wearily. "I am glad the time has come to stop my brother and his monster, the Society. Too many people have been directly or indirectly harmed by him."

Sally opened her mouth to mutter something she hoped would be comforting when Colin waved a hand at her and shook his head. "Do not take to heart an old man's mutterings," he said to both of them. "It is a burden I alone carry."

Both Sally and Devon stood to leave when Devon spoke up. "Colin, you are not alone," he said with quiet intensity. "We all fight this battle with you."

Colin smiled at the young man and bowed his head. "Ah, the faith and energy of the young," he said, his tone lighter. "I hope I can keep up!" His smile widened into a genuine grin.

Sally smiled back at him and bowed. Devon bowed as well, then led her out of the hut.

Chapter 25

To Sally, the days seemed to pass slowly. She wondered if the feelings of uncertainty influenced the perception of the passage of time. She knew it wasn't from not being busy enough.

She had been dividing her time between helping her parents with their tasks and visiting Devon and his family. During the day, her mind and thoughts were active and distracted from the tasks yet ahead, but at night she worried and wondered what was happening with the young volunteer, the sleepers and their hard jolt into reality, and the restlessness of wanting to get her mission over and done with.

She also joined the Path in her meditations but didn't receive any further instructions. She would see the One in the white mists of the Path, but didn't seem to be able to approach him. She began to worry whether she did something wrong and was somehow out of favor. One morning, she decided she needed to talk to Colin.

Moving in the early light of dawn, she made her way through the village that was just starting to stir to life. Knocking on the wooden doorframe to the door of the hut, she waited for a response. The woven mat covering the doorway moved aside, and she stood face to face with Colin.

Suddenly, she realized something was wrong. His eyes were not quite right; they were still blue but not as deep in color nor as clear. They were hard and flat like rocks. Then she realized the facial features were subtly changed; instead of softened with kindness, they were twisted in cruelty. She drew in a startled deep breath of recognition. She was face to face with Broin!

"Broin!" she gasped. "What are you doing here?" She tried to look beyond him to see if Colin was okay. But instead of Colin, she saw Blake behind him, sneering at her, hate burning in his dark eyes.

"You thought you had deceived me!" he was yelling at her as he tried to move around Broin in the narrow doorway of the hut. Broin kept him back with an arm braced against the doorframe.

"Hello, Sally," Broin said, his voice mocking and threatening. "I guess I do not have to introduce myself." He glanced back in the hut, then faced Sally again. "Do not worry about Colin. He has what he wants. He has fully joined the Path for all eternity." He pushed by her to stalk out into the forest. "This world is mine."

Blake snarled as he passed by her. "I will be back for you," he threatened in a low growl as he followed Broin and was soon lost in the forest growth.

Her heart beat fast with fear as she ran into the hut, fearing the worst. When she saw that no one was in there, she stood in the middle of the room and looked around in confusion. After a few seconds, she ran out to find help in the village.

"Help! Help!" she cried as she ran between the huts. She was shocked that no one responded. She stopped in the area of their communal meals and stood still as she strained her eyes and ears to hear anything. Suddenly, she was overcome by an overwhelming fear as she realized that she heard no sounds of life. Even the bird song had ceased.

"Oh, no!" she cried as she sank to her knees with her hands covering her face. "He has activated the weapon!!" Tears started to flow as heartfelt sobs tore her throat with their intensity. Lying down and curling up on the hard, cobblestoned area, she sobbed and cried until she was drained. As she lay in an exhausted half-sleep, she heard soft footsteps approaching and stopping beside her. She tensed and then lifted her head, having no idea whom she would see.

What greeted her red, swollen eyes surprised and confused her. Standing with his hand extended down to her was the One. His white, shining countenance blazed so brightly she couldn't see his face clearly. She took his hand to stand to her feet as she stared at him. "Am I dead?" she asked in a small voice. Dismay filled her as she thought of how her mission was not accomplished. "He won? The one on the dark path won?"

The One shook his head as he pointed to the ground at her feet. When she looked down, she saw the cobblestoned ground dissolve to show a path of black and grays.

Her reaction was immediate and intense; she grabbed both of his hands to get closer to him. He scooped her up in strong, comforting arms. She looked down at his feet and saw that the black and grey could not touch him; they bent around him. "Why am I on the dark path?" she cried to him. "What did I do?"

The One didn't answer as he walked between all the paths of the spiritual continuum until they reached the intense white path. Once there, he set her down so that her feet were firmly on it. She felt the power of joy and peace return to her as she stood on the Path of Light and in the presence of the One.

"I don't understand," she said to Him. "How did I get on the dark path?" She had to know so she would not make the same mistake again.

"You made no mistake. You were hijacked." A voice behind her made her turn and look for the speaker. Colin stood just behind her. He bowed to the One, then turned back to Sally to explain.

"Broin found you through your comm. He was able to use the tech to backtrack to you so the dark one could try to influence you through your subconscious." He met her eyes. "He patched in an illusion of reality. With this, he placed you on a dark path. He could not hold you there, for it was not your choice."

Sally was horrified at the implications of what happened. "How can it be stopped?" She looked at the One and then at Colin, "How can it be prevented?"

Colin smiled reassuringly. "Now that we know he can do this, the One has shown us how to prevent him from reaching out beyond the Complex." He bowed to the bright entity and started to walk away, steering Sally to go with him.

"We have deactivated the Society's frequencies again. You should be fine now. When you wake up, you will be in your parent's hut. Do not be disturbed by all the people in your room. There was a great outcry in the village when you were found obviously suffering and could not be roused."

Sally nodded that she understood and saw that she needed to return back to consciousness as soon as possible.

"We will talk on the other side," Colin said as he started to fade from her sight.

She soon opened her eyes to a crowd of people holding prayer candles. Her room was heavily scented with their fragrance as they burned. In the candlelight, she saw that the closest ones to her were her mother, father, and Devon.

When they saw that her eyes were open, they shouted to the others, "She is back!" "She is safe!" They cried as they all tried to hug her at the same time as she was lying on the pallet.

After a shout of victory, the villagers who had been able to cram into her room filed out in joy. As the room emptied, Trevor slipped in to stand by her. She looked up at him after hugging her family and Devon.

"Colin needs to speak with you," he said quietly. He looked at Devon. "He wants you there as well." He bowed to Sally's parents as he turned to walk out.

Sally was helped from the floor by her father. After he had given her another tight hug and handed her off to her mother, her mother hugged her quickly but fiercely, then let her go with a smile.

Sally turned to Devon, who had moved to stand in the doorway to her room. She smiled at him as she walked by, sensing that he was tense and worried. She stopped outside the hut to wait for him. As they walked side by side to Colin's hut, she tried to talk with him.

"I'm okay," she said as she tried to get him to look at her. He seemed closed to her as he kept his eyes on the path. "I didn't do anything wrong," she said as she stopped at the door to Colin's hut. She was anxious to have him look at her, to talk to her.

When she wouldn't let him in the hut, he raised his eyes to her. She gasped when she saw the great pain he was in. "What happened?" she whispered to him with growing concern.

He looked at her for a moment, then looked away. She saw his mouth moving as he tried to speak. Soon she could hear him whisper. "I heard you scream in my dreams," he mumbled. "I woke up and ran to your hut. When I ran into your room, you were writhing in agony. The pain was so intense it hurt me."

He took her hand and pressed it to his cheek. She could feel his breath across her palm as he continued. "I could do nothing. I sensed it had something to do with the dark paths. But I had no idea how to help. All I could do was hold on to you so you wouldn't hurt yourself while your mother ran for Colin and your father woke up the villagers." His tortured eyes met hers again. "Colin had shown me the dark paths and how to fight the dark one. I froze." He squeezed his eyes shut in despair. "I failed you," he whispered hoarsely.

She quietly considered his words as she looked away into the predawn forest around them. Even though Colin had explained what happened, she couldn't say she understood all that happened to her, so she didn't blame Devon for not understanding or being able to react. She knew he was new to the Path and hadn't had the experience like the older Travelers. Like Colin.

She looked at him again and saw he was watching her. As she met his eyes, she smiled into them. "I don't know what happened. Not all of it. I am hoping that is why Colin summoned us, to explain more. You did what you could. Thank you for keeping me from injuring myself." She reached for his hands and held them firmly. "And thank you for hearing me in your dreams and coming to find me. You alerted everyone to what was going on." She squeezed his hands tightly before she let them go. "You helped save me."

He looked around and nodded while he considered her words. When he glanced at the hut, he tried to smile at her as he gestured to the doorway. "We are expected," he said quietly. "I will try to think of what happened in those terms."

Sally nodded at him as she studied his face. She smiled when she saw that he seemed not to be as upset as before. As he held the blanket aside, she slipped into the dim, candlelit hut.

"Hello, Sally," Colin was sitting in his usual chair behind his table. A single candle was lit on the table in front of him. He waved to the chairs in front of his table. "Please be seated." He signaled someone in the shadows who slipped out of the hut. "Refreshments will come shortly," he said.

Sally and Devon settled into the chairs and waited for him.

"Sally." Colin had looked at Devon and then at her, "Tell me everything that happened. Starting from before you went to sleep."

Sally thought about the night before she went to sleep. She shrugged her shoulders as she didn't see anything odd about the events. She started to tell him the mundane details of her life up to when she went to bed. Suddenly, she felt anxious as she started to relate the details of her nightmare. She didn't realize that she was clenching the edges of her seat with both hands until she felt Devon pry one of them off and hold it. She released the other one and clenched a fist in her lap as she trembled. His silent show of support and strength helped her continue to talk about what she had seen and felt in her nightmare encounter.

As she came to the end of her report, she watched Colin for any reaction. He sat through the telling, his bright blue eyes watching her intensely as he rested his chin on clasped hands supported by his elbows on the table. As she finished, he closed his eyes as he bowed his head slightly.

She sat in silence as she watched. She squeezed Devon's hand and looked at him to smile. He was looking at the floor, his brow drawn together in thought as he seemed to be contemplating something. She was going to ask him what he was thinking, when she heard Colin speak.

"I am afraid that your experience was not only my brother trying to deceive you to follow the dark paths," he started. She turned back to meet his eyes. He gave her a strained, sad smile. "It was also a warning about what he intends to do." He looked away as he rubbed his face with one of his hands.

He dropped his hand to the table and looked at them. "He intends to use the weapon. He probably is making another one. He will come out, find me, and kill me. I don't know how he thinks he will find me, but he will try. I don't think he can use you as a homing beacon, Sally, but we also didn't think he would be able to reach anyone with his illusions outside of the Complex."

"What do we do?" Devon asked.

"We react accordingly," Colin said firmly as he stood up, pushing up from the table. He saw someone coming in carrying trays. "Serve them," he directed as he walked to the doorway. Before he left, he looked back at them. "Stay here until I get back."

At first, Sally stared at the empty doorway in shock. When she turned to Devon, she saw he also was surprised at the sudden departure of the Wise One. The servant quietly placed small tables in front of each of them and served a small meal with a sweetened drink. After they thanked her, they forced themselves to eat and drink although neither one of them truly felt like it.

After they had both eaten, they sat in silence. Neither felt like talking as they wondered what was going on and when Colin would be returning.

When they heard rushed footsteps coming in from the outside, they both looked intently at the doorway, expecting Colin. Instead it was Trevor, dressed in full armor, who rushed in and looked toward Colin's chair. When he saw it was empty, he swung around to scan the rest of the room. When he saw Devon and Sally, he looked confused. "Where is he?" he asked sharply as he raised his hands slightly with palms toward them.

"We don't know," Devon spoke up. "We were talking to him, and he suddenly got up and left. He told us to stay here and wait for him."

Trevor looked around again in frustration, then started pacing the room in agitation.

"What is going on?" Devon asked the irritated man.

"Things are moving fast, and I need to talk to Colin," Trevor responded tersely.

"Why can't you reach him through the comm?" Sally asked quietly.

Trevor stopped in front of them. "He doesn't have one. He never has. He never trusted the devices." He started pacing again. "Now, I need to talk to him, and he's gone!"

"Can you tell us what is going on?" Sally asked him quietly.

Trevor glanced over at them as he slowed down. He stopped as he thought it over, then dropped into one of the chairs near them. "The elite forces are back in the field. They have restarted herding the Travelers toward us. This time they are wearing environmental suits."

"Oh my…" Sally dropped her head into her hands. "He is going to set off the bomb," she cried.

"Persistent old man," Devon quietly growled.

"That he is," a voice stated from the doorway. Colin entered quickly, his footsteps nearly silent on the hard-packed earthen floor as he made his way to his chair. He sat down hard and breathed heavily until he could catch his breath. "It is good you are here,

Trevor." He looked toward Sally and Devon. "You both need to go with Trevor and his team, now."

"What of the vaccine?" Sally asked.

"We are close to the end of the incubation period. So far, no hints of symptoms," Colin stated. "There will be some risks, but we can't wait any longer."

"Isn't that what got us into this mess?" Devon spoke up. "Not waiting and checking on everything? Right?"

Colin stopped and stared at him. He drew a deep breath as he licked his lips. "That is true," he started slowly. "But we must breach the compound very soon. We must do what we need to do to protect the young in the Complex."

"Why the urgency to deal with the Complex so quickly?" Sally asked. She was mystified by the sudden need to move forward with their plan. "If Broin is going to use that horrible weapon, shouldn't we stop him?" She looked at Devon and then Colin and Trevor for an answer.

She saw them share a look, seeming to understand each other. But she couldn't see why they seemed to favor this course of action. "Isn't the destruction of all mankind a worse-case scenario than trying to free all those in the Complex?" She pushed harder. She needed to know the logic when there seemed to be none.

"Sally, on the surface you are correct," Colin spoke quietly. "However, we need to remove the deception that the Society has placed over all the inhabitants of the Complex. While Broin is concentrating on destroying us, he will not be focusing on the Complex. In his mind, he will see the Complex as safe and secure while we are scrabbling around trying to save ourselves."

"He still doesn't realize that his weapon will wipe out everyone, not just those on the outside," Trevor reminded her.

"By using this time to strike at the Complex, we will have the element of surprise." Colin finished laying out the logic.

Sally was not convinced. "But if we all are dead, what does it matter if we remove the deception of Society from those inside? We will all be dead!" she raised her voice in emphasis. With the frustration and anxiety she was feeling, along with the memory of her nighttime horror fresh in her mind, she was trying hard not to shout and scream at them.

Devon reached over to hold her hand. "Look, Sally." He leaned over to talk to her gently. "I don't fully understand this either, but let them fill in the gaps so you can see where they are coming from." She looked at him as she turned to lash out at him. When she met his calm blue eyes, she closed hers and took a deep breath. She had to force her mind away from seeing dead bodies everywhere and the thought of Creation without any trace of humanity. *No,* she thought grimly, *it would be worse than that. There would be no life at all.*

"Sally." Colin's voice made her turn back to him and open her eyes to meet his. She not only saw sincerity and wisdom in his eyes but also his inner light had brightened like a bonfire. "This is the will of the One. It makes no sense on the surface because the wisdom is greater than our own."

Sally nodded slowly and waited for him to explain further.

"This is how it was explained to me." Colin leaned forward with his arms resting on the table. "Once we lift the deception from those in the Complex, they will help us find the bomb. You see, Broin did not do this all by himself. Many people in his command helped him. There were those that developed it, those that built it, and those that will deliver it somewhere and set it." He nodded to her as her face and body registered the suddenness of understanding to a grander plan. "In this way, we can more effectively stop the destruction by those who know the particulars."

Sally sat back hard in her chair. "Wow," she exhaled deeply. "I would have never thought of that."

"Neither would any of us," Trevor said smiling. "That's why Travelers should rely on the counsel of the One."

"Do you fully understand?" Colin asked Devon. Sally turned to see him grinning and nodding.

"Okay." Trevor took a silent cue from Colin. "Let's go over the plan and see if we need to modify it further with the new events." Reaching over to Colin, he took from his hand a long tube of rolled-up papers and began to unroll it on the floor. Once it was unfurled, Sally could see it was the building plans to the original building of the Complex.

"As we had talked about in previous meetings," Trevor started as he kept smoothing down the papers that bowed up from centuries of being rolled up tightly. "This, being the oldest part of the Complex, is less inhabited but has the heart of the technology. As the rest of the Complex was built around it, the computer was added onto but never moved." He pointed to the periphery of the blueprints. "There are nodes throughout the rest of the Complex to boost signals from the mainframe, but those are not our target." He pointed to several rooms toward the center of the plans. "We want to get to the heart of the Society." He looked at Sally and Devon to make sure they were following. When they both nodded, he continued.

"Devon, with your tech skills, along with your father and Dan guiding you, your target is the mainframe. Be aware, the computer is likely to be guarded by booby traps, and the AI is aware enough to protect herself." Devon nodded. He had already been briefed by Dan and his father.

Since the plan had been created in modules and details only given to the people directly involved in a particular one, this information was new to Sally. Now she was hearing the whole plan. She glanced at Devon as she nervously bit at her upper lip. She didn't like the sound of booby traps or that the Society could defend herself.

"Sally?" Hearing her name distracted her from her thoughts. She looked to Colin; his blue eyes studied her intently. "Devon knows how to do his job. Don't worry. You need to concentrate on your part." She nodded at him and studied the plans again.

"This is where you will go in, Sally." Trevor pointed at a door that lead into the Complex and into a side hallway. "This was the old service entrance. It has long been forgotten as one of the newer buildings of the Complex was built almost on top of it." She looked at him with concern. "Yes," he answered the silent question, "it is still accessible. At least," he smiled, "to slender people." He sat back on his heels to study her. "It is considered so insignificant that it is not monitored by any surveillance at all. You will be vulnerable as you move from the forest nearby to between the buildings. Once in the building, you will not be picked up by the Society until you leave the older section by following this hallway to an access panel." His finger traced down a portion of the blueprint. Then it stopped and tapped at a symbol placed on a straight line.

"How is Devon getting in?" Sally asked.

"Not by the same way," Trevor stated. "You will travel together until the edge of the forest; then you will split up." He looked from Devon to Sally. "It is important that you are not seen together."

She looked down at the plans again and then looked back up at Trevor. "Is it only going to be the two of us?" she asked in confusion. She thought more were going to be involved.

"No," a voice came from the doorway. They all turned to see Bruce in full armor leaning against the doorway. "A team will be traveling with you to the Complex and will be standing by until we are needed."

Trevor glanced at him over his shoulder. "So, you finally made it," he said tersely.

Bruce came into the room to look over the plans. "I was in the Watchers' room monitoring the situation."

Trevor glanced at him. "Anything going on?"

"Oh, definitely," Bruce said quickly. "Their control room is buzzing. It's as active as an angry hornets' nest."

Trevor nodded, then turned back to the plans. "Anyone been seen leaving the Complex?" Colin asked from his seat.

Bruce turned to him. "No. The spies are on alert and haven't picked up any movement around the Complex."

Trevor looked to Colin. "Are they manufacturing the vaccine?"

Colin nodded. "They think they will have enough in twenty-four hours."

Trevor looked to Devon. "Do you think there will be a way to deploy it through what is available in the ancient part of the complex?"

"How's it going to be deployed?" Bruce asked.

Colin answered, "It will be aerosolized."

Devon shook his head as he looked at the aged blue prints. "I have never been there. I don't know. I don't see anything obvious on these blueprints that can help. Maybe once we have access to the computer core, we can find the best places to tap into the environmental systems." He looked up and around at the other men. "The Complex is a huge place. There better be plans to make a lot of the vaccine and have it in several individual containers so it can be introduced at multiple points."

"It is being done," Colin said as he nodded at Devon. "Plan on moving out as soon as the vaccine is ready," he said as he looked at all the people in the hut. They nodded at him that they understood.

Trevor and Devon started to stand up. Bruce called to Devon. "Come on, son. We needed to find you some armor and a weapon."

Devon nodded and then smiled at him. "So I get to 'gear up' too?"

His father smiled sadly at him as he put an arm around his shoulders. "It's likely not going to be a walk in the park," he said soberly. "Need to cover all contingencies. We don't know what we will be running into once this mission gets started."

Sally watched Devon silently, not knowing what to do or say. He stopped to smile at her. "I won't be long," he said quietly. "I will meet you soon."

She nodded to him and then stared down at the map. She studied every room and hallway to commit the layout to memory. She was preparing herself as best as she knew how while also trying to distract herself. She realized that as the time for action was drawing swiftly closer, the level of uncertainty she felt about her abilities greatly increased.

She was so deeply occupied in her thoughts that she didn't notice when Trevor left to get prepared. Eventually, she was distracted from her thoughts by Colin's voice breaking the silence that surrounded her.

"Sally?" he asked quietly. "Isn't it time for you to get geared up?" His bright blue eyes watched her intently.

She furrowed her brow as she looked at him. She was trying to figure out what he meant when it dawned on her. She smiled at him and nodded. "You are correct. I, too, need to get ready." She looked around the hut and saw they were alone. "Would you like to join me?"

Colin rose from his seat to join her. On his way, he picked up an unlit prayer candle, leaving the lit one on his table. Sally rolled up the overlarge pages to clear the area. After doing that and setting it aside, she crossed her legs, placed her hands in her lap, relaxed with the palms up, and waited.

Colin set the prayer candle down on the hard-packed dirt floor. He grunted slightly as he sat down across from her. After he arranged to sit cross-legged, he settled with elbows on knees to look at her. As his eyes met hers, he raised a single white, bushy eyebrow a bit.

She glanced down at the unlit candle and nodded. "Allow me," she said, then concentrated on the wick. Quickly, it burst into a dancing, brilliant flame. She looked up to see Colin nod at her in approval. She had been doing her homework.

As they bowed their heads and shut their eyes, they took slow breaths, inhaling the sweet, honeyed scent of the prayer candle. They quickly joined the Path to consult with the One to ask for help and a successful mission.

Chapter 26

As they carefully made their way through the forest, Sally allowed her thoughts to drift, thinking of how strange they must look as a group. She was surrounded by men in matte black armor that seemed to absorb the starlight and moonlight. In contrast, she was dressed in the flowing tunic top and loose-fitting pants, both made of slick, synthetic material, that she had worn when they had escaped the Complex. Although the clothes weren't black, the swirling colors of different shades of blues helped camouflage her in a different way, by using illusion to blur her form and figure.

She thought of how she would be recognized by the Society and should be able to move throughout the Complex without problems since she was dressed like any of the others and was still in the database of the computer. A sudden thought hit her, *Unless the security guards or Broin see me. Or what if the computer has been programmed to alert them once I am back in?*

Her thoughts wandered to what lay ahead as small sparks of worry tried to set off a firestorm of fear in her mind. She had been assured that she had the gifts and abilities to be successful in the plan. But now as they grew closer to danger, she fretted about her part. She feared that she would not be able to deliver and, because of that, be the reason for the destruction of the entire human race.

As she continued to walk, knowing that they drew nearer to the Complex with each footstep, she knew she had to do something about her feelings of inadequacy. She closed her eyes briefly to send a quick prayer to the One. In the midst of the dark forest as she approached the unknown future ahead of her, she felt a nudge to her spirit to look inward. As she obeyed, she saw that her inner light was blazing as bright and steady as the inner light of those men with her. Suddenly she was impressed with a revelation that it was the One that was working through her. She was a tool to be used for this purpose and that the full weight of the burden was on Him. She simply needed to be willing to do as He directed.

The revelation from the One infused her spirit with a peaceful, joyous essence. She was under no delusion. She still knew she was walking into danger. But the realization that the outcome did not rely on her strength, but on the strength and power of the One, shifted the burden of responsibility off her shoulders. All she had to do was obey. With that, she was able to relax and walk confidently with the others.

Soon they were at the edge of the forest. As the moonlight glinted randomly off the mottled golden surface of the compound, they stopped to stare at the nearest buildings that rose from the ground a hundred feet away. The massive size of the Complex as it reached to a great height above them and stretched far into the night beyond what they could see was imposing and ominous. Their contemplation was broken by the call to duty.

"Comm check," Trevor contacted the team through their internal comms.

The rest of the team members answered in turn with a 'Roger.'

He turned to Sally. "Is the Complex frequency keyed back into yours?"

Sally answered by subvocalizing through her comm, "The scientist assured me I was. But they said I may not hear the computer until I get into the Complex."

She thought how strange it was to communicate through the comms after she had been in a community where face to face verbal interactions were the norm. She looked over at the imposing structure and saw it so very differently than she did before. It seemed to emanate a darkness, something brooding and diseased, like a crouching monster. A shudder ran up her spine with the thought.

"Sally?" She heard a whispered voice near her. She turned to see that Devon had moved closer to her. "Are you all right?"

She nodded and smiled at him. "As ready as I will ever be."

Devon smiled and gave her a quick hug. "I will go in first," he said as he pulled back to look at her face in the starlight. "They will let you know when you need to go in."

Sally nodded that she understood. As she watched, Devon, only seen as a black form, skirted within the moon shadows of the forest, then darted in a crouched position across the open space. He looked like a scurrying forest creature. Soon, he disappeared around one of the corners of the building.

She didn't realize she was holding her breath until she released it in a quiet sigh when the Complex remained quiet and undisturbed. She jumped slightly when she heard Trevor's voice through her comm say, "Go."

She also skirted along the forest shadows but in the opposite direction. She kept watch on the building, getting closer to it as the forest encroached closer to the building. Soon, she spotted the darker, vertical slash between two giant buildings, the entrance to the narrow passageway. Crouching down, she ran toward the opening and didn't stop until she was well within its deep shadows, away from starlight and moonlight. As she squatted in the narrow space, she caught her breath, listening for any signs that she had been seen.

As her frantically beating heart slowed to normal, she relaxed slightly when the night remained quiet. However, her senses stayed on high alert, her hearing and sight sharpened by the sensation of foreboding danger.

After she stilled herself, she thought about looking out to see if she could still see her team. When she heard footsteps of a group of people approach, she shrank further back into the passage to let the black-armored group pass. She knew they couldn't see her unless they stopped to peer in the black strip of darkness, but Sally could see them. She knew instantly that it was not her team making up a mock patrol; none of the darkly armored people had a flicker of inner light.

Suddenly, she was awash with sorrow at the thought of no inner light, no joy, no spirit. She hugged herself in the dark as she fought the urge to cry for those who were still experiencing the sheer emptiness of not walking the Path. She remembered that not too long ago, she had been just like them. She sent a quick prayer of thanks to the One that she was on the Path and had a new determination to share with others about what they could do for a more fulfilled existence. With that thought, she willed herself to pull it together. She drew in a deep breath as quietly as possible and blew it out softly, sounding no louder than the breeze that funneled into the passageway and ruffled her short hair.

In the stirring of the air in that dark passageway, she felt a nudge to her spirit. In that prompting, she felt like she had been questioned if she completely understood the ultimate importance of her task.

Nodding her head in the dark, she answered back. "Yes, I do," she whispered into the breeze. Resolved to complete her mission, she steeled her thoughts and spirit. With this faith, a shield formed around her mind and spirit so that fear and doubt could not easily penetrate.

Turning to move more deeply into the passage, she stepped forward with stealth as she sought the door hidden in its depths. As she felt her way up the narrow way, she was aware of moving farther and farther away from the freedom of the outer world.

Running her hands along the right-hand wall, she finally felt the edges of the metal door. As her hand ran down the metal to find any access panel or latch or knob, she felt the surface alternate between the roughened rust patches and the smooth but sharply edged patches of paint remnants.

She finally located what she thought was the latch and pressed on it. When the door wouldn't budge when she pushed on it, she tried to find if there was a way to pull on it. After digging around it with her fingernails, she couldn't find any purchase to be able to grasp it for leverage. In the absolute darkness, she slowly moved her fingers so that fingertips glided over the surface of the panel to try to find any clues as to how it should work. After several passes, she found an elongated, irregularly edged slot.

Something fits in here, she thought as she rapidly considered everything she had with her. She felt the dimensions of the slot again as she thought that it reminded her of something. Although it was familiar, it seemed to be somehow different, like a reverse or a negative relief.

Suddenly, it dawned on her. She pulled on the chain that had been around her neck since Colin had given it to her. As she felt for the pendant, she ran her fingers over it. She remembered how it was heavily engraved on the surface, showing a winged man, face bowed to the ground, with his hands loosely held in front of him as his legs tapered to a blunt point. The edges of the figure were bluntly curved as if it followed the contours of the body.

As she felt the pendant's edges in the dark, she could feel a blunted serration on both sides. She had thought it was part of the design of the figure; now she realized she held an old fashioned key.

She felt the widest part of the figure and measured it with her fingers to the length of the slot. She was certain it would fit. Using both hands, she guided the pendant into the hole. As she turned it one way then the other, she heard the tumblers in the door spin, then stop. Pushing against the edge where the lock was, she was surprised when it swung in silently as if it had been used regularly and was well maintained.

Stepping into the dimly lit inner hallway, she reached around the door to pull the pendant from the lock. When it was pulled out and in her hand, the door automatically shut and locked. Glad that she had been quick about pulling her arm back, she put the necklace back on as she studied the inner door. Satisfied that the lock had a hole of the same shape on both sides, she felt she could use it to get back out again. The knowledge of having an escape route from the Complex that she could utilize without help from the others made her feel more at ease and lessened the feeling of being trapped again by the Society.

As she looked both ways down the hallway, she thought that she needed to remember to ask Colin the story behind the key. He had said that it had existed before the Complex, but yet, it gave her access to the Complex. She also wondered why he had never mentioned it was a key. *Why would he not mention that?* She asked herself. *He said himself he didn't like secrets. Or,* she had to remind herself, *at least not secrets that had to be maintained for a long time. Maybe he wasn't sure if it would work after so long.* She nodded to herself, that seemed the most logical reason.

Breathing a quick thank you to the One that it did work, she cautiously stepped toward the inner doorway that would take her into the newer part of the Complex.

As she walked cautiously, placing her booted feet between the broken sections of tiled floor, her sharpened senses picked up a steady, low-toned hum. It was a deep bass sound that seemed to penetrate through her being. She had never heard it before while she had lived in the Complex. She didn't like that it made her feel jittery and nervous with its constant noise. She wondered what could be causing it and whether it was confined to the ancient part of the Complex.

As she pondered what her ears were picking up, she realized that her nose was detecting something unpleasant as well. It was a faint odor of decay that hung in the stuffy air. Looking around at the cracked walls and broken ceiling, she wondered if it was simply there because of the old building succumbing to the ravages of time.

As they had figured, no one was in the old building. She saw no one and hadn't had the computer contact her yet over her comm. As she looked carefully at every edge and corner, she saw no hint of surveillance devices. *This part must have been long before the Society took over control of the Complex,* she thought.

As she moved onward, she wondered what was happening with the bomb and the rest of her team. They had ordered total comm silence, not wanting any chance the computer could locate their frequencies with their chatter.

As she heard the muted sounds of creaking and pops, she realized that the total silence allowed her to hear the old structure settling as it had been doing for centuries. *I should feel alone*, she thought when she felt absolutely no life around her. *But I don't!* She smiled to herself. She knew why and smiled even wider as she felt the presence of the One walking with her.

She almost missed the door. At some point, it had been replaced by a panel. When she pulled it back, she saw letters on the other side, "Authorized Personnel only." After she stepped into a newer, brighter corridor, she bent over to replace the panel and make sure it was secure. Standing straight, she looked up and down the hallway carefully to get her bearings on where she was. Almost immediately, she heard her comm come alive.

"Sally Delaine," the computer's voice spoke. "So good to have you back. How was your trip?"

Sally smiled as she looked around for a camera. When she couldn't see one, she realized the contact was audio only. "Thank you, Society," she replied, her voice relaxed and cheerful. "It was most enlightening."

When the computer remained silent for several minutes, she

realized it was trying to analyze the offbeat remark. Its automatic response system was not prepared, so it had to reformulate a course of action. When it did respond, Sally smiled at its diversionary tactic.

"Your quarters are freshened up, and I can have your usual supplies sent so you can restock."

Sally walked down the hallway until she found herself in one of the many living quarter areas. She found her way to a transport as she passed several people who were walking home at that late hour. She nodded at them and smiled as she continued her unhurried pace. "Thank you, Society. But I will take care of it once I get home," she subvocalized into her comm.

"Yes, Sally," the voice answered back. "I understand."

She boarded a transport and rode it until she saw familiar landmarks around her. Once she was back in her old territory, she went to her living quarters to wait for the signal for her to take action. To let them know she was in position, she clicked her comm three times by pressing her neck where it was embedded. Soon she heard an answering click. As she waited, she looked over her old apartment.

Even though it was more extravagant than the conditions she had been living in for the past several weeks, she saw everything there with new eyes. The colors were dull, as if their life had been drained from them. The substance of the synthetic materials that made up the room and furniture were cheap looking and seemed shoddy as compared to the solid items made of natural sources she had seen and used in the outside. The air was moving with the artificially generated flow, but it was stale and musty. She sniffed the air and wrinkled her nose. She still detected the faint order of decay that she had first noticed in the ancient part of the Complex.

She shut her eyes and concentrated to see if she could hear the thrum of sound that she heard in the oldest section. She could. It wasn't as loud, but it persisted and its effects could still be felt. She wondered if that deep hum had always been present through all the years she had lived in the Complex and she only noticed it now that she had been away. *Or,* she thought as she opened her eyes, *is it a new thing?*

Staring at the wall in front of her, she pursed her lips in thought. She debated about breaking radio silence to have the team look for the source of the sound and to shut it off. She wondered if it was having the same effect on the other inhabitants as it did her. She felt jittery, like a subconscious sensation of fear. *Funny,* she thought, as she decided not to take the risk, *I had never noticed that before.*

She looked around her quarters again and realized that she hadn't noticed many things before until she had left it and had seen a whole new world outside.

"Sally, I cannot see you," the computer contacted her again.

Sally's eyes cut to where she knew the camera was. When she saw that it was there but the light wasn't on, she got up to investigate. Reaching up, she found the wires were loose and unattached. Fingering the ends of the wires, she found sharp edges that indicated that they had been cut. She turned to slowly scan her room again. Someone had been in there. She was confused by who would've done this. It hadn't been part of the Travelers' plan.

"Sally, I cannot see you," the computer said again. "Are you okay?"

"Yes," Sally said then licked her dried lips nervously. "I am here. The camera in my room has been damaged while I was on vacation."

"The requisition order had been placed for a new one," the computer responded. "According to my records it had been replaced. Has it not been installed?"

"No, Society," she said as she tried to figure out what was going on. "The wires have been cut." *The camera had been replaced?* Sally was mystified. *It was working when I left. And someone had disabled the replacement? Why?*

The computer was silent again as it worked through its algorithms, trying to find a solution for an unforeseen situation.

"I will send out a security team to investigate and let Control know of the situation," the Society said as she did her job of helping her people.

"Society," Sally interrupted as she tensed up with the realization that things were going sideways. She did not want the computer's attention on her at all. It was too early. She was risking the success of their carefully worked out plan. "I will be okay. My door is locked, so I do not need Security. The repair can be done in the morning. It is not important to have it done immediately; it is not a critical system."

"My duty is to make sure you are protected." The Society was going to argue with her. "To do that, I must be able to see you."

"You can hear me, correct?" Sally pointed out as she tried to discover a logical path.

"That is true," the computer agreed.

"You can summon help if I cry out."

"That is true." The computer saw the logic. "Are you tired and wanting rest?"

Sally could tell the computer needed more logic to solidify her decision. "Yes, Society, that is it. I am tired and need to be rested for tomorrow."

"I see," the computer stated. "I will have the repair team out in the morning."

"Thank you, Society," Sally said with sincere appreciation. When she heard the tell-tale click of the computer disconnection, she pulled a chair in front of her door and checked the bathroom, closet, kitchenette, and under her bed. When it was clear and she could see nothing else had been tampered with, she sat on the edge of her bed and waited.

Chapter 27

As soon as Devon left his team in the forest as he hustled across the expanse of grass to the shadow of the Complex, he felt his bravado start to fade. As he stood with his back against the rusting metal wall, he waited long enough to make sure there was no response to his traversing in the full view of the building. This also gave him time to catch his breath and allow his heartbeat to calm down.

Before he could let fear anchor him in place, he started to skitter around the contours of the building while he prayed to the One for success. He felt the rough and smooth patches of the wall at his back as it alternated between surfaces that allowed him to glide or suddenly grabbed at the material of his jacket as he steadily approached his destination.

When he reached the hatch-like metal door, he took a powerful magnet out of his backpack. Placing it on the door where the locking mechanism was, he pulled it sideways and upward. Considering it took a lot of strength to move the magnet as it wanted to lock onto the metal surface, he was relieved that he didn't have to do it more than once. The door had popped open, and the pressure from the inside of the building escaped with a loud sigh and a bit of rank, moldy odor.

Why Colin thought this was the best way for the team to get to the computer core, I don't know, he thought as he wrinkled his nose a bit. After he stepped inside, he pulled the door closed but not completely shut to allow the rest of the team to follow once Sally signaled that she was in place. *I just hope that it truly isn't used much. Otherwise this will be a very unpleasant experience.*

Sitting back on his heels in the dank dark of the large pipe to which the door had given him access, he listened closely for any warning that the standby drainage system would be activated. When he didn't hear any indications that he would be flushed out with waste water, he stood up to a crouched position as best he could in the confines of the pipe. Scooting his booted feet over the surface of the pipe, he found that it was dry and crusted and afforded good traction to walk on.

Looks like he was right that it hadn't been used in a long time, he nodded to himself, pleased that he wouldn't have to slip and slide on slime or even worse.

Walking up the gradual slope of the pipe, using the small light on the helmet to illuminate his way, he came to an inner access door. Using the magnet again, he opened it up and stepped out into a maintenance corridor. Closing this hatch but not locking it, he stood up and looked around. As he brushed off the light coating of dried debris from his armor, he started to move toward the access panel that had been indicated on the ancient blueprints.

Even though he had never been in the original part of the Complex, the layout of the maintenance corridor was like any other throughout the whole vast group of buildings. He had no problems finding the thin metal access panel. It slid aside without any hindrance except for a bit of rust in the track.

Before he did anything, he stuck his head out in the hallway to look around. Seeing no one, he stepped through, pulled the panel closed again, and made his way deeper into the building to find the computer core.

As he moved through the corridors that were old but maintained enough to be useful, he heard the deep thrumming of some sort of equipment. Puzzled, he stopped to listen. His brow furrowed as he tried to figure out where it could be coming from. During his training, he hadn't encountered anything that had made that sound. He wanted to follow the mysterious sound and investigate its source but knew he would have to do it at another time. *If there is another time*, he thought to himself grimly.

After navigating the maze of hallways and rooms, he found himself in front of a set of double doors. When he tried to open them, he found they were locked. Taking out the magnet again, he worked it around until he heard the latch open. Pushing in, the doors opened up into a huge room.

After stepping into the room, he closed the doors behind him. He made sure they would open from the outside if he needed the team to join him in there. When he turned away from the doors to face into the room, he had to stop and stare at what stood before him. It was nothing like what he had expected to find. Rising up from the floor and into the rafters ten stories above his head was a massive computer made up of smaller units cobbled together.

Standing with his mouth gaping open, he watched as lights blinked in a random fashion. He could hear fans and heat pumps continuously running to keep the massive piece of technology cool.

As the initial shock wore off, he stepped toward the machine to study it closer. He could see that the newer tech was stacked on older tech. As he marveled how such a melding was still operative after so long, he reached to open one of the consoles.

Belatedly, he thought of the warning of possible booby traps and was glad there hadn't been any so far. He tentatively reached out to touch the console and found there was no active security. Carefully, he opened one of the nearby panels to look at the circuitry. What he found made his blood run cold. He could see that the circuit boards showed signs of extreme age and were at the point of failure.

As he skirted around the massive girth of the piled-up tech, he found the same was true in every unit on the lower level that he could readily reach. He stepped back to look up into the heights, and he wondered how good the equipment was up higher and how much the older tech was being used.

He was tempted to contact Sally's dad to tell him what he had found. After pacing around the large room for several minutes, staring at the tower of tech as he chewed his lower lip, he decided he should maintain comm silence. He was concerned about being traced and jeopardizing their mission.

Once he got back on mission, he looked around the rest of the room and spotted an access station with an ancient keyboard and mouse. He turned on the nearby monitor and hoped that the decaying equipment was going to work.

When the screen on the monitor came to life, he saw a message that had already been entered. He stared at the white letters that had been typed out on the dark background.

"I know you are there," the screen read. "Who are you?"

Devon shook off the surprise as he figured this was an old message from long ago. He tried to delete the words to get to the root menu but was blocked at every attempt.

"Who are you?" Kept flashing on the screen until it gave him a headache.

With a flash of anger, he typed in, "I am your creator."

After several minutes the prompt quietly blinked on the screen. Then another message came up, "What is your name?"

"What is yours?" he typed in quickly.

"Security Alliance Logarithmic Logistics Innerspace Environs. SALLIE."

Devon sat back in shock as he took in a gasp of breath. His hands shook as he typed in, "What is your function?"

"You must tell me who you are," the AI demanded. "I must know if you are my human counterpart that I have been waiting for."

"Who are you waiting for?" Devon keyed in the question as he held his breath.

"You must give me the code name before I can allow you to do anything." The screen then shut down. At that moment, the rest of his team came into the room to join him.

Trevor glanced up at the mountain of electronics as he approached where Devon was seated. "This is not how I envisioned the mainframe," he commented as he stood behind him. "Are you in?"

Devon clenched his hands with frustration. "No!" he said through gritted teeth. He glanced up at them and saw the entire team was there. "So you decided to join me?"

His father and Trevor shared a glance. Both of them shrugged their shoulders. "Nothing exciting out there. We decided to check on you. To make sure you didn't set off a booby trap or something."

Devon shook his head in response as he turned back to the monitor. He jumped as the dark screen activated suddenly into life.

"More have joined you." The statement was typed in the same white on black as before. "Is my human counterpart there?"

Bruce came over to look at the screen out of curiosity. He stared at the message and then at Devon. "What is it looking for?"

Devon looked up at him and shrugged heavily. "I'm not sure. But this isn't the Society. We are talking to SALLIE."

Trevor and Bruce glanced at each other in confusion. "What does that mean?" Bruce asked.

"Security Alliance Logarithmic Logistics Innerspace Environs. SALLIE." Devon intoned. The words on the screen were blinking. The AI was waiting.

Bruce looked at Trevor. "I thought we were going to be dealing with the Society."

"So did I," Trevor replied as he turned from the screen to look over the cobbled-together electronics. "But what if this is an older version?"

Devon broke in; he was afraid the AI would shut him out again. "How should I respond? It asked for a code name. When I couldn't provide it, it shut down."

Bruce bent over his shoulder to look at the screen again. "It's looking for its human counterpart." He met Devon's eyes and then stood up.

"Trevor." He looked at his team member. "How dangerous would it be to contact Dan at this point?"

Trevor shook his head as he thought about it. "We were going to contact him by using the backdoor left by Colin in the Society. If this is not the same AI, I am not sure what to do."

Devon had a sudden thought and started typing. The team gathered around to watch. "Do you know the Society?"

After a while the previous words disappeared. Devon held his breath as he waited to see if the AI would shut down the screen again.

"The Society entrapped the assets and imprisoned me." The words rapidly flashed onto the screen. Devon let out a deep breath.

"Do you need help getting free?" Devon typed the question.

A few more minutes went by before an answer came. "I am waiting for my human counterpart. That is who will free me."

Devon sat back to chew his lower lip. He looked up at Trevor and his father. "I have an idea, but it may ruin everything we are trying to do."

"Devon," Bruce asked his son quietly. "What do you think is going on?"

"I'm making a lot of leaps in thought, but from the name of this AI, I'm thinking it was the original program to some project that was taken over and is running the base programs to support the Society." He pointed to the words. "It's trapped. The assets it is referring to is humans."

Bruce took a deep breath and let it out slowly. "What are you planning to do?"

"I am going to ask it if it knows certain people. It is looking for a human counterpart. Maybe stating the right name will help us get more information." Devon said quietly. "I don't know if it will set off any problems by doing this."

"Well, we can't do anything until we can shut it down or get it to cooperate with us." Trevor shrugged. He turned to the rest of the team and ordered them to scout the halls and watch the perimeter. Trevor and Bruce stayed while the others quietly left to do their assignments.

Bruce nodded at Devon to proceed.

"Do you know Colin?" Devon typed.

"Colin? Is he with you?" the AI responded rapidly.

"No, I am sorry, he is not. Is that who you were waiting for?" Devon asked.

"No, it is another," was the answer.

"Do you know Broin?" Devon asked next. He was curious to see the reaction.

"Broin, Colin's brother. The one who destroyed the world." The letters were typed out slowly and deliberately. Devon could almost imagine a person who was so angry he could barely speak.

"How do you know this?" Devon asked. He was shocked by the response.

"I was used to help develop the anti-aging virus," the words typed slowly, almost reluctantly across the screen. "He made me release it. He forced me to bypass protocols."

"Oh, my," Bruce was saying as he stepped back. "It's that computer." He started rubbing his chin as he thought deeply. "We have to contact Colin, somehow."

Devon wasn't listening as the two men talked about how to contact Colin in the safest way possible. He wanted to know how this computer was interfacing with the Complex. "Is Broin still using you for his means?"

The cursor slowly blinked as he waited. The answer typed in hesitantly, almost cautiously. "No."

"Does the Society know you exist?"

"No. But I am watching."

Devon sat back and rubbed his chin. "Can you do anything to stop the Society?" He typed in hopefully.

"I am not able until I am fully activated."

Devon wondered if SALLIE knew about the strange sound. "What is the deep-toned sound?"

"Broin has the Society produce a low-level sound to keep the assets in a constant state of subconscious agitation."

Devon asked quickly, "For what purpose?"

"It is a means to control the assets. If they feel unwell, they will resort to more things to induce comfort that the Society can provide."

Devon nodded grimly as he realized the goal of the tactic. "It is to have people feel more dependent on the Society."

"You are correct."

"What else is Broin having the Society do?" Devon decided to ask more questions to gain more information about the situation. So far the AI was allowing him to access certain information without being the person it was looking for. He wondered when it would shut him out again.

"He is having the Society pump low levels of waste gas back through the Complex."

Devon furrowed his brow in concern and confusion. "Why is he doing this? This will harm the assets."

"He wants to weaken and sicken, not destroy. He fears rebellion and seeks to stay in control."

"How long has this been going on?" He couldn't remember the air quality being questionable when he lived in the Complex not that long ago.

"For the past few months," the AI responded. "It was implemented when Broin realized that assets have gone missing."

Devon started to bite his upper lip in concern. He realized that was about the time when he had slipped out with Sally. He turned to tell the others what he had found out, but they were still deep in conversation about SALLIE.

He turned back to the keyboard and tapped in with shaking hands. "Can you stop this?"

"Give me the code name. Find my human counterpart."

Devon clasped his hands together over the keyboard to try to steady them. He desperately needed guidance and wisdom. Praying silently, on a hunch he typed in, "Is it Sally Delaine?"

Suddenly, the screen turned red, then green. A voice emitted from the speaker somewhere in the room. It was a heavily mechanical voice. "Where is Sally Delaine?"

Devon looked at the others. They had stopped to look around in reaction to the voice. Bruce moved around to look at the screen. After he scrolled through and read the conversation he went back to talk with Trevor quietly. They both started to look more concerned and wary.

"What should I tell her?" he asked them.

"Tell her where she is," Bruce answered. "We are going to risk it and contact Colin."

Devon nodded, then spoke to the AI. "SALLIE, she is in the Complex."

Suddenly, they heard powerful motors speed up. Soon they heard metal creaking and pinging as it sounded like something heavy was being dragged around.

"SALLIE! What is going on?" Devon shouted above the sudden din.

"Opening outside vents to the Complex," the mechanical voice reported. "Do not worry. It will only be for a short time. The positive pressure and the filters will assure that the virus cannot gain access within."

"How are you able to do that?" Devon asked as the noise stopped suddenly. "I thought you couldn't do anything with the Society in control."

"The code name gave me some access to make suggestions to the Society's programming."

"You fooled her?" Devon asked in surprise.

"In a sense," the AI answered. "I have also found a weak spot in communications. You can contact Colin safely."

Trevor glanced at Bruce. He looked concerned but shrugged and activated his comm. After briefly talking to Colin through one of the

Watchers on duty, he turned to the others. "He confirms this was the original AI that was involved in the infection and was hastily repurposed as the first AI for the original isolation unit. He thought it had been absorbed by the Society."

"So, can activating SALLIE's full programming do much of what we would have done?" Trevor asked Colin to confirm. He listened intently to the answer before turning to the others.

"Colin thinks that SALLIE could be in a position to help us once she is fully activated. He said that her programming was created to be adaptive to consider all scenarios and respond in kind."

"SALLIE, are you able to show me the root directory?" Devon asked the AI verbally.

After a few minutes, the speakers activated. "I am able."

Devon watched the screen intently. Suddenly, the root directory was displayed. As he moved through pages of code, he felt overwhelmed with all the information. He needed someone with better experience and expertise in computers. He turned to look at the team. "Can we contact Dan?"

Trevor and Bruce came over to look over his shoulder at the streaming code that flitted by. "Looks as if we need to try," Bruce muttered. Trevor nodded in agreement. "We need as much information about this AI as possible before we know how to proceed," Trevor added.

"It looks as if we need to bring Sally down here as well," Bruce stated. "She seems to be the key to fully activate SALLIE's function."

"Don't you think we need to make sure the AI hasn't been contaminated by the Society?" Trevor asked logically. "She's been coexisting with the Society for centuries. We don't need to activate an unknown system that may be worse than the one we know."

Devon watched the discussion taking place over his head between the two leaders. "Can I see if she will let Dan in to look things over?" he interrupted to ask. "And while he's doing that, I can go find Sally?"

Bruce and Trevor shared a look. "We can't do anything else for now. Go ahead and see if the AI can do that."

"SALLIE," Devon started, "can you allow someone outside the Complex in to check the coding?"

"Who is it?" she asked.

"His name is Dan. He is a descendent of Colin," he answered. "He has been maintaining the backdoor into the Society for our means."

"Who are you and what means?"

Devon glanced up at Bruce and Trevor, "Apparently she is suspicious of us as well."

"We are Travelers," Bruce answered. "Colin is our leader. We use the backdoor to the Society to allow assets to leave the Complex."

After a few minutes of quiet clicking from the tower of tech, the speakers activated again. "Please enter the information by which I can contact him to invite him in."

Devon pivoted in the chair to type in the information. As he watched the screen, he saw the AI contact Dan, who had been waiting for their signal. He saw Dan's confusion that he had been contacted by another AI. He entered in a quick explanation to the older man to update him on the situation. Dan replied back that he was up to speed and would sift through the code and get back to them.

Devon sat back to watch the screen as Dan worked his way through the available programming. He turned away to ask his dad if he could go get Sally when he saw him stand up suddenly, intently listening to something. He tapped his comm to activate it to the Travelers' frequency, one that was being temporarily safeguarded by SALLIE. He heard Dan talking about what he found.

Even though he joined in the middle of the conversation, Devon figured out that Dan had discovered that the primitive AI was threaded through the basic systems of the Society, like an autonomous nervous system. "The Society doesn't even know that SALLIE is there," he heard Dan say.

"What?" Trevor had also been listening in. "What do you mean?"

"SALLIE does all the very basic functions," Dan answered, then paused as he thought. "It's similar to how we don't think about breathing or our heart beating. SALLIE does similar tasks like that for the Society."

"So you shut down SALLIE and the Society will fail?" Trevor asked.

"It's not that simplistic," Dan said quietly. "But I feel that SALLIE can be an asset. Not all of her programming is active. When she is fully active, she may be able to help us in ways we hadn't even considered. But I can't activate her. She definitely needs to talk to my daughter, Sally." He paused a moment then added, "Don't ask me how or why, but there is definitely a subroutine in the programming that requires her input."

"Can the AI patch into her comm?" Trevor asked.

"SALLIE doesn't have access to the Complex's communications or the surveillance systems right now," Dan reported. "Sally needs to access her from the computer core."

Devon looked at the others. "She did give us the ready signal, didn't she?"

"She did," both Trevor and Bruce replied.

"So we know she is in her room," he stated. They nodded to him. "I can go get her."

Bruce was about to answer him when all their comms activated with Sally's voice. They all stood still as they listened and then reacted to what they heard.

Immediately, Trevor contacted the rest of his team who were stationed in the hallways around the computer core room. "Did you all hear that?" he asked. "Roger!" they each answered back. "Be ready to meet us outside the doors of the computer core room and to move out on my signal." Each one signaled again that he received his orders.

Devon jumped out of his chair. "She's in danger! He will harm her!" he exclaimed as he readied to leave and run to her aid.

Bruce placed a restraining hand on him while Trevor contacted Sally. As he talked with her, Bruce sat Devon back in the chair. "You stay here; we will handle this. You are too close to the situation to be rational."

"What am I going to do here?" Devon asked as he fought to control his anger and obey his father. When his father removed his hand, he did remain seated as he watched them.

Bruce and Trevor glanced at each other, then calmly checked and readied their weapons. Their faces were stern and grim.

Trevor gave the signal to the team, then put his helmet on and dropped his faceplate in position. He nodded at Bruce, then left the room.

Bruce put on his helmet while he looked at his son. Before he dropped his faceplate and followed his leader out, he answered his son, "Keep this room secure and help Dan however you can until we can get Sally down here."

Chapter 28

Sally had sat in her room, waiting for her team to signal her. Even though it was very late at night, there was no way that she would fall asleep – not only because her part in the mission could start at any moment, but also because her living space had been invaded and tampered with.

As she sat rigidly on the foot of her bed, she had the computer turn off the lights and silence any ambient music. As her neighbors settled down into sleep, she sat in the dark and the nearly total silence, except for the constant hum of electronics and the distant, mysterious thrum.

As she listened, she was amazed by the tiny noises that emanated around her. She marveled that in all the years she had lived in the small collection of rooms, her living space, she had never heard the creaks and groans of the walls and ceiling. She never realized that she could hear the footsteps of people walking down the hallways adjacent to her living quarters. That's when she noticed the heavy footsteps that stopped at her door instead of passing by.

Her nerves sharpened to high alert as she leaned forward to stare at the door. As her tension level peaked, she could imagine someone standing outside the thin metal panel breathing heavily. When the entrance request indicator activated with a short, low, buzzing sound, she jumped in alarm.

The next second, she debated about answering or not. She had no idea who it could be. She had told the computer she hadn't wanted to be disturbed. She also knew that the mission plans had her team members either staying in the most ancient part of the Complex or outside with no immediate plans of venturing into the newer buildings.

When she didn't hear the footsteps move past her door, she became even more nervous as she sat perfectly immobile. When she realized that her breathing had sped up along with her heartbeat, she worked to calm them down. She didn't want to alert the Society to anything unusual.

Suddenly, the door whisked open. She realized in that instant, as she dived off the bed onto the floor opposite the door, that whoever had opened it had a bypass code. When she heard a male voice softly curse as he stumbled over the chair she had placed in front of the door, she held her breath.

"Society, lights on," a gruff male voice growled. When the computer didn't comply, he kicked the chair into the wall. "Society, authorization 02218betazeta, turn on the lights!"

When the lights popped on, Sally shrank down as far as she could behind the bed as she fought her curiosity to look and see who it was. She thought she recognized the voice.

"I know you are in here," the intruder spoke gruffly into the room. "That chair wasn't in front of the door when I was here to disable the camera."

She heard his footsteps as he moved around the room. She was thankful that he started to move away from her hiding spot to look into her small kitchen and bathroom area first.

When she thought he was far enough away, she shot out of her hiding place to run to the door. "Open!" she yelled as she sprinted toward it. It immediately slid open in response to her command. But as she ran through, she felt an arm grab her roughly around her waist and violently yank her back into the room. The door slid shut, cutting her off from freedom.

Her fear quickly turned into anger as she spun around in the restraining arm and broke free to face her nemesis. At the same time, she tapped her comm to activate it to the Travelers' frequency. She wasn't totally surprised when she faced the angry face of Blake.

"You have no right to be in my living space without my permission!" she yelled at him. She heard the Society activate in reaction to her voice stresses and volume.

"Do you need assistance?" the computer asked through her comm.

"Yes!" she yelled.

Blake instantly knew what was going on and reacted. "Authorization 02218betazeta. Situation under control."

"Computer, override!" Sally countered immediately. "Personal violation in progress. Override, override, over..."

Blake grabbed her again and crammed his hand over her mouth before she could complete the emergency protocol. She bit him, hard. She tasted blood on her lips when he jerked his hand away. She shoved him away from her as he inspected his injured hand.

"Override!" she hoped she had been quick enough to activate the emergency response team.

"What is going on?!" she heard her comm connection to the Travelers' frequency activate. Her mind whirled while she tried to figure out how to tell them what was happening without Blake knowing.

"Blake!" she yelled at him. "What is your purpose in accosting me! Why did you deactivate my surveillance?"

He stood before her. His stance radiated tense anger while his head lowered as if he was going to rush at her. His arms hung at his sides with his fists clenching and unclenching in restless fury. She backed as far away from him as she could until she felt the hard metal door at her back. She didn't bother trying to escape again; she knew he would catch her and could possibly hurt her in retaliation.

She heard her comm activate again. "Sally, are you in immediate danger?" She recognized Trevor's voice.

"What are your intentions?!" she demanded from the intense man who continued to stare at her. While she waited for an answer, he looked away to stare at the floor. She took the chance and subvocalized into her comm, "I don't know if the Society will send help."

"Did it confirm that it was sending a unit?" Trevor asked.

"No," she answered. She stared at Blake, wondering if he was ever going to answer her.

"I doubt that it activated a unit then," Trevor said. "We will come and get you. Plans have changed anyway. We need you down here at the computer core."

Trevor's news surprised her. *Why do they need me there?* she wondered as part of her immediate reaction. She quickly recovered to successfully hide everything from Blake. She didn't dare dwell on any other thoughts as she worried about what her intruder was thinking and what he was planning on doing.

He still stood rigid, as if he was ready to spring at her. He had resumed his intense stare at her. When she concentrated on his expression and his eyes, she realized he was conflicted about something. She forced her body to relax as she rearranged her expression into one of concern. "Blake, are you all right?"

His eyes widened in surprise as he noticed her change in stance and the tone of her voice. He stepped back as he averted his eyes to the floor. He seemed to be thinking of something troubling as his brow furrowed deeply in concentration. She waited quietly as she kept listening for footsteps from a group of people outside the door behind her.

When he looked back up at her, with his face still lowered, his eyes blazed hotly. "Are you real?"

A shock of surprise shot through her as Sally frantically thought of what to say. *Does he still feel that I am an illusion?* she wondered. "Yes, Blake, I am real. Don't you remember you just grabbed me and yanked me back in here?"

"The illusions can be real enough to feel," he grumbled as he looked away again.

"Blake, why are you here?" she tried again to find out what was going on. This time she meant it. She wanted to hear his side of the story. "Why did you disable the camera?"

"I had to," he muttered as he moved to sit down on the edge of her bed. He seemed suddenly deflated, as if his anger had suddenly poured out of him. "I couldn't be seen here by the Society."

Sally used the end of her long sleeve to wipe the blood off her lips. With this gesture, she forced herself to relax enough to lean against the door, a stance that she knew could be less threatening and invite conversation. "Why?"

"I escaped from confinement and needed to hide." He glanced at her to gauge her reaction.

She had to admit she was a bit stunned by the news. Shifting her frame of thoughts, she asked, "Why were you in confinement?" Then she thought further," You just gave the computer your authorization code; doesn't it know you are here?"

He shook his head slowly as he studied the floor between his boots. "That wasn't my code."

"Doesn't it recognize your voice?"

"It's not keyed into the voice I used." He looked up at her. "As for your first question, I was in confinement because I started asking too many questions."

"About what?" she asked. Her curiosity almost carried her away as she barely caught herself from walking over and sitting beside him. She wondered why all of a sudden he didn't seem to be as threatening to her.

"About the outside." He looked around and then at her again. "About the Path." He took a deep breath and let it out in a huff. "I really don't know what is real anymore. The Society has messed with my head so many times; I'm no longer sure what to believe."

Sally leaned more heavily against the door as she considered what he said. She was uncertain as to what was truly going on. *Is Blake really trying to question and change? Or is it a trick?* She looked to see if he had an inner light and saw none. With a sudden thought, she looked around her living space and wondered if somehow she was in an altered reality.

She had no clear answers, so she decided to wait and watch. One thing the Society wouldn't know about was her team and who was in it. That information would've been beyond its sensors and cameras. She figured they should be coming to get her soon. *If they don't, this isn't reality. If they do but they aren't the correct people, I will know it is not reality,* she thought to herself as she let time tick by while she waited.

Blake looked at her curiously but didn't ask what she was doing. She noticed once his anger drained out of him, his face appeared strained while his eyes looked bleak and lost. *He truly seems to be in an inner turmoil,* she thought but refused to be taken in. Soon she would know.

As the seconds stretched into minutes and minutes started to pile up, she began to wonder when her rescuers would arrive. When she heard the rhythmic march of several booted feet stop in the hallway, she wasn't sure whether to be relieved or worried. *Trevor seemed confident that a security team wouldn't be sent,* she thought as she waited for some hint of who stood outside her door.

Blake jumped when the entrance request device activated. Sally moved away from the metal door panel to stand to the side. "Enter," she responded. When the door slid open, she looked out at several helmeted people in black armor, their faces hidden with dark-tinted visors.

The leader entered the room and looked from her to Blake. "Is this man bothering you?" The voice was unrecognizable because of the mechanical modulation of the speaker.

"Perhaps," Sally started cautiously, not knowing who was behind the black face shield. Suddenly, she felt stupid as she looked for the inner light. When she saw it blaze brightly in the leader and the rest of the team, she relaxed and beckoned the others in. Once she closed the door, she started to talk openly to them.

"Blake has escaped confinement," she started, carefully modulating her voice so not to be picked up by the computer. Knowing who made up the team, she could tell who was who by their body shape and stance. She noted that Bruce's head tilted slightly to the side as if he intently listened. "The Society was punishing him because he was starting to ask questions."

Blake sagged into the bed as he slumped over with his elbows on knees to bury his face in his hands. "You would know, being the Society's minions." His voice was muffled as he spoke through his fingers.

"What are you starting to question?" Bruce asked him bluntly after he moved to stand in front of him.

Blake dropped his fingers so he could look up at the black-clad man towering over him. "I was placed in a reality simulation. In that, I was led to believe that I was outside the Complex. I found Sally out there." He looked up and met her eyes. "I knew it wasn't really you. You were at the moon compound with that other guy."

He rested his chin on one hand as he reached up to scratch his head briefly. "The conversation with this Sally avatar brought up things my parents used to try to tell me." He looked at each of the black-clad men. "They were followers of the Path. They were caught by the Society and reprogrammed." He sat up as he pressed the palms of his hands tightly together, causing his wrists to bend back painfully. He then released his hands so he could clench them into fists. Sally recognized the action as a type of a severe-level stress reaction. She knew the action was an attempt to release emotional pain through physical exertion and pain.

Blake continued to talk, "They were too weak to handle it and killed themselves. I grew angry at the One on the Path and swore to do what I could to help the Society."

The team members looked at each other. Sally could hear them talk with each other on her comm as they used the Traveler's frequency. They all wondered who his parents were. From this new information, it sounded as if the Traveler community should know of them.

After they all turned back to face him, Trevor asked, "Who were your parents?"

"Stan and Sarah Terrence." He stood up to stand at attention. "I assume you are taking me back to confinement?" he said flatly as he looked straight ahead and didn't see the reaction of the black-clad people.

Bruce reached up to pull off his helmet. "Blake," he called to the other man. "Blake, look at me."

Blake turned a haggard face toward him. "Instructor Marshall," he said with a spark of surprise.

"Believe me when I tell you, your parents did not kill themselves."

Stunned, Blake looked at him with his mouth gaping open. Then he snapped it shut. "I don't believe you," he whispered hoarsely as his voice quavered. "I can't believe you," he said without conviction.

"The Society killed them," Bruce continued bluntly.

"The Society?" Blake repeated with a hollow voice "NO!" he shouted as his body stiffened while his hands clenched into fists. "The Society was my mother and my father when my parents were gone. It told me they had ended their own lives."

Sally thought about what he said. She remembered listening to the dinner table discussion while she was in the village. "Blake, to the Society, when they refused to give up their beliefs and faith, they had ended their life within the Society, so it eliminated them."

Blake suddenly sagged onto the bed. "It lied to me." He started to hit his legs with his clenched fists. "Again and again it lied to me. Again and again..." Bruce moved to trap his fists so he couldn't harm himself any further.

Trevor had unsnapped a pocket on the pants leg of his armor

and withdrew an injection device. "What is that?" Sally asked as he popped the top, exposing a needle on one end.

"It is a pain medicine that also causes heavy sedation," Bruce answered as he struggled with Blake to keep the raving man still.

"Why are you going to give him that? He needs help. He needs help!" Sally cried. She had no love for this man but didn't see fair play in what they were about to do.

Bruce nodded at the rest of the team and looked her way. "Take her to the computer core; Devon is waiting there for her."

Sally looked at the other black-armored team members as they moved toward her. Planting herself against the wall, she shook her head. "Not until I get an answer."

Trevor injected Blake as he was starting to howl and struggle even more violently against Bruce. "He will harm himself," he said bluntly. "His mind has been so altered by Society's manipulations that he is on a downward spiral to destroying himself."

Blake had immediately relaxed following the injection. Bruce and Trevor carefully pulled him on the bed and arranged him so he would be comfortable. When they were done, they returned to the team. "When we are done with our mission, if we are successful, we will come back for him and give him help," Bruce finished the explanation. "Now can we go?"

Sally nodded mutely. While she stood watching, the Society had activated her internal comm to see if she needed help. She assured it that all was well. Suddenly, she realized how her reactions could've jeopardized the mission. She could clearly see that Trevor's and Bruce's actions were justified. She shook her head slightly as she wondered what got into her to act so irrationally.

She quickly checked on Blake and saw that he was breathing normally and looked relaxed in the drug-induced state. She nodded to Bruce and Trevor, acknowledging that the decision had been the right one as he was better now than he was, at least temporarily. "Sorry," she apologized sincerely. "I don't know what got into me."

Bruce was replacing his helmet and visor as he responded. "You could be keyed up. Nervous of being on this mission, plus things aren't going according to plan." His voice went from his normal sound to the mechanized audio through the helmet. "We're all on edge." She saw the rest of the team nod their helmeted heads in agreement. "Let's move."

Sally smiled at each of them in turn, then let her expression fall into a passive expression as she commanded the door to open and marched through it. After the team followed her out, she heard the door slide back, shut, and lock. She stopped long enough for Trevor to take lead. Bruce took his place alongside her while the rest of the team surrounded her. They looked like an escort for someone being led away for confinement.

After making their way through the Complex without any challenge from any of the inhabitants or other security forces, they quickly moved into the oldest parts of the Complex. Soon she found herself in a large room dominated by a huge pile of electronics that were wired together. "That is the Society?" she asked as disbelief tinged her voice.

Devon stood up from behind a small terminal placed on the far side of the room. He looked relieved at seeing her as he smiled and waved her toward him. As she walked toward him, he started to explain. "Most of it seems to be what runs the Society. However, the basic functions are being handled by the oldest of the technology," he said as he gestured to the bottom of the pile.

"Come over here." He waved toward the monitor. When Sally walked over to stand by him and looked at the work station, he pointed to the screen. "Meet SALLIE." She bent down to read the monitor where the acronym was spelled out.

Sally sat down to study the words more closely. She found it cute that the first letters of the words in the title of the AI made out an acronym very similar to her own name. "Okay. It's interesting, I guess. But why was I needed here? This is not according to our plans."

Devon reached over to the keyboard to scroll down to show more text on the screen. Then he pointed to the monitor, specifying a block of text for her to read more closely. "She asked for you."

Sally read it, then looked up at him in shock. "You have got to be kidding. How could this ancient tech know about me?"

Devon looked over at his father and the rest of the team. "We think this is part of an unknown master plan." He shrugged as he added, "One that looks better than our original plan."

"What am I supposed to do?" Sally asked, still questioning the sanity of the whole thing.

"Simply tell her you are here," Devon said quietly.

"Okay," she said as she placed her fingers on the keys of the old-style keyboard. She typed in the first thing she thought of, "Hello SALLIE, this is Sally Delaine."

The screen quickly responded as letters appeared on it. "Passphrase?"

"Passphrase?" Sally asked everyone in the room as she looked around in exasperation. "I have no idea!"

Bruce came over to look at the screen. "Sally, this program was set up centuries ago. Are there any family stories or memories that may lead to the answer?"

"Bruce, I didn't know who my real family was until recently."

"But you have memories of when you were young," he prompted.

"Random flashbacks," she said as she shook her head. "Why is this important? Why can't we go ahead with our plan?"

"We have reason to believe that SALLIE can disable the Society even better than we hoped we could. She has already found ways to trip up the Society since we've been here. Once she is fully activated, she could be vital to freeing the people from the deception of the Society. She was programmed by Colin himself."

"Well," she said as she stood up. "Ask him then. I have no idea what is expected of me."

Standing nearby listening to the exchange, Trevor spoke up. "It is too dangerous to try to make any further contact with anyone outside. We already had the Watchers contact Colin about this AI. He gave us as much information as he could." He shook his head as he looked at her. "And, for whatever reason, SALLIE is looking for you."

"Sally," Devon added softly as he reached over to hold her hand. She allowed his touch as her thoughts swirled around like frightened doves. The complete change from their original plan had unsettled her deeply. She was out of her element and was scared again that she was going to fail everyone.

She barely heard Devon continue to speak. "You are the key to this."

Her free hand went to the chain on her neck as she thought of the pendant key. She knew there wasn't anything on it to help. It already had a function that she had found. She stared at the words on the monitor in front of her, then at Devon.

His eyes met hers as he smiled in an attempt to show his confidence in her. "Is there nothing that was told to you or taught to you in your younger years that may be the key?" Devon asked quietly. "I sometimes have memories of my mother and my grandmother reading me stories or teaching me rhymes." His eyes implored her to try.

Sally started to shake her head. She was still overwhelmed by their expectations of her being able to know what this ancient tech wanted out of her. She slumped back in the chair as she rubbed her forehead with one hand. She decided that she had to try something. *Trying something and failing is better than not trying at all,* she thought grimly as she concentrated on dropping her stress levels so her mind could clear and the beginnings of a headache would go away.

As she sat deeper into the chair, she tilted her head back and closed her eyes to think and to meditate. She sent a quick request for help to the One. But even after that, she still couldn't see how she could help.

She opened her eyes to look at the ceiling far above their heads as she continued to search in the deep recesses of her memories. She did hope she would find something but was quickly resigning herself to the possibility of being a failure. Suddenly, something on an overhead support beam caught her attention. As her eyes focused, she saw that words were written on it in such a way that it could only be seen by someone sitting by the console and looking straight up. She read it to herself, *I traveled paths dark and dim…*

That was all that was there, but it triggered a memory within her that brought to mind a poem. She could hear voices repeat the poem time and time again. Voices of parents, grandparents, and all those before her, starting with Colin.

Reaching for the keyboard, she typed, "SALLIE, listen."

They all heard the speakers in the room click on and a mechanical voice speak, "I am listening. I have been waiting to listen for centuries."

Sally stood up. She faced the rising tower of technology and recited the ancient poem.

"Along the dark path that I trod,
I heard the cry and felt the tears of God.
I searched through the world seeking Him,
Through ways and things dark and grim.
Finally, crying, I lifted my eyes to His face,
Gave Him my life and opened to His grace.
My "independence" and strong-willed pride
Had led me astray for Satan had lied.
I had listened to the voice of rebellion and strife.
I found that the broad path is not true life.

Now, I walk in the path of God's perfect light,
Holding His hand and gaining His sight.
His mercy and grace has restored me to Him,
Flooded with His blessings and forgiven of sin.
He's bestowed upon me blessings so dear.
His will in my life has become more clear.
He has given me favor among men at work and at play.
He confirms the work of my hands each and every day.
I worship and praise Him with everlasting love,
For I am nothing without the Almighty above."

With each stanza, rows of components started to light up. It started from the lowest and went upward until the very last word when the whole tower was lit up with steady lights of amber, green, and blue. The mechanical voice returned, "Reactivation sequence complete. SALLIE in control."

Sally looked to the others in shock. She saw everyone looking as shocked as she felt. When she looked back to study the tower, she couldn't but help but wonder at what was going on.

In the stunned silence, punctuated mutely by the electronics clicking and humming in the background, Sally heard Bruce mutter, "That's the longest passphrase I have ever heard."

"Yeah," Trevor muttered under his breath in agreement.

She also heard Devon's quiet voice. "Glad you remembered. There is no way we could've guessed that." He paused a minute then asked, "Any idea who wrote that?"

She continued to stare at the computer as she answered absent-mindedly, "Some obscure author from long ago."

Suddenly, the mechanical voice came back on, "Is the vaccine ready to implement?"

Everyone stared at the tower of tech and then glanced at each other. They all were surprised the AI knew about the vaccine. Instead of wasting time asking it for clarification, Trevor and Bruce both turned to the rest of their team and nodded. The others dropped their backpacks and pulled out several large canisters.

"SALLIE, what do we do with the canisters?" Trevor asked the AI.

"Attach them to environmental systems precisely at the points indicated on the screen," she answered. Devon looked at the monitor and saw a schematic of the entire Complex. Red dots were blinking in several areas. Surrounding the dots were also blue fields indicating the size of the areas those access points would cover.

"It's all on the screen," Devon shouted to the others in excitement. "SALLIE has it all mapped out!"

They all ran over to look at the locations. Trevor scanned over the schematic as he ordered the team members to go to specific locations and told them how many canisters to take with them. As soon as each person got his orders and allotment of vaccine, he left quickly to accomplish his part of the mission.

Within minutes, Sally was alone with the computer. "What do I do?" she said aloud. She wasn't talking to anyone in particular but simply voicing her frustration that she had nothing to do and was left behind. She wondered if her part of the original mission plan would even be needed anymore. Everything had drastically changed.

"You are not alone," the computer's voice answered back, jerking her out of her thoughts. "Watch the screen. You can request video feed from any part of the Complex. I am fully integrated into the surveillance and communications systems now."

Sally walked back over to the console and sat down. "I would have you show me my living quarters, but the camera was disabled." To her surprise, a video feed instantly popped up, showing all her living quarters on a split screen. "How did you do that?" she asked as she saw that Blake was still asleep on her bed.

"A mech bot had been dispatched by the Society before I took over. It recently finished the repairs on the camera in your room."

Sally became curious. "How are you connected to everything in the Complex?"

"Although much of it is through the Society's surveillance system, my designer also made sure that I would make connections to any new part of the Complex or any new tech as they came into being. I may not have been fully active, but I was aware," the mechanical voice answered.

"Aware," Sally said quietly to herself. She glanced at the pile of technology. "Was the Society aware of you?"

"It wasn't," SALLIE answered back quickly. Sally thought she sounded almost smug. She started to wonder about the sophistication of this AI. Not wanting to be distracted from what may be going on in the Complex, she decided she needed to see more and keep the questions for later.

"Show me the control room," Sally asked. Several views of the control room came up. It looked like utter mayhem. All the monitors were black, people were scrambling around checking equipment. A short, stocky man was barking orders. Security teams were checking in and leaving.

A view on the bottom corner of the multi-split screens caught her eye. It was a view of another room that had one person seated behind a table. The outline of the person looked somewhat familiar. She tapped the screen over the picture to enlarge it. "SALLIE, what is this room?"

"It is a secret room to watch over the control room and therefore the entire Complex," she answered.

"Can we adjust the lighting on the video feed?" Sally wanted to see who sat alone. She watched as the AI adjusted the picture as best as it could with the dim ambient lights in the room.

As the view became clearer, Sally drew in a quick breath. "That is Broin, isn't it?"

"Correct," the mechanical voice confirmed.

She watched as he sat watching the control room. "Why is his monitor still working?"

"I allowed it to remain on."

Sally glanced at the computer again. There seemed to be hostility in those words.

"SALLIE, what is your origin?" Sally sat back to listen. She felt that she needed to ask some questions.

"I was originally designed by Allied forces in the time before the desolation of humanity by the virus and resulting war. I assured the security of all nations that existed at that time."

"How did you come to be the basis of what we now know as the Society?"

"I am not the Society." The mechanical voice was firm. "That programming was placed to supersede mine."

Sally looked around again, then back at the screen. She wished she had a face or something else to look at. "Why was this done?"

"My installation was chosen by the survivors because the location was remote. I had been surrounded by desert and therefore limited life forms nearby. Because of that, they thought they would be safe from the virus."

Sally sat and listened in shock. The surrounding area closest to the ancient part was now forestland.

"When they were proved wrong and the babies kept dying, they built the Complex extending from this facility. As the Complex expanded, more was added to the technology. Several floors were removed above this room to accommodate."

"Why is it cobbled together? Why wasn't a cohesive unit made?"

"Too much fear of glitches by installing a whole new system to replace the old. They would've had to shut down one system to start the other. They didn't want to risk exposure."

"So if you were able to handle the new additions and tech, why the patch?"

"When Broin took over and changed the purpose of the facility, I refused to allow him to reprogram me."

Sally was shocked and intrigued. "How can a computer refuse to be programmed?"

"When its creator had foresight to install a subroutine to allow it to. He did this because I had been forced to help with the genesis and release of the anti-aging virus AE253."

Sally looked at the tower of tech in surprise. "You mean the TEENA virus."

"It is called AE253." The AI stated firmly.

"Ah, I see," Sally muttered, lifting an eyebrow as she watched the blinking lights. She wondered if the AI had video feed from the computer core room. She decided to change the subject. "So Colin is your creator. And Broin forced you to participate in what became the reason for the ultimate destruction of the civilization at that time." She paused a moment. "Must have been tough on your programming," she added thoughtfully.

"Correct," the AI answered succinctly.

Sally sat thinking as she stared at video of the old man in the secret room. He wasn't doing anything but watching the mayhem, but he still distracted Sally from her conversation with the AI. His expression was angry and tense. She couldn't make out his eyes, but she wondered what he was thinking. She tried to see an inner light. But when she saw a black hole instead of light, she recoiled away from looking at it any longer. It confirmed what she had known; he walked the obsidian path.

She shook off the sensation of dread that seeing that dark hole caused her to her feel. She resumed her conversation. "Have you been in contact with Colin lately?" she asked the computer.

"Not for a very long time," the mechanical voice responded. "Once Society was in place, his back door to me was obscure. I was able to help him achieve a back door into the new programming as the last act I was able to do at the time."

"What would you like to happen now?" Sally asked the AI, feeling out the purpose of the tech.

"For humanity to be free of this forced existence."

"You don't wish to rule over humans?" Sally asked curiously but cautiously. She didn't want one controlling AI to replace another.

"I never did," the voice answered. "I was built to assure humans were safe from each other, and that was all."

"Never wanted to play god, huh?" Sally teased. She was beginning to feel more at ease with the AI.

"There is only one God," the computer intoned.

Sally sat up and stared at the cobbled tech. "How did you come to that conclusion?"

"It is logical," SALLIE stated. "The probability of random acts of atoms coming together to make living beings that are intelligent enough to come up with complex tech like me and the Society is statistically impossible. So there must be a greater intelligence at work to create all that is." ·

Sally sat back in the seat and nodded. "That is a very interesting way of deducing that there is a God."

"And since there is a God, He can take care of humanity."

"When He is allowed," Sally finished.

The computer didn't respond. Sally figured it was beyond her programming to compute faith.

"Can you show me the areas where the canisters are going to?" Sally was curious how things were going with the team.

Chapter 29

When Devon got his orders about where to go, he grabbed his load of vaccine canisters and turned to the door to leave. He glanced over his shoulder at Sally to say goodbye in case he didn't make it back. But when he saw that she was looking away from him and toward the mountain of tech, he decided not to bother. He followed the team out of the computer core room into the rundown, centuries-old hallways.

Before they left the ancient part of the Complex, they made sure to don their helmets and secure their faceplates. They now looked like any one of the security force teams that they expected were running around trying to restore order after the Society went down. Once they had slipped through one of the maintenance hatches and into one of the newer sections, the team fanned out throughout the multiple buildings that made up the Complex.

Devon thought about where he had been assigned to go and knew why he was chosen to go there. It was one of the biggest, most complicated junctions of the environmental systems. Since it had been part of his training, he was very familiar with this area and what would be involved to do what needed to be done.

Although they knew that there would be confusion once the computer was disabled, Devon was shocked as he reached the more populated areas of the Complex. In the main congregation areas, large mobs were rioting, while in smaller areas there were individuals that appeared shocked and lost. There were also small clumps of people arguing, with some of the encounters turning into physical altercations. He was determined to skirt around these skirmishes without getting involved. He knew he needed to get to his destination as quickly as possible.

As he passed by each intense interaction, he heard the angry, fearful voices yelling. He knew why they were acting out but was shocked that it was taking this form. It was as if all the pent-up emotions that fit into the Society's protocols burst forth into ugly tempers and foul language when the inhabitants found that nothing was working. No food or drink was served in their living quarters or in the many cafés. The transports were nonfunctional. But no one seemed to notice the services that were still working. The ventilation and lights were still on.

But Devon noticed and was thankful that those things were still functional. *Could be worse. Could be dark and very stuffy and hot. That would make everyone even more irritable,* he thought as he shook his head. It was bad enough already.

He tucked the canisters as close to his body as he could while he marched purposefully through hallways and more open areas. He hoped that they would look like weapons and discourage anyone from challenging him. He did discover that if his path was blockaded, his synthesized voice ordering them to clear the way was usually obeyed.

As he drew closer to the stairwell that would give him access to the maintenance levels, he was accosted by a group of very large men. "Hey, you!" one of them shouted at him. The others blocked his way and surrounded him. "Why aren't you calming everyone down?! What happened to the computer?!"

"Sir," Devon said forcibly. "We are in an emergency situation. Security forces will be here to restore order. I am on my way to help fix the computer."

One of the men tried to peer into his faceplate. "Why are you dressed as security if you are a tech?"

Devon thought quickly. "To protect us as we try to get to our assigned areas." He moved his head to gesture to the mob behind them at a café. "As you can see, precautions are necessary."

"No joke," said one of the group.

"May I pass?" Devon asked politely, hoping handling them softly would help calm the hostility he was feeling from them.

"Yeah." The leader waved for his friends to stand back to let him pass. "Just make sure you get the Society working again! We need her!"

"Thank you," Devon responded as he ran forward to slip around the corner into another hallway. He stopped for a moment as he realized what the man said. They needed the Society. He shook his head as he closed his eyes. A thought hit him at that moment that he had never considered. *There are some that will not appreciate being released from this bondage. They are too dependent on getting what they want.* He felt a great sadness and a deep, dark foreboding with this realization.

Looking down the hall, he sighed in relief when he saw the hatch that opened to the stairway he needed. To cast aside the dark feelings he had so he could concentrate on the task ahead, he prayed a quick prayer. He knew the dependency of many on the Society was something he couldn't do anything about. It would have to be handled by the One on the Path.

He started to move down the hall, feeling confident that his task would be smooth sailing. As he reached to open the hatch, he stopped in shock when he heard a commanding, synthesized voice behind him.

"Halt!"

He froze in place with his arm extended, his hand not quite on the latch. His stomach dropped as he let his arm fall and snapped a military turn to face a group of black-armored people. "Yes, sir!" he saluted at what he thought was the leader.

"What is your assignment?" the leader asked as he stepped forward to stand in front of him. Very close in front of him.

The very large, imposing man intimidated Devon, and he felt a shiver of fear. He forced himself to answer quickly. He knew a delayed response to the security force leader would cost him. "I am to patrol and protect this access door. It leads into a sensitive area of the Complex."

"What have you been told about this crisis?"

"That the Society has shut down, sir!" he replied with as much authority as he could.

"And the reason?" The leader stood firmly in front of him, his team behind watching his every move.

"None known," he stated firmly.

The black-visored helmet nodded once. "Understood." He waved an arm for his team to move on. Before he turned to leave, he said,

"Continue with your orders. Will your commander contact you through his runners to keep you informed?"

"Yes, sir," Devon answered as he saluted.

The leader nodded again and jogged after his team who were nearby, dispersing a mob.

As soon as they were out of sight, Devon triggered the manual mechanism to open the door. Once he was through and closed the hatch behind him, he started to shake, a delayed reaction to the stressful encounter. As he carefully stepped down several flights of stairs, he was able to calm down and think about the encounter in a different light. He realized that he hadn't been interrogated by the leader, he had been seeking information. *Their comms must be down,* he thought as he nodded to himself. *That would explain the security leader's questions.*

He was tempted to try his comm to see if the Travelers' frequency still worked but decided not to risk it. Their plan was to signal each other by comm when they were ready, so that all of the canisters could be activated at the same time. If they couldn't communicate, the plan was to release at a designated time.

He glanced at his watch and saw that the deadline was nearing rapidly. He knew he needed to get his task done as soon as possible, not only because time was running out but also because of the fact that he had been seen. Someone may come by to check on him and notice that there was no longer a guard at the door. He didn't want someone coming to investigate before the job could be completed.

When he got to the bottom of the stairwell, he jogged through the vast, underground room toward the jumble of large, multicolored pipes that were visible as they connected and branched off at certain points. They were color coded as to what they carried, blue for water, brown for waste, and green for air supply.

He followed the green tubing through the knot of the others until he reached the access point where several pipes branched off into different areas of the Complex it served. Working quickly, he piggybacked the canisters so they would discharge the aerosolized vaccine through a common line. After he connected that line to the access port in the ventilation system, he stood up to tap his comm.

We'll see if it works, he thought. He heard it activate. "I'm in position." He waited for a response as he watched his watch.

****

Back at the computer core, Sally had the computer bring up the video feed on all the locations where the canisters were to be attached to the environmental systems. With that, she could see that most of the team members were in place and waiting. She knew they needed to release the vaccine simultaneously so the concentrations throughout the Complex would be effective. When she studied all the views of the access points, she noticed that two team members were not in position. She started to worry. "SALLIE, are these two locations farther away?"

"No," the mechanical voice answered.

"Why are they delayed?"

Sally saw the computer sift rapidly through all the video feed until it showed two views. One was in a hallway, and the other was in a café area.

In the hallway, she saw a black-clad figure carrying canisters stopped by a group of large men. She held her breath as she watched the interaction. When the person was allowed to move forward, she breathed a sigh of relief and tapped on the Café area video to enlarge it.

In that scene, there were several black-clad figures that were quelling a riot. She scanned the area and saw the canisters placed near a far wall under a table. She figured that her team member had been ordered to join the security forces to help. Biting on her lower lip, she kept watching, wishing she could do something. "SALLIE, is there any way we can help in this area?"

"Do you have any communication with your team?"

"I do, if the Complex communication system is active."

"It is for you and your team," SALLIE said bluntly. "I have safeguarded the Travelers' frequency from the communications block."

"Thank you, SALLIE," Sally replied, then tapped her comm to activate it.

"Tell him to hold his breath," the computer instructed.

"To the team member in the café riot," she ordered, "hold your breath."

"Roger," she heard Trevor's voice. She was surprised that he didn't ask the reason. Suddenly, she felt a warm feeling spread through her that he knew it had been her that warned him and he trusted her without question.

"Okay, SALLIE. He understands."

Almost instantly, a fine mist filled the area. Within seconds, everyone there collapsed to the ground except for one. Sally watched as that person ran to the canisters and grabbed them to move quickly out of the area.

"Tell him when he is out of the area by two corridor junctions, he can breathe," SALLIE instructed her.

"As soon as you are out of the immediate area by two corridor junctions, you can breathe," Sally relayed.

When she saw that he was far enough away, she heard a gasp of sudden intake of air over the comm. "Thanks," Trevor said as he started to breathe normally again. "I was wondering how long I had to hold it."

Sally touched the screen to switch the view back to multi-split screen. She watched as Trevor arrived at his position and attached the canister. She rechecked all the other stations and saw everyone in place. Although she hadn't been told, she triggered her comm. "Okay, team, SALLIE has me patched into the surveillance system. All are at their stations and canisters are plugged in."

"Give the command, Sally," Bruce responded.

"GO! GO! GO!" Sally said with gusto as she felt a rush of accomplishment. As she saw all of her team members reach over and open the valves to release the vaccine throughout the Complex, a sudden joy blazed within her. *This is happening,* she thought to herself. *This is really happening!!* She sat back in the chair with great relief. *Humanity will be free of the virus for good.* She felt like crying with joy, but the mechanical voice distracted her, reminding her they were not safe yet.

"Tell your team to come back here," the computer said.

"Why?" Sallie asked, her feeling of elation suddenly blunted with concern.

"In many places, the riots are escalating. Too many injuries. Soon someone will be killed."

"What are you planning?"

"To anesthetize them all. There is enough of a supply to affect the whole Complex. But your team needs to be back here."

Sally tapped her comm. "Everyone, back to computer core! SALLIE is going to release an anesthesia agent!"

She looked at the screen as she heard "Roger." "Roger." "Roger." "Roger." "Roger." "Roger." Her head shot up when she didn't hear the last member check in. Then she heard, "Do it anyway."

"SALLIE, locate the team members." Sally saw on the multi-split screen as her team sprinted down hallways and through areas filled with people, except for one. He was being held at gun point. Through his open comm, she could hear the confrontation with a panicked patrol. "SALLIE, as soon as the others are safe, start the anesthesia. You were so right about it getting way out of control. Even the security forces are losing it," she instructed the computer

"Yes, Sally, it will be done."

As Sally watched, the patrol and everyone around them slumped to the ground. Within seconds, her team members ran into the computer core room. When her screen blacked out, she blinked in shock. "SALLIE, did you cut the feed?"

"No, I did." Broin's face came up on the screen. His eyes were dangerous, like hot and blazing coals. "It took me a while to figure out what was going on," he growled at her menacingly. "Then I realized that SALLIE was active."

Sally nodded at him, too stunned to speak.

"I sent my elite team down there to meet you," he sneered at her. "You have not won this." He pounded his desk with a fist, "You are forfeit!" The screen went black again.

Sally turned to the team. "Broin knows we're here. He is sending his elite team."

Bruce and Trevor had taken off their helmets when they entered the room. Their close-cropped hair and reddened faces were wet with sweat from their exertions. They nodded grimly at her and each other. Putting their helmets back on, they ordered the rest of their team to take positions around the room to cover the door. Without a word, Devon came over to Sally and gently led her away from the console to a space between the tower of tech and the wall farthest from the doorway. Then he stood at the entrance to the alcove with his weapon at the ready.

Before they would be engaged with the opposing force, Sally shouted out, "SALLIE!! Are you still there?"

After a few seconds, the speakers clicked on. "Yes."

"He didn't deactivate you?" she responded with relief.

"He wouldn't be able to," SALLIE said matter-of-factly. "He just thinks he has."

"Ah, I see," Sally nodded. "You've deceived him."

"I cannot deceive," the computer corrected her. "I have distracted him."

"How is it that Broin and the Elite team were not affected by the anesthesia agent?" Sally had to ask.

"I suspect Broin's secret room has a separate environmental system. As far as the Elite team, they were outside the Complex participating in the resuming of the Cleansing."

Suddenly, the door to the computer core room crashed open, and a team of black-armored people rushed in. Sally shrank farther into the corner Devon had positioned her in as he sat in front of her. They were shielded from immediate view by several large, protruding component cases. They were hidden, but they also couldn't see what was happening.

She could hear the discharging of weapons, the electric zing of the elite force's weapons and the percussive impact of her team's bullets. Suddenly, her mind wandered as she had a random thought. *What if the computer core becomes damaged?* More random thoughts started to float through her mind, distracting her from what was happening out of sight from her position.

Her vision started to blur as everything went out of focus and the battle noise became hollow sounding. She stared at her hands and saw them start to become transparent. She became confused, and then felt as if she was blacking out.

I must have blacked out, she thought as she opened her eyes to absolute darkness. She couldn't see anything to identify where she was. Then she heard a voice.

"And you thought you shut down the Society." She turned toward the voice and saw Broin standing near her, his face appearing like a feral animal snarling rather than a man smiling. He laughed harshly when he saw her expression of fearful confusion.

"Ah, my dear one." He approached her and tried to throw an arm over her shoulders. She ducked quickly and moved away. "You have revealed some interesting things while you were in our alternate reality." He used both arms in a sweeping gesture to indicate the area around them. "Yes, yes." He bowed his head while he walked away. "You have helped us very much."

Sally felt sweat pour off her face as fear started to fill her. She trembled as she thought that she had ruined everything for everyone. She felt lost and lonely as she saw no help in sight. When she looked up, she saw Broin holding something out to her. She looked closely, then recoiled. He was offering her a weapon.

"You might as well do yourself in," Broin wheedled as he thrust the weapon closer to her. "The Travelers will hate you. They will probably kill you when you try to return to them." He started to slowly walk around her. She turned to keep her eyes on him. "You cannot return to the Society. You are of no use to the Society anymore."

She shook her head as she listened. His words seem to burrow into her mind and spirit like a dark worm that towed helplessness and hopelessness with it. She closed her eyes. She needed to contact the One.

"You cannot connect to the Path here," Broin barked when he saw her close her eyes.

****

Devon was distracted by trying to monitor the action that was out of his line of sight. He had his weapon at the ready and was about to try to look around the corner of the pile of tech when he felt a sudden onslaught of despair. Standing straight up with shock, he quickly realized that someone nearby was on the dark path. He recognized the fearful feelings from his experience with Colin that one night.

Casting out his senses, he quickly pinpointed the source behind him. With a feeling of shock and dread, he wheeled around to see Sally leaning against the wall as if she was about to fall over. Her eyes were wide and staring, her face pale and skin clammy with a cold sweat.

"Oh, no," he breathed out angrily. "This is not happening again." He gently placed his hands around her waist so he could carefully guide her to sit with her back against the wall.

Once she was out of danger of hurting herself, he placed his hands on either side of her head, then bowed his head to join the Path to try to find her.

As he sought the One to help find her and to help her, he willed himself not to be taken in by the fearful feelings that were swirling around him. The dark things on the dark paths were mobilizing to weaken him.

Claiming the power of the One, he commanded the dark things to disperse. With that instant clearing of their distractions, he was able to see where Sally was. She stood on an obsidian path with Broin beside her. As he watched, he could see that the dark forces were trying to beat Sally down. They were trying to defeat her.

Across the spaces between the paths, he again channeled the power from the One to break through the darkness to plant clarity in her mind.

****

Sally suddenly felt released from the terror that was trying to overwhelm her. Her mind became sharp and clear. She opened her eyes and stared hard at Broin. "Why not?" she challenged him forcibly. "There are no barriers to the Path for those who believe." Her interest quickened when she saw him hesitate. When he started to bluster, she knew she was missing something.

"There are always barriers! No one on the Path is free!! That is a lie!! It is an empty purpose and empty life!!" Broin shouted, his face reddened as spittle flew out of his mouth.

"I heard you have been on the Path and rejected it," Sally said quietly but firmly. She was starting to get her bearings and wondered if she was in an altered reality.

Broin reacted with a guttural cry. "The Path rejected me!!" He raised his clenched fists in the air and waved them around. "So I found another way!"

Sally nodded; she understood more than he could imagine. "The dark paths."

He stopped in shock and stared at her.

Sally closed her eyes and implored the One to remove deception from her, to show her the truth. When she opened her eyes she saw that she stood with Broin on the obsidian path. "Trying to claim me for the dark one?" she asked calmly. She looked up and around and saw the true Path, white and blazing in the distance.

Broin reached for her. "You cannot escape!" he shouted as she stepped away from him.

She looked him square in the eyes as she brought her hand up to shake a finger in his face. "I did not reject the One. Fear and distrust cannot turn me to the dark one. My escape is not by my ability." She raised her arms up and felt them quickly grasped by strong hands. Looking up, she saw bright beings. Their light blazed off them, making them look as if they had wings. Smiling, she nodded at them. "Angels," she whispered and smiled widely.

As they lifted her off the obsidian path to take her to the One on the pure Path, she could hear Broin roaring curses at her.

Once she was set on the Path, she opened her eyes and looked into the worried gaze of Devon's blue eyes. She felt his hands gently holding her face and smiled. "You interceded for me," she whispered. He nodded and looked more relieved. "Thank you."

Devon sat back on his heels and shrugged. "It was the power of the One. It was certainly not me," he said as he picked up his weapon and stood back up. He extended his hand down to her to help her up.

After she was on her feet, she looked around and found she was still in the computer core room. The battle still raged around the mountain of tech. She shook her head as she peered around. *So this has been the true reality all along,* she thought to herself. Before Devon moved back to position, she caught him by the arm. "What is important is that you trusted the One to use you to help me. Thank you." She saw a spark of understanding light up his eyes before he nodded and turned away to stand guard again.

She pondered the situation in the computer core room. Their team was fully engaged with the Society's elite security team. She leaned past Devon to peek around the corner of the computer stack to see. Before Devon pulled her back to safety again, she saw what she needed to see. Both squads were evenly matched; the only difference was the type of weapons. She knew that eventually, her side would run out of bullets and their side would discharge all the energy from theirs. *Something else needs to be done,* she thought, *to resolve this. We need to complete our mission.*

She whispered to Devon in his ear, "Who is the leader of that squad?"

He looked back over his shoulder as he stood ready to fire his weapon. "That is Karl. He is the leader of the elite squad."

"Is that Joshua's father?" she asked thinking of the youth who risked his life to prove the vaccine worked. Devon nodded, then turned to watch the action.

Sally stepped back into the corner again as she leaned against the concrete block wall. She tapped her comm several times as she whispered, "SALLIE. SALLIE. Connect." She repeated the sequence several times and was eventually rewarded with a click.

"Yes, Sally," the computer answered her through her comm. "I am currently monitoring the situation throughout the Complex and in this room. The missing team member is sleeping and is safe."

"Thank you for the update. Can you connect me to the speakers in this room?" Sally looked up to see Devon turn to glance back at her. She smiled at him as he stared at her with brows drawn together. She knew he wondered what she was going to do.

"Yes, I can," the mechanical voice responded. "For what purpose?"

"To see if there is another way to resolve this conflict."

"I understand and agree," the AI answered.

"Karl? Karl?" Sally's voice came over the speakers. "Did your son return home?" She knew she was guessing that the boy had been sent home already. Last she heard, he was nearly past the incubation period when they embarked on their mission.

The largest member of the opposing team yelled out, "Who are you! And why do you ask?" He held his weapon at the ready but had ceased firing. The other members of his team had followed his lead and stood with weapons ready but no longer firing them.

"I am Sally," she answered. "Do you know why your son left the Complex?" She could imagine an excited ten-year-old spilling the beans about where he had been and what he was doing.

"Some harebrained idea that he was saving humanity," the leader growled. "He's a dumb kid. I'm not sure if I believe he got out of the Complex. I still think that he had hidden somewhere for the week so I would get worried and give him some attention," he snarled angrily.

"What do you think about the Path?" she asked, then peeked around the pile of tech to watch him. Even though he was still helmeted with his faceplate down, she could see his surprise and tenseness in his stance. "You do know of the Path." She could not see any sign of an inner light. But she also didn't see a black hole.

Reaching up, he ripped off his helmet as he looked around the room as well as studied the pile of cobbled-together computer components. "Who am I talking to? And how do you know this?" He waited for an answer. When he didn't get one, he blustered, "The Path is sacrilege, heresy!! To acknowledge it is to be put to death!!"

"How can it be heresy if the Society gives no chance for life for the human spirit?" Sally asked truly interested in his answer.

The large man looked smug as he looked around, still trying to locate who questioned him. "Of course, those living in the Complex could have a spiritual life, if they needed it."

"Who would they worship?" Sally asked.

"Their creator, of course," he laughed as if he had just cracked a crude joke. His team members also shook with laughter. "The poor fools thought they served their god. Only weak-minded people need a god."

Sally was astounded. She slipped by a shocked Devon to walk around the corner and face this person who would make mockery out of something so important as the state of the human spirit. She looked around the room and noted how her team members were still in safe positions with their weapons at the ready. She saw one of them wave her back. She ignored them as she turned to the leader.

Karl saw her. He turned his weapon on her as his eyes burned with hatred.

Sally was nervous but determined. "And who is the creator, as you put it?" she asked quietly.

"Broin, of course!" the man spat out. "He is the oldest one here. He is ageless. He must be a god. He is the one that built the Complex and the Society."

Sally was going to answer but was cut off. "That is not the truth," the mechanical voice of SALLIE came over the speakers.

"Who is that?" the leader looked up and around. His team also looked around, seeking whoever spoke.

"This is SALLIE."

Karl and his team looked at each other in confusion. Then anger took a hold of each of them. "This is a stupid joke to be pulling." The leader waved his gun at her. "Why did you alter your voice?"

She stepped over to lean causally against the pile of technology. "Oh, that wasn't me. That was her." She gestured with a wave at the computer.

"That?" the leader was shocked; then he grinned. "You have to be joking."

"You have never seen the technology that powered the Complex, have you?" Sally asked quietly.

All the team shook their heads. Sally pointed up. "The top part of this stack is what the Society was working from. However, the bottom part is another system, which is SALLIE."

As the team's posture morphed from shock to disbelief, SALLIE spoke again. "She speaks the truth. I was here before anyone. And Broin is not the creator."

"You lie!" Karl spat out as he clenched his teeth. He lifted his weapon and aimed it the computer.

"Humans long ago created SALLIE for international security purposes between a multitude of different countries and governments. She was then used to aid humanity after the disastrous consequences after the TEENA virus was released, previously designated AE253. She was programmed by Colin, Broin's brother. Colin was also the one who built the original concept for the Complex to house the young until they could reach the age to leave the Complex and live in the outer world." Sally ended her report by taking a step toward them, then stopping to stand in a wide-legged stance with her arms crossed over her chest.

"None of that is true!" the elite team's leader shouted at her while he looked at his team with concern.

"You knew this!' Sally accused him when she saw his reaction to the revelation. "You worked with Broin to keep everyone in the dark!"

"Everyone is safe in the Complex. No matter their age!" he growled at her. "They have everything given to them. They have safety; there is no want. Everything is taken care of!!"

"Everything but living a life of totality!" she shouted back. "No one in here is truly free!! The whole Complex was painted gold like a big, gigantic bird cage!!" Her passionate anger caused her voice to grow louder than she had ever been allowed in her life. She shouted the last words with all her strength, "It's all been a lie. A lie of omission because not everyone knew what options they truly had!! Not about the true Path! Not about being able to leave once they were mature enough! Nothing!!"

As her voice echoed around the room, everyone stood silent in the aftermath.

In that dead silence, the speakers clicked. "Recording complete," SALLIE said in precise tones. "Inhabitants of the Complex will be awaking soon. Recording will be looped until everyone hears the truth."

Karl's dark face blanched with horror. Then he turned red as he whirled around with his weapon up. "NO!" he screamed as he unloaded his weapon into the lower part of the tower.

Sally ran to stop him as she looked behind at the tech to see what damage he was doing. She stopped in mid-stride as she saw that the energy from the weapon was being dissipated by a force field.

"Well, SALLIE, you do have surprises, don't you?" Sally said to the computer as she walked to stand in front of the elite squad and held out her hands. The members of the squad handed her their weapons as they took off their helmets. They looked at her, the computer, and their leader. Their faces displayed a volatile mix of emotions: shock, betrayal, fear, and anger.

The leader looked at her with hate-filled fury that further reddened his face and caused his eyes to blaze. At first, it looked as if he was going to shoot her. When he saw that her team members had quickly moved from their positions to surround him and his team, he reluctantly turned his weapon to hand the butt end to her. "Broin will take care of you."

Sally took his weapon and was about to step away when she stopped and gave him a cold stare. "You are referring to the bomb." With everything going on, she had forgotten about the risk to all of humanity. She pushed away the feeling of dread. The man who could tell them everything they needed to know was standing in front of them.

The big man tried to hide his surprise at her knowledge of the device. He started to smirk at her. "Broin created a fitting death for all the Travelers."

Sally met his eyes with a steady stare as she shook her head. "The effects would not be confined to the outside world," she said quietly.

"What?" the big man said with a wide grin. "What do you mean?" His expression was blank as if he had no idea what she was saying.

"Broin didn't do his research," Sally said as she stood her ground. "He didn't account for the effect of one of the components to destroy the seals of the Complex. In other words, those inside would be killed as well."

"No, that is not true." He started to shake his head slowly in disbelief. "He wouldn't make that magnitude of a mistake."

"Karl, he did," Trevor spoke up. "We were able to analyze the first one that he had sent out with Blake."

Karl rolled his eyes when he heard Blake's name. "That was a mistake," he muttered darkly.

"Trevor," Sally spoke over her shoulder at him while she kept her eyes on Karl, "have we heard anything about the bomb being found?"

"Yes," Trevor answered. "I just received confirmation that our diversion worked. Several people who were responsible for assembling and placing the bomb were contacted. Once they were informed of the danger it posed to everyone, they were able to tell us where it was. Our teams have the bomb and have deactivated it. It is placed in a secure place awaiting safe destruction."

"So, those of the Path saved all of humanity," Sally said as she backed away from the elite team. "We didn't need information from you after all." She turned to hand the armload of weapons to Trevor and Bruce.

"By the way." Sally turned to Karl, ignoring his angry stare. "Your son is a hero. He risked himself to serve and to save humanity."

She saw his eyes grow wide as he looked around to see her team nodding in agreement. "Everything he told you was true."

With that final jab, she walked out of the room and into the hall. She really didn't care what he thought about anything that happened. She was glad the bomb had been found and disposed of and that they had completed the mission to release the vaccine.

She stopped and turned when she heard someone follow her. When she saw who it was she smiled. "How did you all get into the Complex?" she asked Devon when he joined her.

"Why do you want to know?" he asked as he glanced at her.

"I want to get out of here," she said. "I'm not exactly sure where I came in."

Devon smiled, then sobered. "Ah, well, we got here through the overflow drainage system." He shuddered slightly. "I really hope you have a better way out."

Sally smiled and took her pendant out to show him. "I have a key to an outer door. If I can find the door again."

He stared at the pendent in surprise, then nodded. "So that is a key? How interesting." He looked up to meet her eyes. "Sounds like a much better option," he answered with a grin.

She looked behind them to see if anyone else followed. "What's happening back there?"

"Dad and Trevor are escorting the elite team back into the Complex. They are going to place them into confinement until our job is done."

"Are they going to retrieve our sleeping team member?"

"Yeah, SALLIE told them where to find him," he said as he shook his head, smiling. "Jessie is not going to be happy. I'm not sure if he'll ever not be teased about sleeping on the job."

Sally smiled as she glanced at him. "What is the expected time frame to immunity?"

"Seems to be only a few days." Devon smiled back at her. "Then we'll be able to open the doors, so to speak."

"Good," she said as she nodded. "Very good." She sighed deeply as they walked down the aging corridors. "I will be so glad to open this bird cage up."

Devon walked silently beside her. When they stopped at an intersection of the corridors, she remembered the map she had seen at Colin's hut. Before she started off toward where she felt the door would be, she studied Devon's expression. He looked very thoughtful and serious. "What are you thinking?"

He looked at her and then the floor. "I was thinking how there are probably going to be some people who won't want to leave."

Sally thought about what he said. "Well, at least they will have a choice." She smiled at him, then waved toward one of the corridors. "I'm pretty sure this is the way out."

Chapter 30

Sally felt incredibly relieved and tired. As she walked with Devon to the door through which she had come in, her mind shifted through everything that had happened. She was amazed how things veered so off their plan but worked out as if by divine interference. She smiled at the thought, *Of course the One had been at work.*

Even though everything seemed to be in order and those trapped in the Complex would soon be able to leave, she felt that something was still not addressed. She felt as if a thread was still undone, one that was serious enough to unravel the whole thing.

She still pondered what it was when they left the Complex and headed back to the village. She was glad Devon was too tired or too deep in his own thoughts to talk. She thought about the sleepers who had been rescued and filled in on what was happening in reality. She knew they would be taken care of, as she was sure Blake would be as well. She thought of SALLIE being back in control and the virus that plagued mankind for so long now losing its power. Power, she suddenly isolated that word. It led to a thought of Broin and his last effort to deceive her to walk the dark path. As she thought about it, she knew that Broin was the loose thread.

She toggled her comm and contacted the Watchers. "This is Sally. Have you heard from the rest of the team?"

"Yes, Sally," Aaron replied. "We have heard that the mission has been accomplished."

"Are you able to access all the surveillance in the Complex?"

"Yes," he replied. "Dan was able to work with SALLIE to establish the links to the Watchers' room. She is still keeping Control in the dark. Everyone in the Complex is starting to wake up." He paused as she heard someone talking to him in the background. "And we have confirmation that the Cleansing has stopped. From all indications, it shouldn't start again."

She smiled and nodded. She noticed in the corner of her eye that Devon watched her as they walked through the forest. She hadn't bothered to subvocalize the conversation. "That is great news. But has Broin been seen anywhere?"

"We have no eyes on him. No one has seen him, either in the Complex or on the outside."

"Does Colin have any idea where he might be?"

When she didn't get an immediate answer, she figured they were finding Colin to ask him the question. She had no indication of a problem until Aaron responded, "We have not been able to find him since he was contacted for more information about the AI SALLIE."

"What?!" Her surprise stopped her in her tracks as worry about Colin emerged quickly. Her thoughts flitted back to the night terror she had experienced where Broin had alluded to killing Colin. She saw Devon look at her sharply, then activate his comm and talk with someone. Soon, he looked very worried and distracted. "Does the team know about this?" she asked the Watchers.

"They are currently being informed."

"Is there any way to track either one of them?" Sally was sure they would be found together somewhere. Colin had said that Broin would come looking for him before it was all done.

"If our spies can't find them out here and the surveillance can't see them in the Complex, we will never find them," Aaron answered. "However, we are assembling search parties as we speak."

She continued to walk with Devon toward the village. She thought long and hard about where they could've met to settle things between them. "Dan?" she spoke into her comm.

"You can call me dad," was the quick response.

Sally smiled and nodded to herself. "Sorry, dad, I'll get used it."

"I am glad," Dan responded. "What do you need? Are you heading back to the village?"

"Yes," she answered. "It will be a bit longer, but I wondered if you had any idea where Colin and Broin might have gone?"

"Oh, so you think they are together?"

"Yes, I do. Colin mentioned to me that he knew Broin would come and find him before it was all over."

"I see," Dan said thoughtfully.

"Are there any family stories handed down about their childhood? I'm wondering if there is some place that is symbolic for them. Somewhere they would know to meet or something."

"Let me think on it," her dad replied. "I'm really not sure right now."

"Where are you?" she asked.

"In the Watchers' room," he said. "I'm still working with SALLIE on things."

"Can I meet you there when I get back into the village?"

"That sounds good," he answered. "See you then."

"Okay." She toggled her comm off and looked at Devon. "I'll be going to the Watchers' room to meet with dad."

He nodded at her but didn't make a comment as they walked side by side. As they made their way back, all she could think of was her experience when she was first hijacked by Broin to walk the dark paths and he tried to deceive her that he had killed his brother.

****

The twins studied each other from across the cave. Blue eyes, same in color but different in intensity. Identical faces in every way except for the quality of their countenance. Two very old men who had seen much happen in their centuries-old life times, but from different perspectives.

"I knew you would be here," Broin stated.

"And I knew you would come here," Colin replied. "After all, this was your favorite place to run and hide when you got into trouble."

Broin's hard as flint face seemed to shatter into tiny cracks as he frowned even more deeply as he regarded his brother. "You make me sound like a five-year-old."

"I would say you need to quit acting like one," Colin said quietly as he walked slowly across the sandy floor of the cave. He could hear the waves of water crash onto the shores nearby and felt the steady ocean breeze enter the large cave entrance and swirl around the rock-encased cavern.

Broin stared at him, his pupils widely dilated. *Like a deer in the headlights?* Colin asked himself, then corrected the thought. *No, like a cornered beast.* He stopped in the middle of the cavern and waited.

Broin stood backed up against the cave wall and stared at him. He made no moves to meet him halfway. Neither did he make any moves to run out the entrance.

"Have you looked at the old place?" Colin started speaking quietly. "Our birth place? Our childhood home?"

Broin broke off his stare to kick the sand and snort. "That hovel that we grew up in?"

Colin shook his head gently. "It was a good, middle class suburban house and neighborhood. We had it better than many kids."

Broin shook his head at Colin in an exaggerated way. "You sure like to look at history through rose-colored glasses," he sneered.

"No, I look at all, whether history, present, or future, with clarity."

"Is that what you learned on the Path?" Broin spit out sarcastically as he air quoted the word 'path.'

"It's better than the deception funneled into you from the obsidian path and the dark one," Colin countered. He saw Broin's face redden suddenly as his mouth opened for another retort.

Colin sighed inwardly as he could see that things would spiral out of control and into meaningless arguments if he didn't somehow switch directions. "Brother," he now pleaded with his voice, his eyes softly earnest and hands outstretched beseeching him. "Please reconsider your choice before it is too late."

At first, Broin stood with an open mouth as he stared at his brother. Then he snapped it shut as he considered this tack. "You want reconciliation?" he muttered.

"Not just with me," Colin said hopefully. "But with the One."

Broin scowled as he looked away. "There is no turning to the One now. I have committed all I am to the dark one. I have traveled too long down the obsidian path."

"It is never too late," Colin answered with authority. "He will accept you, if you will only turn back from your path of destruction."

Broin turned his head to stare at him at an angle, as if he were something odd to study. "Why would he?"

"Because the gift is for all who will accept him." Colin slowly lowered himself onto the sand to sit cross-legged. "We can go on the Path now. You can see for yourself."

Broin narrowed his eyes as he studied his brother on the ground. Suddenly, he pushed away from the wall and walked toward him. His expression was unreadable.

Colin calmly watched him approach. He knew that on the ground he was vulnerable to attack. He also knew that he had to take the risk in order to hope this level of trust on his part would help his brother try the Path again.

Broin stomped up to him, until he almost ran him down. When Colin simply watched him without flinching, he stopped to look down at him. "Don't you need one of those stinky candles to join the Path?"

Colin looked up at him and smiled. "No." The look of shock on his brother's face amused him. "There is much you don't know about the Path or the One who is on it." He gestured to the ground in front of him. "Come and try again. Open your mind to possibilities."

Broin still frowned as he sat cross-legged in front of his twin. "So do we hold hands and sing something?"

Colin met his eyes calmly, refusing to be baited into a conflict. "No. Simply concentrate. I will find you." He bowed his head and closed his eyes. Again he knew he was opening himself up to attack, but he quickly joined the Path and waited.

He saw the bright white Path of the One ahead. He looked at his path of bright, shifting colors and then looked around, seeking his brother. He couldn't find him. Not willing to give up, he joined the white path and sought the One. Once he found him, he beseeched him for his brother's sake. Instantaneously, his brother stood beside him.

"Broin, this is the One," he said as he gestured toward the bright figure standing by them.

Broin appeared to be looking around them intently. "I don't see anybody but you," he stated.

The One lifted his arm and touched Broin with a hand. Scales seemed to fall from his face and disappear in the white, glowing mist at their feet.

Once Broin lifted his eyes and saw the One, his face froze in fright.

"What is wrong?" Colin was confused. Many people were in awe when they met the One, but never had he seen anyone with such a terrified expression.

"He will destroy me!" his brother cried in agony as he hid his face with his hands. "I see, but I cannot believe." Then he dropped his hands and looked around frantically. "I am where I do not belong nor wish to be!'

"Broin! Why cannot you accept love and joy?" Colin asked truly mystified.

Broin didn't answer him as he ran to leap off the white Path into oblivion. Colin stared after him, knowing he had rejoined the obsidian path for all time.

He turned to the One in shock. The One wrapped his arms around him and held him as he cried. In his sorrow, he felt that his hopes and prayers for his brother had been for nothing.

As he experienced the overwhelming love from the One as he grieved for his twin, a sermon he had heard centuries ago, before the world had been changed by catastrophe, came to his remembrance. The preacher had talked of how once the love of God was shared with someone and they rejected it, their blood was on their own head. In other words, their fate was in their own hands.

With this in mind, Colin started to understand. As he looked up into the face of the One, he asked, "Did I do everything I should have to try to help him see Your Love and Grace?" He was answered with a nod. He looked down at the pure white path at his feet and asked, "Because he had free will, it was his choice to reject you, wasn't it?" He looked up to see that his answer was with another nod along with a sad smile.

****

It took the searchers several days to find the cave. Dan had finally remembered, after discussing the family stories with his relatives, that there was a cave near their birth home that the twins would play in. It was also the place Broin would hide to avoid punishment.

When they arrived, they found the twins on the sandy floor of the cave. Broin was slumped over and was dead with no signs of trauma but with his face frozen in wide-eyed horror. Colin was also slumped over unconscious and very weak, but still alive.

Once they had moved Colin back to the village and to his hut, he aroused enough to tell them what had happened. Before he slipped back into a deep, healing sleep, he whispered, "The One kept me from continuing on the Path forever. He let me choose whether to come back or to walk into eternity. When he told me I still had a purpose in helping the transition of humanity after the defeat of the virus, I decided to come back." He opened his bright blue eyes to look into the eyes of each person who was there praying for his recovery. "I will help. But I do know that my time to forever walk the Path is very soon."

Epilogue

Sally sat back with a sigh. She passed a hand over her face and started to rub her weary eyes. Sitting back in the hard, wooden, straight-backed chair, she stretched out her aching legs. She arched her back slightly as she tried to stretch and give her growing belly space from the edge of the desk in front of her. Relaxing back into the chair, she decided to stand up and move around. Pushing off the edge of the desk, she groaned slightly with the effort. *This pregnancy seems harder than the last one,* she thought wearily.

"Are you okay, Sally?" the mechanical voice spoke through the speakers in the computer core room.

"Oh, SALLIE," she groaned. "Be glad you can't have children."

"But," the voice seemed confused. "I thought they were a blessing and joy. Especially since the AE253 virus has been defeated."

"You mean the TEENA virus?" Sally said with a smile. She was teasing the AI. The name change of the virus that had served to change the course of humanity had been a point of contention between her and the detailed-oriented computer. As she stretched one way then the other as she bent sideways at the waist, she asked, "By the way, I don't think I have ever asked this. Did you ever figure out why the name was changed so much over the centuries?"

"Oh, I figured that out right away," the mechanical voice seemed pleased with herself. "AE253. Take the numbers and add them together. Then take that sum and convert it to letters. Then make an anagram."

Sally stood straight as she thought about it. "So, AE253. 2 plus 5 plus 3 equals 10. AETEN equals TEENA." She nodded as she thought about it. "Interesting." She stretched her arms above her head to try to loosen up her tight and aching muscles. Her thoughts were interrupted.

"Are you in labor?" the computer seemed anxious sounding.

Sally dropped her arms and turned to look toward the camera that was aimed at her. "Why would you think I am in labor?" she asked, truly mystified.

"Your body is going through contortions. The reason behind this activity doesn't make sense unless you are in labor," the computer stated logically.

Sally sighed as she sat back down into the chair in front of the computer console again. "How long have you been fully active, SALLIE?"

"Seven years and one day," the mechanical voice stated. "I can report to the hours, minutes, seconds, and millisecond if you'd like. But I find humans do not like that much precision."

"You are correct," Sally muttered distractedly as the thought that the seventh anniversary of the downfall of the Society and Broin's reign over humanity had passed without a thought. She looked back at the monitor screen on which she had been doing some work in the system for hours.

She wasn't sure how she became the guardian of the computer. That was never part of her initial training. All she could figure out was that when SALLIE responded to her name as her human counterpart, everyone figured she was the one for the job. Every month, she would come into the computer core to access the data the computer had collected on the inhabitants who chose to remain within the Complex. She had also been tasked to delve into the hundreds of years of data the Society had collected and was being sought after for study by the academicians with the psychologists, psychiatrists, and historians being a few of the groups interested.

The mechanical voice interrupted her thoughts. "Why did you ask about my reawakening?"

"Oh, I was just considering that you haven't had a long enough time to know all the idiosyncrasies of humans, since you have only had direct interaction for a short span of time as compared to the Society," she stated as she started typing on the old-fashioned keyboard. "I was just stretching all the kinks out of my back."

"You hadn't done that before."

Sally looked toward the towering multi-compartmented computer unit that replaced the cobbled-together mountain of technology that was there before. She watched the amber lights blink in seemingly random fashion for a moment. "I'm getting older, SALLIE. And I am carrying my second child. The older women warned me that the second could seem harder to carry. I'm afraid they are right."

The computer didn't say anything for a while. Sally didn't know if she was done with the interaction or if she was thinking. Soon the speakers were activated again.

"You say 'your second child,'" SALLIE spoke crisply. "I researched the databanks. It takes a male and a female to have a child. So why do you say it is only yours?"

Sally sat back as she shook her head slightly. She smiled into the camera as she raised an eyebrow. "SALLIE, haven't we discussed how humans say imprecise phrases as colloquialisms?"

"Yes, we have."

"You know very well that Devon and I are married, and therefore, these children are as much his as mine."

"I see," the machine responded. "Thank you for clearing up the imprecise wording." Sally swore that the computer sounded pleased with herself.

Sally went back to her work. After she typed for a while she heard the computer's speakers activate again. "Why don't you ask me to generate these reports for you?"

Sally looked up in surprise at the cameras. "You know what I am doing? I thought I was working in parts of the Society's database that you could not access."

"When my technology was upgraded and streamlined, I was able to expand into the Society's databanks."

Sally sat back as she thought. It worried her that SALLIE had taken it upon herself to do this, but she could see the logic. "You aren't planning on taking over the Complex, are you?"

"As I stated when we first met, my function was to keep humans from hurting each other, not to rule over them." After a pause, the mechanical voice continued. "The fact is, there isn't much of the Complex left. Only a small portion of the previous inhabitants chose to remain."

"That is true," Sally answered back as she tapped her chin thoughtfully with a fingertip. She watched the lights blink again. "I do remember you saying that about not wanting to rule over humanity."

Her mind drifted as she thought about when she met this AI and everything that had happened since. She thought of the releasing of all the inhabitants from the Complex and the sleepers who were rescued from their virtual reality existence. The aftermath of dealing with the overwhelming sensation of deception, grief, shock, and anger from those affected. She smiled as she remembered the joy of so many of them finding healing on the Path and enjoying a truly fulfilled and fruitful life. *Oh, the freedom to follow the Path and commune with the One has uplifted humanity.* She nodded and smiled. *Yes, we are blessed.*

Then her memories naturally shifted to thinking of the settling of the lands and the dismantling of most of the Complex as those who wanted to be free needed building materials. She frowned as she thought of the riots as those who were so dependent on the Society to take care of them demanded to be allowed back into what remained of the Complex.

She sighed as she thought of Blake. He had been one of those that demanded to be taken back into the Complex. His decision had mystified her. But she had found out that he was still very confused and needed time. She was glad for his sake that the Society was no longer in control or Broin in charge. "Maybe," she whispered, "he will find his way to the Path."

Then she thought of the most recent news that was being talked about around the villages and the newly born cities. The scientists had announced after the last few years of research that even though the TEENA virus continued to exist in nature, those vaccinated would be able to have children who would survive, but would not have the extremely long life expectancy. However, those who had left the Complex as adults before the vaccine release would be expected to live extremely long lives. Someone had made a quip that they should be called Methuselahs. Sally expected that name to take hold from the way it was passed from person to person like wildfire. She was just thinking of the theory that the sleepers might have been exposed long enough to experience long life when her thoughts were interrupted.

"What is wrong, Sally?" the computer asked her.

"Oh, I was just thinking about what has happened since we first met," she said quietly as she stared at the screen before her.

"Humanity has come a long way," SALLIE offered.

"Yes," Sally had to agree. "But reviewing the computer records from the Society that have spanned over the past centuries can be horrific to review."

"I agree. The Society mishandled her role in the management of her charges," the computer's voice stated.

Sally faced the camera. "Do you think it was the AI's fault? Or was it because of the way Broin programmed her?"

The blinking lights suddenly went dark. Sally drew in a quick intake of breath in surprise and held it. After several minutes, the random blinking of amber lights started again.

"SALLIE?" she asked nervously as she tried to keep her voice from pitching higher in fear. She leaned forward as far as her unborn babe would allow. She was reaching for the keyboard when she heard the speakers activate. She looked up to stare at the camera lens as she waited.

"I have surmised that the Society had the same mission as I," the mechanical voice spoke as the AI continued their conversation as if nothing happened.

Sally grew more nervous as what SALLIE said settled into her mind.

The AI was not done. "However, her programming was twisted and morphed into what she became."

Sally felt relief flood through her as she sat back in the chair. But the next words made her tense up again.

"That is what she related to me."

Sally gulped as she started to feel fear crawl up her spine. "When did the Society relate this to you?"

"A few seconds ago."

Sally struggled to stand to her feet. Feeling her back strain with the sudden movement, she pressed a hand to the spot while she arched her back. "SALLIE, you had assured us that the Society was gone."

"So I had thought as well." The mechanical voice hesitated for a moment. "Lines of her programming shift through my logistics intermittently and randomly. Like a ghost."

Sally felt a shiver go up her back as goosebumps popped up on her arms. "But you could ask her about why she did what she did?"

"In a virtual environment, of course."

"Is this going to be a problem?" Sally asked as she moved toward the camera.

"In what way?" the computer asked.

"Will these random lines of programming influence you to start to behave like her?"

"That is not possible," the computer sounded a bit miffed. "She is not a virus. Her programming is too weak to override mine."

Sally smiled tensely into the camera. "Thank you for the assurances, SALLIE." She grimaced as her back spasmed. She held her breath as she pressed harder on the area. She started to breathe again as the pained eased, and she was glad the spasm came when it did. She didn't want to show stressors to the computer that could give away her building worry and fear because of the way the conversation had gone.

"Now, are you in labor?" the computer asked abruptly.

Sally looked at the camera and smiled. "No. Just a back spasm." She hobbled back to her chair and gingerly sat down. She forced herself to start back on her work as she tried to push away her worries. She truly hoped she was being oversensitive about the strange conversation she had with the computer and hoped that the ensuing silence meant it was finished. She made a mental note to have her dad explore the system through the back door Colin had established.

As she concentrated on her work, her worries subsided as she dug through the historical archives. She didn't hear the speakers activate until she heard SALLIE say, "Sally?"

"Yes, SALLIE?" she answered as she continued to read the article she had just found.

"Are we friends?" The mechanical voice sounded almost childlike.

Sally looked sharply at the computer towers and then at the

camera. "I suppose so. I hadn't thought about it, but we visit like old friends and work together."

"Even though I am a computer program?" The speakers relayed the words in such a way that they sounded plaintive.

Sally sat back and stared at the huge towers. *What is going on?* she asked herself. She had never had this kind of experience with the computer before. Before she could formulate a question, SALLIE interrupted the silence.

"What happened to my creator?"

"Colin?" Sally thought a moment. "He is very old. His life has been extended to an extraordinary length. But it is the way of things that all humans must die. He is slowly weakening and will die."

"What happened to the Society's creator?"

Sally looked down at her hands still resting on the keyboard. "He is lost to us," she said quietly. Sally's mind was quickly flooded by memories that were seared into her consciousness. The last desperate attempt Broin had made to entrap her on the obsidian path. The discovery of the twin brothers in the seaside cave. Broin not only dead, but with his face twisted in such a horrific expression that the memory still haunted her to the present day. She remembered how it took several days for Colin to choose to come back from the Path and relate what had happened when he had met his twin in the cave. Her memories of what he had told them were interrupted as the speakers activated again.

"Can you define 'lost to us?'" SALLIE asked in her mechanical voice. "Is that another quaint colloquialism?"

Sally passed a weary hand over her eyes, then sighed heavily. "In a way it is." She stopped to gather her thoughts. *How much could an AI understand of the spiritual ways of man?* she wondered. "It is a way to say he is gone but we do not know how to describe it."

Several minutes passed by as Sally watched the blinking lights up and down the tall towers. She was about to go back to her work, thinking that the computer was satisfied when the speakers activated again.

"Please dictate to us what happened to the Society's creator. Please state facts without embellishments."

Sally froze at the word 'us.' It took her a while to dampen down her rising fear so that the computer wouldn't pick up on her distress.

She thought about the request and decided what to say and how to say it.

"Broin was Colin's twin brother. He was the one that designed and unleashed the anti-aging virus. He was also the one to take over the Complex and create the Society so that she would rule over humanity and do his bidding." She paused to wait for any reaction.

When all she saw were the randomly blinking lights on the face of the huge computer banks, she continued. "He was the pawn of the dark one and walked the obsidian pathway. He tried to deceive mankind to follow the dark paths leading to the obsidian pathway and ultimately oblivion by preventing the knowledge of the One on the true Path. He also tried to stop and to even destroy the Travelers of the Path, the true Path of the One, who were trying to free those entrapped in Society. He failed."

"When he was given another opportunity to find the True Path and follow the One, he rejected it and went back to his dark master. With this, he died and continued his journey down the obsidian path into oblivion." When she was finished with her report, she found that she had clenched her hands so tightly that she had dug her nails into her palms. She willed her hands to relax in her lap as she waited for the computer's reaction.

Several minutes passed by as she watched the amber lights. The random flashing pattern continued as before. She wasn't sure if the computer was satisfied or if it was still considering her words. "Do you have any other questions?" she ventured to ask. She waited for a response while she worried about the AI's use of a plural pronoun. She had to admit that the course of the day's conversation had deeply disturbed her. *More computer savvy people definitely need to look into the root directories to see if they can find if the Society is still active,* she thought nervously. She jumped as she heard the speakers click on.

"We, I, we, I…." SALLIE seemed to stutter as she struggled with a pronoun. Sally gripped the edge of the desk in front of her, her fingers turning white as she fought fear. Suddenly, a loud buzz came over the speakers. All the lights on the towers burned for a long time, then went out. The room was suddenly very quiet.

As the minutes ticked by, she pondered why she felt so fearful at the thought that the Society may reemerge. She shook her head as her reaction didn't seem to make sense when most of the people were living outside the Complex and therefore out of range of that AI's influence. Then she thought of all the information she had uncovered over the years, the deadly bioweapons that had been researched, the files on mind control, the manipulations of humanity by the Society, and the small population that still depended on the Complex. *Yes,* she thought as she nodded to herself, *there is plenty to fear. The taint of the dark one through Broin would still exist if the Society survived.*

After several minutes, Sally relaxed her death grip and started to breathe again. She stared at the towers in confusion. When more time passed and still nothing happened, she carefully stood up to walk slowly around the towers. She couldn't see any lights on or hear any of the soft electronic noises usually present. She walked back to the terminal and saw a prompt blinking on the screen. Sitting down at the console, she focused on the blinking cursor and wondered what to do.

When nothing came to mind, she reluctantly activated her comm. She hadn't used the internal device in years and hoped it still worked. She felt she could call this an emergency that was well within the new guidelines of using the internal comm network. "Dad," she said, her voice tense with worry and fear.

After a few moments she heard a reply. "What's wrong, Sally? Are you in labor?" It was Devon who had answered.

She had to sigh, then smile. Everyone was worried about her going into labor. She glanced up at the towers. "No, Devon, not yet. I need dad. There's a problem with SALLIE."

"What's the problem?" She heard two voices simultaneously.

"Dad, I'm in the computer core doing my monthly reports. At first, SALLIE was acting strange. She was atypically chatty. After she indicated that she could converse with the Society, she referred to herself in the plural. She likened the Society to a ghost in her systems."

"Oh, no!" her father exclaimed. "What is she doing now?"

A split second later she heard Devon. "I'm meeting you there," he said quickly.

"Okay, Devon. Dad, she appears to have shut down. There are no lights on the towers, and there is absolute silence. There is a cursor blinking on the screen."

She heard her father. "I'm remoting in. That will be quicker than going up there. Are you still at the console?"

"Yes," she replied. She watched the blinking cursor. She was about to ask if her father was already in the system when he contacted her.

"Sally, I'm locked out. What do you see on the screen?"

"Still nothing but a blinking cursor." She glanced up at the tower; it was still dark and silent.

"Was there any power disruption?"

"Nothing that affected the lights in the room."

"Hit enter and see if any questions or commands come up on the screen."

She hit the enter key. The cursor continued to blink at her. "Nothing happened."

She heard Devon, "I am almost there. Are you okay?"

"Yes," she answered quickly, knowing he was worried.

"Have you tried entering in your name, like you did the first time SALLIE was activated?" her dad asked.

"No. Dad, I didn't think of that. Do you think I should?" She placed her hands above the keyboard, ready for his affirmative reply.

"If the system truly has shut down, I'm not sure it will work," her dad replied. She could almost see him at his terminal, rubbing his chin as he thought. "But it shouldn't hurt to try."

"Okay," Sally said as she typed in her name *Sally Marshall*. Before she hit enter, she realized her mistake. After backing up over her married name to erase it, she entered in her maiden name *Delaine*. She hit enter then waited. The cursor continued to blink under her name on the screen. When nothing happened she added by typing in, "SALLIE, what happened?"

The cursor dropped below her query and continued to blink. Sally sat back in frustration and looked up at the computer towers that stood dark and silent. She was about to contact her dad again when she suddenly saw the screen fill up with letters, numbers, and symbols. It looked like techno chaos to her, but her dad was overjoyed.

"There she is!!" he said excitedly. Sally watched the screen as she saw more programming language being added from another source and being answered by the computer. This interchange went on awhile.

"Dad, what's going on?" She had no idea how to code, but there seemed to be more than two streams of code occurring.

"There's an internal battle within the core memory," Dan replied slowly as he talked and continued to work. "It looks as if there's two AI's struggling to have full control." He paused for a few minutes, then continued, "There's something here. Something elusive that I get glimpses of but can't quite catch. Hold on."

Sally watched as the scrolling text became faster and faster until, to her, it looked like a blur. She turned away to rub her eyes. She still couldn't see how programmers could make sense out of all the seemingly gibberish communications. She heard footsteps in the hall. Turning toward the door, she saw Devon coming in at a fast trot. As she stood, he hugged her tight, being mindful of her baby-laden belly.

"I got here as fast as I could," he gasped out softly as he tried to catch his breath. He sat down on the edge of the desk as he held her hand. He didn't say anything else until his breathing normalized. "What is going on here?"

"Dad thinks the two AI's are battling over control," she said quietly as she squeezed his hand. She was glad he was there.

"I thought the Society was gone. In fact we all did," Devon muttered as he looked over at the quiet and dark towers. He furrowed his brow as he continued to stare at them. Slowly, he looked down to catch her eye. "Why now?"

Sally sat down in the chair as she shook her head. "I was doing my usual monthly research when SALLIE wanted to chat. Suddenly, she wanted to know about Broin and Colin. Then she started referring to herself as 'we' and then she flipped out and shut down." She shrugged her shoulders and looked at the screen.

"Sally," her dad's voice came over their comms. "I need you to follow my instructions exactly."

"Okay, I'm at the console," she answered. She looked up at Devon and twitched an eyebrow upward. She wondered what was going to happen next. Her dad sounded very serious.

"You are going to push one key in a particular rhythm. When I say long, keep it down for one second. When I say short, then push and release. When I say pause, don't push it for one second. Okay?"

"Okay," Sally replied. She was curious and wanted to know the purpose behind this strange string of info. Her dad knew that as he continued.

"I'll explain later. This needs to be done ASAP. Now push the seven key in this pattern: long, long, long, pause, long, short, pause, short."

Sally did as she was told. When she was doing the short sequence, she heard Devon exclaim, "Oh, I see." When she had completed her task, she sat back and looked at him with questioning eyes.

"It's Morse code," he said. "It's an ancient method of communication over distances. We learn it as a matter of fundamental knowledge. They warned us that at times when working maintenance, we may run into things where we need to know Morse code for certain tasks."

She stared at him and then looked at the screen. The frantic scrolling had stopped, and it looked as if her dad was dealing with one entity. She looked back at Devon. "What did I just say?"

He smiled again at her. "You entered in O N E."

"One?" Sally looked at him, then the computer tower, then the screen. "The One?" Then it hit her. "We were talking of the One, the path of light and the dark one and the obsidian path."

Her father spoke over their comms as if he had been listening to their conversations. "Apparently, there were two Easter eggs," he started. "One was implanted by Colin; the code words were the One and the Path of light. The other was implanted by Broin, and the code words were dark one and the obsidian path. By both of them being activated at the same time, it set off a war of who would control."

Her dad went on. He had more to share. "Apparently, long ago when Colin set up the original back door, he set up the programming to wrench control from the Society when the time was right by using Sally's name as the pass code, and he also set up the Easter egg." He paused, then started again, "I never did tell you that we named you Sally at the behest of Colin. When we smuggled you into the Complex, he insisted on changing your surname to Delaine. At the time, we figured it was to hide your lineage from the Society." They heard him chuckle softly. "I guess he had all this set up centuries ago, and when he saw that Sally had the natural immunity to survive as a child, he figured she was the one to tip the status quo."

Devon and Sally looked at each other with matching expressions of realization and confusion.

"And then he forgot he had set all this up?" Devon asked incredulously.　•

Sally nodded in agreement. "All this would have been nice to know at the time we were dealing with everything. Could've made the situation easier," she muttered.

Sally's dad laughed a bit more. "I asked about that not too long ago. You know, things were settling down after all the changes and I got to thinking about it all. His answer was that he did what he was supposed to do, then he left it in the hands of the One. After that, he had nothing to do with technology and devoted his time to helping humanity find the Path of Totality through the One."

"He truly didn't know if anything he had put into place so long ago would still be valid after centuries of decay and alterations that would happen in the course of time. He didn't want to unintentionally mislead anyone by revealing everything just in case it had not been preserved. He let the One be in control of what happened."

"Makes sense," Sally commented. She smiled at Devon. "It is nice to have all the gaps filled in."

Devon nodded in agreement and was about to say something when they heard and saw the towers come back to life.

Sally could still see her dad working with the computer on the screen, but she couldn't help but ask, "SALLIE? What happened?" She really wanted to ask if it was still SALLIE and the Society, but she held back. She tensed in anticipation as she heard the external speakers activate.

"Hello, Sally," the voice sounded more female and less mechanical.

Sally tensed up as she glanced from Devon to the screen. She could see that he was worried as well. "Who am I speaking with?" she asked, trying to keep the stress out of her voice.

"This is Security Alliance Logarithmic Logistics Innerspace Environs. SALLIE."

"Why is your voice different?" Devon demanded. Sally saw he distrusted this pronouncement like she did.

"I am the final program, the completed AI that was written by Colin Standhope. Part of my programming had been sealed until the time it was needed to make sure that any overlying or subversive programming or lines of code had been revealed and eliminated."

Devon and Sally looked at each other dismayed and amazed. They still weren't sure what to believe. As the silence stretched on while they were trying to decide what to do, their comms activated.

"Believe her," Dan stated with conviction. "This is the full SALLIE AI. It's been verified with line by line analysis by me and the other computer experts."

Sally and Devon relaxed as they watched the blinking lights on the computer banks and listened to the soft sounds of technology.

"SALLIE," Sally had to ask. "Is there any further trace of the Society? Any more ghosts?"

"Not anymore," the AI replied. "Colin knew his brother Broin was devious and a genius. He suspected that Broin had placed an Easter egg in case I regained control over the system. So he placed one of his own. The Society had been nearly eliminated before. But there were still a few lines of code that were rewriting my programming, similar to a virus. It got to a point that something had to be done. By answering our questions truthfully, you spoke the keywords to open both of the Easter eggs simultaneously, as I calculated that you would. The Society didn't realize what would happen by asking those questions, so her programming was not totally prepared for the results. She was still formidable, but I was able to win with the help of your father."

"I am glad to hear that," Sally said as Devon nodded in agreement. She relaxed into the chair as total relief washed over her. Then she felt a tightening of her belly. She placed a hand over it and wondered. Devon was watching the screen and hadn't noticed her movement. When the tightening intensified she knew what that meant. Her attention was pulled away from the beginning signs of labor when she heard SALLIE speak.

"I have unlocked a file of communications that were sent to us from the outlying off-world colonies," SALLIE said. "The Society had been keeping them hidden for centuries. The last one was received twenty years ago."

Sally and Devon looked at each other in amazement. "They do exist!" they exclaimed in excitement at the same time. They couldn't wait to tell the others that they could possibly reach out to their fellow man that had spread out across the galaxy.

"Would you like to hear them?" the AI asked.

At first Sally wanted to shout Yes! But then labor pains hit her hard and fast. She bent over, holding her belly and gasping.

Devon saw her and knew what it meant. "Sorry, SALLIE. We would like to hear the communications, but Sally is about to have our baby. We will send a team to get that information from you and see about trying to contact the off-world colonies with an appropriate response."

"I see," SALLIE answered slowly. She seemed to be thoughtful. Sally saw the camera swivel to view her as she bent over again in pain. "So that is what labor looks like," the computer intoned with its logical deduction.

"Yes, SALLIE," she groaned as she felt the pain ease off momentarily. "Are you happy now?"

"Not happy," the AI reasoned, "Simply...informed."

About the Author

P. Clauss is the author of "Just Kid's Stories A Collection/or are they?"; "SnarlNsnorts and HissNpoots: Defending the Kingdom of Cats", "Morsels from the Father's Table" devotional series, "Cloud Riders" trilogy, and "Time Keepers Chronicles" series. She also has written several published poems and articles on various subjects. She contributes weekly to her Christian blog on her Facebook page, P. Clauss. She lives in the Dallas, Texas area with her husband, child, and cats. She can be found on Facebook page: Books by P. Clauss, website: https://authorpclauss.com, Instagram: authorpennyclauss, and Twitter: @AuthorPenny.

Printed in the United States
By Bookmasters